icy secrets, scandalous lies

A Michelle Kilpatrick Mystery

Book Three

sharon kay

the michelle kilpatrick mysteries

Book One: The Peculiar Case of the Petersburg Professor (setting: October, 1974)

Book Two: Fashionably Fit, Fatally Flawed (setting: December, 1974)

Book Three: Icy Secrets, Scandalous Lies (setting: April, 1975)

icy secrets, scandalous lies

who's who

The University of Petersburg

Commuter Lounge Gang

Amy Brown (works as a waitress)

Billy Carson (musician)

Jimmy Gordon (political aspirations)

Lawrence Jackson (Vietnam Vet/works at Police Station)

Michelle Kilpatrick (works at Mae's Gift Shop)

Rick McGuire (works at his mother's fitness center)

Tasha Constantin (free-spirited hippie)

Todd Spratt (Beatles fan/sci-fi nerd)

Yash Sharma (party-lover, business major)

T.J. Wilson (Michelle's best friend)

***

The Kilpatrick Family

Michelle's parents: *Brice and Nancy Kilpatrick*

Michelle's siblings:

Crystal Kilpatrick Weston (spouse—Mel Weston)

Mike Kilpatrick (spouse—Suzie Stewart)

***

The Peterson Family

Chauncey Peterson (father of Anne and Mae, founder of Petersburg Lumber Company and co-founder of Petersburg)

Anne Peterson Ladd (Mae's sister, married to Burt Ladd)

Mae Peterson Romano Miller Emerson (Owner of Mae's Gift Shop, previously married to Anthony Romano, Johnathan Miller, and Nathan Emerson)

Craig Miller (published mystery author & grad student, son of Mae Peterson and Anthony Romano, adopted by Johnathan Miller after Anthony's death)

Steve Goodright (son of Chauncey Peterson's sister, cousin to Mae and Anne)

Barbara Braxton Goodnight (married to Steve Goodnight)

Danny Goodnight (Steve and Barbara Goodnight's son)

Linda Goodnight (Danny's sister—in Europe)

***

The Skating Team

Charles Wyatt (coach)

Olga Nicolaus (choreographer)

Cherie and Ethan (skaters—pairs team)

Eric (singles skater)

Katie (singles skater)

Naomi and Jason (skaters—pairs team)

words to ponder

"A lie can travel half way around the world while the truth

is putting on its shoes."

Mark Twain

chapter one

Monday, April 14, 1975

If I had to listen to one more lecture on the importance of journalism internships before graduation, I just might scream —if only it were that easy!

I glanced at my finger. The mood ring I bought at Mae's Gift Shop last week had turned a deep black, confirming what I already knew. I was stressed.

And why?

Internships, or the lack of one, to be precise.

As soon as class ended, I bolted out the door of my Magazine and Feature Writing class and headed for the Commuter Lounge. I needed to see my friends, to escape from all things academic.

A warm spring breeze brushed against my face as I hurried towards Whitley Hall, and the scent of freshly cut grass wrapped me in memories of carefree childhood summers when I never worried about my future.

But that was then.

And this was now.

I could still feel the sting of the rejection letter from the *Chicago Tribune*: "We regret to inform you…"

My life felt like a jigsaw puzzle thrown into the air, pieces in chaos with no clue how to put them together. Yet amidst that chaos, deep down inside, a flicker of hope sparked reminding me my dreams were not a lost cause. All thanks in no small part to T.J.

I had spent most of the weekend sulking in my room, grappling with disappointment. And I wasn't doing much better when T.J. picked me up this morning for our drive to the university.

"Man, what's up with you?" T.J. switched off the radio and glanced at me as I clicked my seatbelt. "You look like you lost your best friend, but hey, that can't be 'cause I'm right here." His chuckle faded when he saw I wasn't laughing. "Seriously, what's going on? What happened? Did somebody die?"

I sighed and sunk deeper into my seat, staring out my window. "No," I mumbled. "I didn't get the internship in Chicago. What am I going to do? It was going to be my ticket out of here."

T.J.'s hand rested on top of mine, his blue striped shirt sleeves peeking from under his denim jacket. "Hey, it's going to be okay. Sometimes, things don't work out like we want them to, you know? Maybe it just wasn't meant to be. Besides," he added with a smirk, "sticking around in Petersburg isn't the end of the world, is it?"

I tugged absentmindedly at the Eiffel Tower charm dangling from my necklace. "How can you say that?" I huffed, feeling the weight of Petersburg's monotony pressing down on me. "You know how much I want to get out of here. I don't want to end up working on my family's farm like my brother and sister. If that happens, I'll be stuck here forever."

I slouched deeper into my seat. "I'll never see the Eiffel Tower, Buckingham Palace, or the emerald hills of Ireland, or—"

T.J. adjusted his aviator sunglasses, the sun reflecting off them as if he were a cool-guy superhero. "I'm not saying give up on your writing," he said, casting me a side glance, as if to say, *Get real*. "There are newspapers around here you could work for, and besides, I thought you wanted to be a freelance reporter. What's stopping you from doing that? You've already had two articles published in major newspapers in the last few months. That's pretty cool! Just keep writing."

He was right. The editors who published my pieces on Professor Ladd's murder and the failed attempt to close the Petersburg Health & Fitness Center had praised my fresh approach. Even my parents thought I'd done a good job. Surely, if I could impress them, there was hope for me as a journalist.

With each step toward the Commuter Lounge, it was like a lightbulb switched on in my head, and its light kept growing brighter. My goals didn't depend solely on getting the Chicago internship. The only thing standing between me and my dreams was...well, me. Why wait for opportunities to come my way when I could create my own writing assignments? The future I envisioned was within reach. I just needed to work for it. Little steps. Big steps. It didn't matter as long as I kept moving forward. I had two years before graduation. Time was on my side.

I glanced at my mood ring. The stone had shifted to a calming sky blue. It was right—for the first time since opening the letter, I was relaxed.

With the tremendous weight lifted from my shoulders, I bounded down the stairs to the Commuter Lounge. My feet hit the tiled floor and I scanned the room like I was looking for the latest issue of *Rolling Stone* magazine on the newsstand.

My gaze swept over the rows of tables and chairs occupied by students talking and eating. A few were even studying—a very few.

I spotted my friends at the trio of tables we had claimed at the start of the school year, strategically positioned in front of the row of lockers that lined the wall. As I navigated through the crowded space, I danced around errant chairs and scattered backpacks, weaving my way toward my safe haven.

As I drew closer, Rick spotted me, his face lighting up with a broad smile and gestured to the empty chair beside him. "Hey, Michelle! How's it goin'?"

"You know, another day in the neighborhood," I said, returning a smile as I slipped off my suede jacket and settled into my seat.

"Don't I know it?" He laughed, running his fingers through his tousled brown mullet.

After arranging my books on the table, I glanced past Rick's shoulder. Billy and Jimmy were engrossed in an intense card game...again. Amy was whispering into Billy's ear as he shuffled the cards. Her eyes sparkled with mischief as a rosy flush crept up his cheeks.

Rick and I shared a knowing glance and a silent laugh, fully aware of Amy's flirty antics as she attempted to disrupt Billy's focus. But he remained resolute, dedicated to the cards in his hand.

The scene was classic for our table: the guys were absorbed in their world of cards, and Amy was just being her flirty self, all big eyes and innocent giggles. But all that changed when Todd walked in and plopped a hefty brown paper grocery sack onto the table with a resounding thud, arousing our curiosity.

"Whatcha got, man?" Rick leaned forward in his seat, trying to catch a glimpse inside the bag.

Todd, his eyes twinkling, swatted Rick's hand away. "Wait, dude. This is top-secret stuff. Gotta make sure Alice isn't around."

As if on cue, our heads turned to scan the room for any sign of Alice, the matron of the Commuter Lounge. She was a stickler for enforcing the rules of her domain—our cherished home away from home—no smoking, no loud conversations, no music, no profanity, and certainly no leaving messes for the janitorial staff to clean.

With Alice nowhere to be found, Jimmy straightened his tie and declared, "She must be in her office."

Even though Alice could pop out any second for one of her legendary surprise inspections, we were in the clear for now. We turned our attention back to Todd, who was digging into the brown paper bag and looked like a magician getting ready to pull out a rabbit.

It was a coffee maker.

He plopped it on the table while keeping a vigilant eye on Alice's door for any hint of movement.

"A coffee maker?" I asked, flipping the box around to read its contents.

"Yeah. I'm sick and tired of paying a fortune for a cup of coffee at the Student Union. It's highway robbery what they're charging. I did the math the other night, and it hit me that we could brew our own coffee for a fraction of what they're charging." His frustration underscored each word.

Rick, Amy, Billy, and Jimmy nodded while echoing their complaints about the exorbitant prices they were paying at the Union for their daily caffeine fix.

I sat there, listening attentively, but as someone who disliked coffee and always opted for a can of diet pop from the vending machine, I had no idea about coffee prices. Raising an eyebrow, I asked, "How much do they charge for a cup of—"

Todd answered before I could even finish my question. "They've jacked it up to fifty-five cents, and there's no way I'm going to line The Man's pockets when I can make my own for twenty cents."

He stowed the coffee maker back in the bag and placed it on the floor beside his feet before pulling out his chair and sitting down. With the faces of the Fab Four—the Beatles—

staring at me from his t-shirt, he continued, "The big problem is Alice. She'll never let us make coffee down here if she finds out. So, we've gotta do it on the sly. I figure she won't spot the coffee machine and supplies if we keep them under the table during the day. Then, when the last person leaves at night, everything goes into my locker. If we all pitch in twenty cents for each cup we drink, we'll have enough money to keep the joe flowing." He leaned in his chair, balancing on its back legs. "No more getting ripped off by The Man!"

Lawrence, our resident Vietnam vet, walked in just then, interrupting Todd with a hearty laugh. "What's all this talk about price gouging?" he teased, nudging Todd's chair further back, causing Todd to scramble to regain his balance. "Didn't your mama ever warn you about tipping your chair back?"

With his eyes gleaming with mischief, Lawrence sat next to Todd, clearly enjoying Todd's battle to maintain self-control as he went from indignant surprise to amused resignation.

"Touché, man," Todd grinned, rubbing the stubble on his chin as he was finally stable in his seat once again.

"Did you hear? Todd's our hero," Jimmy declared, slapping his cards down dramatically. "He brought in a coffee maker, so the Union can't keep robbing us blind for a cup of coffee."

Billy gazed at the cards Jimmy had thrown down and sighed in defeat, his curly auburn hair falling across his forehead. He brushed the hair out of his eyes as he gathered the cards into a tidy stack and added, "Yeah, he says it'll only cost us twenty cents a cup."

Lawrence shed his camo jacket, draping it over the back of the chair. "Sounds like a good idea. Count me in, man."

Concerned about potential problems with Todd's plan, I spoke up. "But what about Alice? What do we do if she finds out?"

Todd smirked. "We do what we gotta do to make sure she doesn't find out."

My brows furrowed with skepticism.

"Relax, it'll be easy," Todd reassured me. "We just need to be careful and not brew when she's around."

I tilted my head, peering at him through narrowed eyes. "But what about the smell...I mean, aroma?"

Billy chimed in, his brown eyes wide with excitement. "We can keep a couple of cups of coffee on the table. If anyone asks, we'll say the smell...*or aroma*...is coming from them. I say we give it a shot. It's worth it to save some money."

"Yeah," Lawrence nodded. "What's the worst she can do? Kick us out?"

We exchanged concerned glances around the table.

"Look, guys," Lawrence said, playing the role of our group's elder statesman. "She'd warn us first. Alice isn't going to kick anyone out. I mean, have you ever seen her do it in all the time we've been here?"

He had a valid point. None of us had ever witnessed Alice banish anyone from the Commuter Lounge. Threaten? Absolutely. Evict? Never.

"Great, then it's settled," Lawrence concluded with a satisfied grin.

Todd nodded. "Cool. I'll stash the coffee maker in my locker and bring the supplies tomorrow. Our coffee operation begins at 8:00 in the morning." He stood, hoisted his grocery bag, pivoted toward his locker, and tucked the machine inside.

Lawrence leaned over the table closer to me. "Michelle. I've got some intel on those guards who were supposed to be watching Sarah's cell the night she died."

After months of dead ends regarding Sarah's mysterious death while in police custody, there was finally some news. In December, when Sarah was arrested for Shelly's murder at the fitness center, she accused a mysterious man of ordering the hit on Shelly and the destruction of Caroline's new business. At first, Sarah insisted on keeping his identity a secret, but then she had a change of heart and agreed to speak with Detective Douglas. Tragically, she was found dead in her cell the night before her meeting with the detective.

Officially ruled a suicide, her death never made sense, especially after Detective Douglas discovered the guards weren't where they were supposed to be that night. Since then, he and a few of us, including Lawrence, had come to suspect that the guards and the unnamed man played a role in her sudden demise.

"What did you find out?" I leaned in. My curiosity heightened.

"We knew the Chief of Police placed the guards involved on indefinite leave, but we didn't know what happened to them. Then, Detective Douglas found a memo ordering the chief to transfer the dudes out west. And get this—the department footed their relocation expenses in full."

I leaned even further. "How'd Douglas get hold of the memo? Someone didn't just hand it to him, did they?"

Lawrence's voice dropped to a whisper. "Actually, you're kind of on the right track. Some officers who worked with the transferred guards had their own suspicions about Sarah's supposed suicide. Now, whether that's because of their own intuition or something the guards confided in them before they left, I'm not sure. But regardless, we think it was one of them who slipped a copy of the memo onto Douglas's desk."

Lawrence surveyed our table, focusing on Todd, Rick, Amy, Billy, and Jimmy, occupied with their own conversations. Confident they were not listening to us, he clasped his hands and continued. "When Sarah died of *suicide*, the higher-ups ordered Douglas *not* to investigate her death— said it was a closed case. But like us, he didn't buy it, not when she was ready to name the man responsible for ordering Shelly's murder. But gathering intel without tipping off the wrong people has been challenging, to say the least."

"Does Detective Douglas have any idea which officer left the memo?" My gift of imagination kicked in as my mind swirled with potential explanations for the clandestine developments.

Lawrence shook his head. "He doesn't know who it was, and, frankly, it doesn't matter at this point. Right now, he's happy to have a lead, especially one that supports our theory that someone is trying to cover up the cause of Sarah's death."

Knowing that Lawrence worked part time in the records department at the police station, I asked, "Can you find out where the officers were transferred?"

"Funny you should ask," Lawrence smirked. "After finding the memo, Douglas knew exactly where to find that info. And, *no*, I can't tell you. But, anyway, he found where they're working. He's going to contact them today and see if they're willing to shed any light on what happened the night Sarah died. Hopefully, they know something about the missing surveillance video of Sarah in her cell that night."

I rested my arms on the table, cupping my chin. "I hope Detective Douglas can find the mystery man Sarah was talking about. She said Mae had to pay for the sins of her husband—just not sure which of the three husbands Sarah was referring to. Regardless, until the police catch this guy, Mae's life could be in danger."

"For once, you and Douglas are on the same wavelength." Lawrence adjusted his round, wire-rimmed glasses. "I overheard him joking about enlisting your help with the case. But who knows? Mr. By-the-Book detective may call you one of these days."

"That'll be the day." I grinned. "Of course, if he ever asked for my help, I wouldn't say 'no.' It would be kind of fun to work *with* him instead of sneaking around behind his back all the time."

Out of the corner of my eye, I spotted a hand pulling out the chair next to me. I looked over, and my smile grew wider as I saw that the hand belonged to T.J.

"So, what's this?" A look of puzzlement crossed his face. "You're working with Douglas?"

"That'll be the day!" I chuckled, shaking my head. "He'd have to be pretty desperate to ask for my help, and I don't think he's there yet. Just as well," I said, glancing at the clock. "Right now, finding out why Coach Wyatt chose Petersburg to train his team at for the Winter Olympics is about all I can handle."

T.J. crossed his arms, leaning back in his chair. "I read something about that in the *Wildcats' Daily News* the other day. It doesn't make sense why an ice skating coach of his caliber would choose to train his team here. I get that it's away from the competition, but plenty of other rinks in the country could do the same thing."

"That's exactly what I'm going to find out." I slipped my arms through my jacket, grabbing my books. "I'm meeting him and Craig in a few minutes at the Peterson Ice Arena."

T.J. groaned. "What's Craig got to do with this?"

"His agent, Suzette, set up a meeting between him and the coach. She represents both of them and thought it would be nice for them to get acquainted. Anyway, Craig invited me to join them. And get this: when I saw Keith—you remember him, the assistant editor of the school paper? Well, when I saw him in class this morning, I told him about my meeting with Coach Wyatt and suggested the story idea. He liked it." I grinned. "I'm taking initiative, just like you said I should."

T.J. shook his head, a mix of concern and protectiveness in his expression. "I didn't say work with Craig, though. Promise me you'll be careful. I don't know what it is about that guy...maybe it's because he writes murder mysteries, but he just seems to push you toward trouble. I mean, even that crazy stunt you two pulled with your fake engagement—look at all the chaos that caused."

Rising from my seat, I waved off his concern. "You've got nothing to be worried about. I'm simply writing about a group of figure skaters and their coach. I'm sure they're all way too busy practicing to cause any trouble. What could possibly go wrong?"

chapter two

With my books tucked under one arm, I tugged open the heavy glass door to the ice arena, my heart pounding like finals week had snuck up on me. I was about to meet an Olympic figure skating coach—exciting, but also seriously intimidating.

As I stepped inside, the bright fluorescent lighting bounced off the white walls, and a wave of unease replaced my nerves. I was suddenly back in Detective Douglas's office, summoned as a person of interest in Professor Ladd's murder.

I bit my bottom lip and took a deep breath, anchoring myself in the present. The shadows of the past belonged exactly where they were—behind me.

I paused at a trophy case and caught my reflection. After I adjusted my glasses and tucked a few strands of my blonde shag into place, I took a deep breath and whispered, "Okay, Michelle, you've got this."

Continuing down the hall, I passed framed photos of the university's hockey team and banners celebrating past victories. I might have lingered, but muffled voices, barely audible above the Eagles' "Best of My Love," drifted down the hall.

Drawn by curiosity, I followed the sound to the end of the

corridor where a large viewing window overlooked a long stretch of ice. I knew the university had a curling team, but this was the first time I'd actually seen them in action.

Two teams darted across the ice in a strategic dance, sweeping furiously in front of a heavy stone while their teammates shouted. I couldn't tell if the cries were encouragement or reprimand, but the energy was electric.

"Curling, huh?" Craig's voice made me jump.

"I didn't hear you come in. You scared me." I whipped around, my heart racing.

"Sorry 'bout that." He chuckled, smoothing out the creases in his blue plaid blazer. "I'll admit, I've never watched curling before. Between the two of us, it baffles me why sweeping the ice to move a stone fascinates people." He shrugged. "But to each their own, I guess."

I smirked, nodding toward the ice. "I don't know. It looks kind of fun. And hey, at least it's not as dangerous as getting beat up while playing hockey."

"Maybe," he said, with that charming grin of his. "But where's the fun in that?"

I rolled my eyes. "You are so warped sometimes."

"What?" He blinked with mock innocence, his green eyes twinkling.

I scanned the hallway and, not seeing anyone other than Craig, asked, "So, where are we supposed to meet this Coach Wyatt?"

"Upstairs by concessions. You ready?"

"Sure. Let's go." I nudged his shoulder as we headed toward the stairs at the end of the hall. "New threads?"

"Yeah, what do you think? Is the plaid too much?" Craig smoothed the front of his blazer, a hint of uncertainty in his tone.

I nodded. "No, I like it. Looks good on you."

"It's a tad avant-garde for some of the establishment types

in the English department, but I thought I'd be a little daring."

"It's good to shake The Man up now and then," I laughed, coming to a halt at the top of the stairs. "Speaking of the man, do you see him anywhere?" I searched the room, taking in the concession stand, tables, and chairs. Other than the lone attendant working behind the counter, Craig and I were the only ones there.

Craig shrugged, glancing around the room with raised eyebrows. "Why don't we take a seat? Might as well be comfortable while we wait. I'm sure he'll be along soon."

I spotted a table by a large window that overlooked the rink. "Let's sit over there. Maybe we can watch the skaters practice until he gets here."

To my delight, several skaters beautifully executed their jumps and spins. Their performances transported me back to the Figure Skating World Championships on TV last month.

The commentators, all former Olympians, passionately explained the intricacies of the required elements for the skaters' routines, especially those for the compulsory figures. They meticulously broke down its technical elements, emphasizing the importance of skaters seamlessly connecting two circles while executing a change of foot or blade edge. A poor score in this event could ruin a skater's chances of medaling.

Yet, despite my new appreciation for these elements, watching them was boring, which probably explained why the network only aired brief clips.

For me, the thrill and elegance of figure skating lay in the newly introduced short program and, of course, the long program. The routines, set to music and filled with multiple jumps and intricate footwork sequences, never failed to mesmerize me.

Whenever I watched a competition, I promised myself I'd take skating lessons, dreaming of effortlessly gliding across the ice. However, I never followed through. My inability to skate from point A to point B without falling remained proof of my inaction, and the idea of me jumping and landing on a slender blade only existed in my dreams.

"Amazing," Craig exclaimed, watching one skater easily lift his partner into the air and throw her into a jump. She landed on one foot with her other leg extended behind her, parallel to the ice.

"And you, my friends, are watchin' the next Olympic Pairs gold medalists," declared a man with the most eloquent Southern drawl I had ever heard.

I turned and gasped. The man standing beside me was the one and only Coach Wyatt. Dressed in his trademark off-white zippered long jacket with a red, white, and blue figure skating patch on the sleeve and a bright white scarf around his neck, he looked just like his pictures in the magazines.

"Coach Wyatt," exclaimed Craig as he extended his hand. "It's nice to meet you, sir. I'm Craig Miller, and this is my friend Michelle Kilpatrick, a reporter for the *Wildcats' Daily News*. Thank you for taking the time to meet with us today."

"When Suzette told me her famous mystery writer was at the university, how could I say 'no'? I've read all your books. They make for excellent readin' while flyin' to competitions."

"Thank you, sir. I'm glad you enjoy them."

"And you, young lady—" he said as he shook my hand with all the charm of a southern gentleman, "have quite the reputation as an investigative reporter accordin' to Suzette. She sings your praises quite highly." Lowering his voice, he continued with a mischievous glint in his eyes, "I suspect if you ever need an agent, she'd be happy to represent you. If not, you just let me know, and I'll set her straight."

My cheeks flushed, and I glanced down. "Thank you," I said, my voice barely above a whisper. Then I drew a steadying breath, lifted my chin, and met his eyes. "How long will you and your team be training here?"

The coach nodded toward an empty table. "Why don't we go sit down? I don't know about you all, but I've been on these dogs all mornin'. A chance to sit would be right welcome. Would you all like somethin' to drink?"

A minute later, Coach Wyatt returned with three cups of hot cocoa.

As the coach settled into his seat, I sipped my hot chocolate and studied him, intrigued. Everything I had read about Coach Wyatt spoke to his reputation as a demanding coach who accepted nothing less than perfection from his skaters. Yet, the man before me appeared relaxed and easygoing. Was this the man behind the façade, or was it the other way around?

Curious, I dove in with my questions. "So, if you don't mind me asking, what brings you to the University of Petersburg? You've been coaching at a rink in California for several years, right? So why here?"

"Well, there's nothin' like getting down to brass tacks," Coach Wyatt chuckled. "I like a lady who gets to the point. None of this wastin' time with needless chit-chat." He took the lid off his cup, letting the steam escape. "If my skaters are goin' to be ready for the Innsbruck Olympics next year, they need access to the ice and the ability to train without fear of sabotage."

I cocked my head. "Sabotage? What do you mean? Were you having trouble at your other rink?"

"Sabotage? Bad luck? Coincidence? Whatever you want to call it…things were happenin' that were unnervin' my skaters, and I can't have that." He swirled his hot cocoa. "They have to focus on their skatin' with no distractions. That's the only way they're goin' to be ready."

Out of the corner of my eye, I saw Craig's shoulders drop as he muttered under his breath, "Not again."

I totally got where Craig was coming from. Only a few months ago, we'd seen a fitness center nearly go out of business after someone tampered with one of the treadmills and a person died. We had seen firsthand how sabotage could unravel lives and leave lasting damage.

I locked eyes with Coach Wyatt. "What was going on?"

"First, it was random stuff like practice tapes bein' erased or goin' missin' or skate guards disappearin' from lockers. Nothin' too terrible, but just enough to make you feel downright uneasy. I thought I could solve the problem by havin' my skaters take their belongings home. You know, not leave anythin' important in their lockers. But when two of my skaters had their apartments broken into and their skates stolen, I said, 'Enough is enough.' And then, out of the blue, Doug Hansen, an ol' friend of mine who manages the rink here, called me. I was flustered and mentioned some of the trouble I was havin'. He said to call him if I ever wanted to change rinks. At first, I thought he was jokin', but he assured me he was not. Well, I thought about it for a few days, and then I called him to see if the offer was still on the table, and if so, what would I have to do to make it happen?"

Craig straightened in his chair, peering at the coach. "And what kind of deal did the two of you work out?"

"In exchange for bein' able to use the ice whenever the university isn't usin' it, my skaters teach in the club's group skatin' program, give private lessons, and put on one or two exhibition skates. I also agreed to help the skatin' club here start their ice dancin' and pairs programs."

I raised an eyebrow. "Sounds like an awful lot of work for some practice ice."

Coach Wyatt glanced around the room and ran his hand through the strands of his salt-and-pepper hair before responding. "Yes, but if my skaters can practice without havin' to look over their shoulders all the time, it'll be worth it."

Behind the coach, I noticed a young man enter, sneaking up with a playful grin. He motioned for Craig and me to keep quiet, and with a broad smile, he placed his hands on the coach's shoulders.

Coach Wyatt jumped and whipped around. "Danny, my boy. What a surprise! What are you doin' here?"

"Figured it was time to face my demons and come home," the young man chuckled.

Coach Wyatt pulled Danny to the side of his chair. "Michelle. Craig. I'd like you to meet Danny."

The mischief in Danny's brown eyes faded as his gaze shifted from the coach to Craig. "Craig Miller, by any chance?"

"Yes, and you are—"

"Danny Goodnight. Steve and Barbara's son. It's weird, but I've known Cousin Mae since I was fourteen, and, in all that time, she never mentioned having a son. I only found out last fall when you moved to town, and you and Michelle linked my parents to Cousin Anne's murder. Isn't that ironic? You repaired your bond with your mother while destroying mine with my parents. What a twist, huh? Almost good enough for one of your mystery novels."

I inhaled deeply, bracing for what might come next.

To my relief, Danny reached out his hand across the table to Craig. "Look, man, no hard feelings. What my parents did was wrong. It's taken me a while to come to terms with the fact that their sins don't have to dictate my future. Besides, we're family, right?"

He then turned toward me with a warm smile. "And Michelle. I know I never shop at Cousin Mae's store, but I've heard a lot about you. She claims she could never run her gift shop without you. I think she secretly hopes you decide to stay in Petersburg after graduation." He chuckled. "I take that back; I don't think she makes any secret of it at all."

Coach Wyatt gestured for Danny to take the seat next to

him. "Sit down, my boy. I had no idea you were comin' back to Petersburg."

"Um," I interjected. "How do you two know each other?"

Danny settled into his seat, unzipped his brown leather flight jacket, and loosened the off-white silk scarf tied around his neck. "Before everything blew up with my parents, I worked part time at the arena while I went to school here—resurfaced the ice, rented skates, sold ice time. You know, stuff like that. I was a business major, and my dad encouraged me to get experience outside the Peterson Lumber Company. Of course, now I know why. He didn't want me to learn about his embezzling."

Danny leaned back in his chair. "Anyway, after that mess with my mom and dad, I had to clear my head and get away. So, I took the winter semester off, and Mr. Hansen set me up with an administrative job at an ice rink out west. That's where I met Coach Wyatt."

Craig's eyes widened as he listened to Danny's story. When he finished, Craig shrugged. "And now you're here, imagine that?"

Danny didn't seem to notice Craig's uneasiness and flashed a grin that rivaled Craig's Hollywood smile. It struck me that these two were second cousins, and I couldn't help but envy those lucky genes that gave them those pearly whites. Of course, I giggled a little, reminding myself that having a bit of cash didn't hurt either!

"Yes," Danny said, "I'm home for a while. Mr. Hansen, the rink manager, offered me my old job. I might even register for classes next fall and finish my degree. But first, I need to find an apartment since—" he stopped abruptly.

As I looked at Danny, the weight of how drastically his world had shifted hit me hard. His parents' arrest for the murder of Professor Anne Ladd had turned his and his sister's lives upside down. When neither Danny nor Linda attended their parents' arraignment, they were only names on a piece of paper, distant and disconnected from me. But now, sitting in plain view, Danny was real, and a pang of guilt washed over me. I couldn't shake the memory of my role in exposing his parents' crimes and the ripple effects their actions had on their children's lives.

Not only did Danny and Linda have to deal with their parent's arrest and its fallout, but there was also the unexpected revelation that Craig—not their father—was the rightful heir to Chauncey Peterson's fortune. That discovery meant Craig was the legal owner of Peterson Manor, the home where Danny and his family lived. Despite Craig's written offer to let Danny and Linda stay in the house, they refused, choosing to move in with friends as they navigated their new reality.

The unfairness of the Goodright children paying a price for their parents' crimes made me tense, and I desperately wanted to change the subject. I anxiously twisted my silver chain around my fingers, trying to think of a way to bring up a new topic without seeming too obvious, but my mind was blank.

Fortunately, Coach Wyatt came to the rescue. "Why don't you stay with me while you get settled? I've rented a large house not too far from here, where my team and I are staying. It's got nine bedrooms, and we're only using eight, so there's a room for you if you'd like."

Danny looked at Craig and grinned. "I'd like that. I'd like that a lot. In fact, it's perfect."

chapter three

I weaved through the maze of parked cars in Commuter Lot #3, my eyes landing on T.J.'s green Nova. He was pacing beside it, arms crossed—a classic sign he was upset. T.J. only paced when he was beyond frustrated. Whatever it was had clearly gotten under his skin.

His rolled-up shirt sleeves were visible, a telltale sign he had been at his car long enough to stash away his jacket and books. Was I late and throwing him behind schedule? A quick glance at my watch dispelled that idea.

Once within earshot, I shouted, "Hey, T.J.! Whatcha doing?"

He jerked his head toward me and snapped, "Waiting for you. Why else would I be standing here?" The bite in his tone caught me off guard.

T.J., short for Timothy James, and I live across from each other just outside the Petersburg city limits. In the thirteen years I've known him, he's never lost his temper with me.

Well, almost never.

He's one of the most even-tempered people I've ever known, and it's one of the many things I admire about him. Sure, he has his moments. T.J. is human, after all, but he's a master at maintaining his cool.

Today felt different, and I debated how to react. T.J. was obviously agitated. Perhaps my first instinct was correct, and he was on a tight schedule. Maybe he was counting on me getting to the car earlier than usual. It was the only thing I could think of.

I hesitated before pulling the car door open. "I'm sorry for keeping you waiting. I didn't mean to," I said, hoping to ease the tension.

"It's not you," he replied, buckling his seat belt. "You didn't do anything wrong. I'm just… I'm sorry for acting like a jerk. It's been a rough day."

"Why? What happened?" I prodded.

T.J.'s gaze dropped to the floor. "It's Meg. We had a huge fight this afternoon, and I don't know what to do about it."

"What about? What'd she do?" I asked, my instincts telling me that this was all her fault. T.J. would never do anything wrong.

It had to be Meg.

I always thought she was bad news for him, and seeing him upset only confirmed my suspicions. T.J. deserved someone who appreciated him, and while part of me wished they would break up, I knew his well-being wasn't the only reason fueling my hope.

T.J. had always been my rock, my confidant, biggest cheerleader, and best friend.

But everything changed when Meg came into his life in the fall. Sure, we still hung out together, but Meg was always with us, even when she wasn't physically. He talked about her all the time.

Sometimes, I thought I wanted more than friendship with T.J. and wondered if he might too, but I never had the courage to discuss "us" with him. What was the point of risking our friendship when I was so uncertain about my own feelings? I just wanted things to go back to how they were—T.J. and me.

No drama.

No Meg.

So I sat, and I listened as his rant continued, his despair rising with each word. "Meg's furious because she thinks I spend too much time with you. I told her we've been friends forever. That's all there is to it. We're just friends."

"Did she believe you?"

"No. Not at all." He paused. "She's convinced you have a crush on me. That you're trying to break us up."

I bit my lip and fidgeted with the charm around my neck. "Why would she say that?"

"She says your engagement to Craig was nothing more than a way to make me jealous."

I shook my head in disbelief. "You know that's not how it happened. Craig and I were never really engaged. We only pretended to be to get information to clear Rick's mom and prove she wasn't responsible for Shelly's death. Craig had a meeting with Mr. Langford to get financial details about his gym, and I needed to be there. The only way we could explain my presence was to say we were engaged. It was supposed to be a secret, but once people found out, we had to keep up the act until we solved Shelly's murder. It wasn't about us. It was about the case."

"I know that, and you know that. But Meg doesn't. She saw us talking at the Christmas party, while we were getting some cookies. She thinks I was trying to talk you out of marrying Craig, that I was jealous. That your plan worked. And then, when you two called off the engagement..."

"What? She thinks it was because of you that we called it off? Craig and I never planned on getting married. We just had to figure out a way to end our engagement and still stay friends, so we told people we rushed into it and needed some space to think things over."

"I get it, but Meg still believes I'm not being honest with her about you and me, and she's kind of right. After all, I knew your engagement was a sham, but I kept my promise to you and never told anyone, not even Meg. I *am* keeping secrets from her."

I didn't know what to say. Despite all my good intentions not to deliberately come between T.J. and Meg, I had inadvertently done so with my unorthodox scheme to catch Shelly's killer.

We rode in silence—no music, no conversation, nothing. The landscape rushed by as it morphed from rows of houses to a bustling array of businesses lining the street. At long last, signs signaled the upcoming entrance to the highway. This trip would be over soon.

Lost in my thoughts as I tried to find a way out of the mess I had created, I twisted a strand of hair around my finger.

I slouched into my seat, feeling guilty. As much as I wanted T.J. and Meg to part ways, I didn't want it to be because of me—because of my secret.

Finally, I placed a hand on his arm. "I'm sorry. I didn't mean to cause you any trouble with Meg. Why don't you tell her the truth? Just ask her not to tell anyone…and if she does, I'll just have to live with the consequences. My parents still think the engagement was for real. They'd be crushed to learn I wasn't honest with them, but as my grandma always said, 'Be sure your sins will find you out.' From the start, I should have come clean and told my family that Craig and I were not engaged and why we were pretending."

I turned away and leaned against the door, staring out the window.

T.J. touched my shoulder. "It's not just Meg being upset that has me on edge," T.J. confessed. "I'm troubled because she can be so vindictive. If I tell her the truth, I'm not sure I can trust her to keep it to herself, and, worse yet, she might use it to hurt you. That's the real problem—a lack of trust. How can she and I have a relationship without trust?"

T.J. pulled his car under the basketball hoop at the side of my driveway.

Before I got out, I placed my hand on his. "What if Meg feels the same way? Maybe she's worried she can't trust you. If you really care about her, be honest with her." I shrugged. "It's the only way you'll ever know if you two can move forward. Don't worry about me. I'll be fine. Just remember, trust starts with the truth."

Closing the car door behind me, I trudged toward the front porch. The burden of contributing to T.J.'s distress weighed heavily on me, as did the fact that I might have just pushed him back into Meg's arms. One bad thing after another. First, the rejection letter for the internship, and now this.

Once inside the house, I started up the stairs to my room so I could change my shoes for work, but the glow of the T.V. screen caught my attention. Instead of hearing my mom preparing supper in the kitchen, she was sprawled on the couch, wrapped in a blanket with a pillow cradling her head.

"Mom, what's the matter? Are you sick?"

I'm not sure why I asked because I already knew the answer. Mom's vibrant blue eyes were barely visible through her half-opened lids. Her skin was pale, and, considering she rarely went without makeup, its absence spoke volumes.

"I think I've got the flu," she whispered.

"Can I get you anything? Do you have a fever?"

I placed my hand on her forehead as she pulled the blanket up to her chin.

"I took something to bring my temperature down about an hour ago, but could you get me some pop? Perhaps that would settle my stomach."

I rushed to the kitchen and returned with a glass of pop and a straw.

"What else can I get you?" I asked as I gently placed a damp washcloth on her forehead.

"Supper," Mom murmured. "Your father will be home soon, and I don't have anything for you all to eat. Can you fix something?" She paused, taking a few deep breaths before continuing. "There's some roast left from yesterday. Maybe shred it and warm it up for sandwiches."

I nodded, glancing at my watch with a sigh. It was already 4:30 p.m., and I was supposed to start my shift at Mae's Gift Shop at 5:00 p.m. "Sure…um, let me call Mae and tell her I'll be a little late."

As I reached for the phone, I calculated that reheating the leftovers and making roast beef sandwiches would take ten to fifteen minutes. Dad would come in from working in the fields around 5:00 p.m., and then he would be home to take care of Mom. If everything went smoothly and Dad wasn't late, I could make it to Mae's by 5:30 p.m. But what if he's late? I can't leave Mom alone.

Fidgeting with the Eiffel Tower charm around my neck, I wished I could let my dad know Mom needed him. Life would be much easier if he had a shoe phone like Agent 86 on *Get Smart*.

Next to the black rotary phone, a message was scrawled on a notepad lying on the end table.

"Did you write this?" I asked, trying to decipher the writing.

Mom turned her head slightly, her words punctuated by labored breaths. "Yes…sorry…I couldn't catch…everything he—"

"That's okay. Who called?

"Craig," she murmured.

"Do you remember what he wanted?"

"Something about a dinner…tomorrow? You should call him. Maybe you two can work things out," she replied weakly.

Mom handed me her glass, and I adjusted the cloth on her forehead. "I'll call him later and find out what he wants."

"Sorry," she mumbled as she rolled over and drifted off to sleep.

Dragging the phone cord, I settled on the steps leading upstairs and dialed Mae's number. As expected, the news that I would be late didn't please her. Tonight was her Bridge night, but circumstances were out of my control. I held my breath, waiting for her response.

"Get here as soon as you can," Mae said curtly before hanging up.

It wasn't the news I'd hoped for, but at least it wasn't as bad as it could have been. I tried to push aside my concerns about Mae and focused on her son, Craig. As curious as I was about his phone call, I knew calling him back would have to wait.

Making my father's supper came first. A quick glance at my watch showed it was already 4:40 p.m. Time to pick up the pace.

***

As I walked into Mae's Gift Shop right at 5:30 p.m., Mae was already in her coat, standing behind the antique brass cash register. I quickly dropped off my jacket and purse in the back room before heading back to face her.

By the time I returned, Mae had moved to the front door, her arms crossed and foot tapping on the tile.

As I grew closer, she pulled the door open, casting a fleeting glance over her shoulder. "Your mother?"

"Not well. I had to help her," I said defensively as Mae waved me away, the door swinging shut behind her.

With Mother's Day still a month away, the shop had a calm, unhurried feel. A few customers wandered in, browsing for birthday cards, anniversary trinkets and retirement gifts, but the steady hum of conversation and footsteps was notice-ably absent.

And the hours dragged on.

Truth be told, I could have used the time to study, but I wasn't in the mood to do homework. Instead, while standing in the cash wrap, I mulled over T.J.'s advice to take control of my writing career.

I opened my notebook and tried to compile a list of story ideas. First up: the Coach Wyatt story for the school paper.

Next? As much as I racked my brain to come up with other ideas, my mind drew a blank—too many emotions swirling around to think clearly.

After half an hour and no progress on my list, I gave up and turned my attention to the skating coach story. I scribbled several questions under Coach Wyatt's name and made a note to call him to set up an interview. Tapping my pencil's eraser against the glass display case, I stared into space, trying to brainstorm every possible angle the story could take.

What would students find intriguing about a coach and his team on their journey to make it to the Olympics? I shrugged. *What would make it a bigger story for a national paper or magazine?*

The phone rang, snapping me from my thoughts, and I smiled when I recognized the voice on the other end of the receiver. "Craig. Hi. I was going to call you tonight when I got home."

Craig chuckled. "I knew my mom had her Bridge game tonight, so she wouldn't be there to scowl at you for talking on the phone. Are you busy? Can you talk?"

I scanned the empty store, gazed at the security mirrors hanging in the corners, and confirmed I was alone. "Yeah, it's cool. I can talk. Nobody's here."

"Great. I mean, not that my mom's store is empty, but that you can talk. Anyway, I wanted to tell you that Coach Wyatt invited us to a Meet-and-Greet sponsored by the Petersburg Ice Skating Club tomorrow night and then to his house afterward for dinner with his skaters. Will that work for you, or do you have plans?"

"No, that should be fine. What time?"

Craig emitted a relieved sigh. "Oh, good. He said about 5:30 p.m. He'd like to talk to us about something."

"Any idea about what?" I asked.

"No clue," Craig admitted. "Just that he needs our help."

chapter four

As Craig and I descended into the basement of the Peterson Ice Arena, I was struck by the lobby's transformation from dingy to festive. The red, white, and blue balloons and streamers cascading from the ceiling infused the room with energy.

The concrete walls, once bare, now displayed colorful photos of Coach Wyatt's team competing internationally. Every detail, down to the decorations on the food tables, reflected the patriotic theme and echoed the colors of the Petersburg Figure Skating Club.

I scanned the crowd for Coach Wyatt but didn't see him. Instead, a group of skaters in matching blue warmup jackets caught my eye. They stood out among the casually dressed crowd. They had to be members of his team.

"Ahem," a voice cut through my thoughts. Coach Wyatt's broad smile greeted me as I turned around.

"Hi," I said as Craig pivoted beside me. "I was looking for you but couldn't find you." I gestured to the crowd in the room. "There sure are a lot of people here."

"Yes, the skating club certainly got the word out," he

chuckled. "Come with me. I want to introduce you to my team," he said, leading us through the gathering. "They should be easy to spot," he grinned, pointing toward the group wearing the solid blue warmup jackets.

We first approached a young man dressed in team attire who was deep in conversation with a couple of wide-eyed teenage girls. He raked his hand through his messy dark brown hair, effortlessly creating that perfect windblown look.

Coach put an arm around him and said, "Excuse me, Eric, can I pull you away for a moment? I'd like you to meet some friends of mine."

Eric nodded. However, his posture stiffened when Coach Wyatt introduced Craig as a mystery writer and me as a reporter for the school paper. The warm smile I had witnessed only moments ago hardened, replaced by a more guarded expression. Eric extended his hand to Craig and then to me, maintaining a steady gaze with his light blue eyes.

Craig asked, "What does your family think about your skating career?"

Eric took a step back, his jaw tightening. "My family has always been supportive, but I prefer not to talk about them. Skating's a full-time job for me. I like to stay focused."

At that moment, three skaters from Coach's team approached us—a guy and two girls. As the petite blonde with a pixie cut, reminiscent of Twiggy's iconic hairstyle, linked her arm with Eric's, his mood brightened instantly.

The other girl smiled warmly, her big brown eyes darting between Craig and me. "Who are your friends, Coach?"

"Cherie. Katie. Ethan. I'd like you to meet Michelle and Craig. Michelle is writin' an article about our skatin' team, and Craig is doin' research for a new book."

Cherie's eyes sparkled with interest. "A reporter and a writer. How fascinating! Not sure how much of a story you'll find here—just a group of skaters working hard and hoping to make it to the Olympics."

"Sounds good to me," I replied.

Ethan chimed in, grinning. "If you have any questions, we'd be happy to help. Just don't make the story for the paper too juicy. We've all got reputations to uphold." He winked at Katie, causing her to laugh.

Coach surveyed the room. "Have any of you seen Jason or Naomi?"

"No. They were here a minute ago, but I don't know where they went," Eric said.

"All right," Coach said, turning his attention to Craig and me. "You'll get to meet them at the house." His face grew solemn. "But, if you'll excuse me, I need to speak with a few people startin' with that gentleman over there." He pointed to a man wearing a navy blue blazer. "He's the president of the skatin' club. I shouldn't be long. Could you meet me in the coach's lounge in, say, fifteen minutes?"

I nodded while Craig replied, "We'd be happy to, but where is the lounge?"

"Go through those double doors, and to your left will be the skaters' room. The coaches' lounge will be straight ahead."

As I tugged at the sleeve of my peach-colored cardigan to check my watch, Craig nudged me. "Let's go grab some food since we've got some time. I'm starving! I didn't have time to eat between teaching and an endless stream of students during office hours."

"Poor baby," I teased. "It must be exhausting being a grad student and teaching assistant dealing with hordes of students all day. Life is so much easier when you can just travel the world doing interviews and pitching your latest mystery novel and having people pamper you."

"If only," he chuckled, rolling his eyes. "Come on, let's see what they have before you smother me with your sarcasm."

Craig led the way to the food tables, where the aroma of baked goods filled the air.

"Look at all these cookies!" I exclaimed, reaching for a sugar cookie decorated with red, white, and blue sprinkles.

Craig chuckled as he snatched one too. "Don't tell anyone, but I can't resist anything with sprinkles."

"Your secret's safe with me," I promised, laughing.

After filling our plates, we moved to a quiet spot in the corner—better for observing the gathering.

As we ate and speculated about why the coach wanted to talk to us, I noticed a tall male skater wearing a blue warmup jacket engaged in a heated discussion with Eric nearby.

In a low but intense voice, the guy who, by process of elimination, I assumed was Jason, said, "I don't like it. He's always playing favorites with them."

After making eye contact with me, Eric glanced around the room before turning back to Jason and muttering, "Keep your voice down. Too many ears in this place."

Jason shook his head, his sandy blond hair framing his face. "Sure, you're not the one who got hurt."

My eyes followed him as he stormed away, joining Cherie, Katie, and a third female skater, most likely Naomi, by the food table. Cherie looked over her shoulder at Eric and then leaned closer to Jason and whispered something in his ear.

Craig tapped my arm. "Let's go find the coaches' lounge."

In just a few moments, Coach Wyatt joined us, closing the door behind him.

"What's up, Coach?" Craig asked. "You wanted to talk to us?"

Coach Wyatt gestured toward one of the two well-worn couches. Craig and I exchanged glances, puzzled. The coach retrieved some papers from a locker and then settled onto the couch opposite us, lifting one of the papers in the air.

"I wanted you to see this," he began, handing it to Craig. "It all started a couple of months ago."

Craig read it, then passed it to me.

I scanned its contents: *You can run but can't hide. It won't be long before the world knows the truth about why your skaters are always winning. Time is running out. Either you come clean, or I will tell the world.*

I laid the paper in my lap. "Coach, do you know what they're talking about?"

He shook his head, concern weighing on his face. "The only thing I can think of is…and this is difficult for me to even give credence to, but there was a rumor goin' round at our previous rink that some of my skaters were usin' performance enhancin' drugs. At least, that's how the story started. Like most lies, it grew until there were whispers I was dopin' my skaters *and* bribin' judges. That contributed to my decision to take my team and leave. The rumors were becomin' too much of a distraction. I hoped that by relocatin', my skaters and I could remove ourselves from all the gossip and get a fresh start, but yesterday afternoon, I received this." He handed another paper to Craig.

Craig flipped it over, absorbing its contents before passing it to me. As I read it, Craig asked, "I have to ask, Coach, are the rumors true?"

Coach's eyes widened with indignation as he sprang to his feet. "I would never jeopardize the well-bein' of my skaters by givin' them drugs, and I hardly need to pay off judges. My skaters are among the best in the world. We don't have to cheat to win."

Craig met the coach's gaze. "I understand that, sir, but to answer my question, is that a definitive no?"

Exasperated, the coach grunted. "I am absolutely not dealin' drugs, and I am not payin' off judges." He took a deep breath and continued. "But as disturbin' as those rumors are, they're not my most pressin' concern right now. This is. I received it yesterday."

The coach handed Craig yet another note. With a heavy sigh, Craig passed it to me, and as I read the words: *You must be punished. Prepare to meet your Maker,* a shiver ran down my spine.

I leaned forward. "Do you have any idea who started the rumors or sent this death threat?"

Coach Wyatt stared into the distance, pondering. After a moment, he replied, "I assumed another coach started the rumors." He took a deep breath. "There's one in particular who has been quite vocal about my women's singles skater beatin' out his for a spot on the podium at Nationals and Worlds. And then there's pairs skating, which is no less cutthroat. I'm sure I've made some enemies there as well. I'm a-sittin' target with possibly three Olympic medalists." He shook his head. "I thought it might be him, but truth be told, it could be anyone. At least, that's what I thought until I received these last two notes."

"Why's that?" I asked, intrigued by the shift in his narrative.

"Because someone left them in my locker," Coach Wyatt said, his voice tinged with tension as a grim expression crept across his face. "This means whoever sent them is here in Petersburg and has it out for me."

He took a deep breath before continuing. "That's why I've asked you here. It's becomin' painfully obvious that the writer of these notes is likely someone from my team. I'm too close to them to see things clearly. I can't believe one of them would stoop so low, but what other conclusion can I draw? Who else would have access to my locker?"

With the death threat still in my hand, I asked, "Have you contacted the police about the death threat?"

Coach paused, his gaze thoughtful. "No, I have not. I know I should, but I am hopin' that durin' this reception and at the house, you'll pick up on somethin' I've missed. You know that old sayin', 'You can't see the forest for the trees'? I admit, it's hard for me to identify the culprit when I have such unwaverin' trust in all my skaters."

As he spoke, his anguish was undeniable. "And as far as callin' the police…if the threat is from one of my skaters, I would rather deal with it myself. The last thing I want is to ruin someone's reputation with an arrest when there's a chance we can clear up whatever misunderstandin' has led to this behavior."

A sudden knock on the lounge door startled us.

"Yes," Coach Wyatt snapped as he jerked his head toward the source of the interruption.

A voice from the other side called through the door. "Mr. Ryan is looking for you. He wants to introduce you and the team to everybody and have you say a few words."

Straightening his tie and inhaling deeply, Coach Wyatt declared, "Well, I guess it's showtime. Shall we go?"

Craig and I trailed behind him into the lobby, finding a spot in the back as the introductions began. We listened attentively as Mr. Ryan introduced Coach Wyatt and his skaters. Taking the microphone, the coach shared his insights into training his skaters for the Olympics and his excitement about starting the pairs and ice dancing programs for the Petersburg Skating Club.

Just as Coach concluded his remarks, a woman he had introduced as the team choreographer approached us with a warm smile. Olga's dark brown hair, fashioned in a ballet bun atop her head, and her fitted, soft black top paired with pink leg warmers over black trousers gave her the air of the dancer I assumed she was.

"Hello. I'm Olga," she said. "Coach Wyatt wanted me to show you another exit to use to avoid all this commotion. He'll meet you in the parking lot in a few minutes."

Craig and I followed her as she skillfully guided us across the rink's slick surface, leading us to a room that housed the ice resurfacing machine. We stopped at the steel door that opened to the parking lot.

"If you'll wait here," Olga said, adjusting the strap of her purse, "Coach Wyatt will be with you shortly. I've got to go and get things ready for dinner." She flashed a quick, knowing smile. "See you at the house."

As soon as she disappeared from view, I blurted out, "How does she manage to walk on the ice in those platform shoes? I almost fell, and I'm wearing loafers!"

Craig chuckled, shaking his head. "I don't know, but I guess working on the ice all day, you learn how to stay on your feet."

True to Olga's word, Coach Wyatt arrived shortly afterward, and we eagerly followed him through the tree-lined streets of Petersburg to the house where the skaters were staying. When Craig pulled up to the curb, I stared out the windshield in disbelief. I couldn't believe what I was seeing.

"Oh, my word! When he said he was renting a big house, I had no idea he was talking about the old Hathaway House!" I exclaimed.

"Hathaway House?" Craig echoed.

"Yeah, in the late 1800s, Charles Hathaway started the glass industry around here. He even built the art museum on campus," I explained, the excitement flooding back as I recalled the stories I had heard growing up. "They used to open the house up at Christmas time, but I was never able to go. Man, I knew the family moved out a long time ago, but I had no idea it was rental property now. That's crazy."

Overwhelmed, I threw open my door. "Come on. I want to see the inside."

As we drew near the house, Coach Wyatt opened the front door and ushered us inside with a warm smile. The soft glow from a brass chandelier lit the entryway, and the faint clatter of dishes drifted in from the kitchen. He took my jacket with a polite nod and carefully hung it in a mahogany coat closet that carried a faint scent of cedar

While Coach and Craig shared stories about their agent, Suzette, I couldn't help but notice how much the coach's leisurely Southern drawl reminded me of my maternal grandfather, who hailed from the deep South. There was a familiar, unhurried grace to his manner—like he had all the time in the world—which made me want to kick off my shoes and settle in, as if we were old friends rather than recent acquaintances.

As the two of them continued talking, I took in the living room: green and gold damask wallpaper lent a formal air, while an antique mantle clock ticked softly above a carved marble fireplace. Yet the elegance had been tempered by function. Ballet barres ran along the walls, portable mirrors were propped up here and there, and yoga mats were scattered across the shiny hardwood floor. The room felt like part old mansion, part workout zone.

"Ah, yes," Coach Wyatt chuckled as he caught my eye. "You've spotted our ballet room. It might not be pretty, but it serves its purpose and gets the job done. This old house has a lot of rooms, but so many of them are small. This is one of the larger ones."

An idea sparked in my mind as I studied the basic setup. "You know," I glanced toward Craig. "Rick's mother might be able to help."

I shifted my focus back to Coach Wyatt. "Rick is a friend of ours from the University's Commuter Lounge. His mother opened the Petersburg Health and Fitness Center in December. There's a room for ballet. It's not all decorated yet, but it's functional. I'm sure Caroline would be happy to work something out with you, and it's not too far from the university."

"Sounds like a good idea," Coach replied, brightening at the suggestion. "If you give me her number, I'll call her. The university offered us access to their dance room, but the hours when it's available don't mesh with our schedule. Havin' an option outside these four walls would be downright nice." He glanced around the cramped workout area. "With eight people vyin' for the same equipment, it can sometimes try everyone's patience."

"I can only imagine. Let me see if I remember who all is on your team." I took a deep breath as I tried to recall tonight's introductions. "You've got two pairs teams and two singles skaters. That's six people. Who am I missing?"

"Don't forget Olga, our choreographer," Coach chuckled. "She likes to map out elements of her programs off the ice before she gives them to the skaters. And then there's Danny. Considerate boy—only said he would use the equipment when no one else wanted it. One big happy family." He paused, and his face sank as he continued. "At least, that's what I thought."

The moment hung in the air, heavy with things left unsaid. But before I could respond, the sharp thud of car doors slamming cut through the silence. Coach's shoulders squared, and he smiled as he adjusted his tie. "Sounds like everyone's home. Time for Round Two."

chapter five

Coach Wyatt returned to the front door, holding it open as his team filed into the house. He held up a hand to stop the last two.

"Jason. Naomi. I didn't get a chance to introduce you to Craig and Michelle earlier. They're the reporters I told you about."

We exchanged pleasantries, and it became clear from the way Jason and Naomi looked at each other that their connection extended beyond the ice.

Jason slipped his arm around Naomi's petite frame, and that's when I noticed his wrapped hand.

I remembered him saying at the Meet-and-Greet, "You're not the one who got hurt." I hadn't noticed the injury then, but now there was no way not to see it.

After a few minutes of polite conversation, Jason said, "If you'll excuse us, we need to get ready for dinner. See you in a few minutes."

The couple disappeared up the stairs, leaving me wondering what, exactly, had happened to his hand and what secrets the team might be hiding.

Alone again, Coach gestured for Craig and me to follow

him into the dining room. "Shall we take our seats? Everyone should be down soon."

He directed us to opposite sides of a beautifully set table draped in crisp white linen and topped with a floral centerpiece of deep red roses and white lilies. Ornate silver candlesticks flanked the arrangement, their tapers already lit and casting a soft, golden glow. I sank into a high-backed chair, the velvet upholstery cool against my fingertips, and let my eyes wander.

The room exuded old-world charm—plush burgundy drapes framed massive windows overlooking the shadowed garden outside. Crown molding traced the high ceiling, and a glittering crystal chandelier hung overhead. A grandfather clock stood in one corner, ticking softly, and a sideboard along the far wall held an elegant silver tea service and porcelain figurines that looked far too delicate to touch.

The setting was far more formal than I'd expected for dinner, and for a moment, I felt completely underdressed. That is until the skaters filtered in, casually dressed in jeans and sweaters, chatting easily as they found their seats.

I toyed with the Eiffel Tower charm dangling from my necklace and then brushed my hair away from my face while trying to decide which fork I should use for the salad.

My thoughts drifted from flatware to whether I should dive straight into asking my dinner partners about the threatening notes or start with something more casual, like the weather?

For me, asking about the sacrifices the skaters were making—being away from family, physically demanding training, and the financial burden of chasing their dreams— was straightforward, easy, and necessary for my article.

However, tonight's challenge was more complex. Not only did I need information for the newspaper, but I needed to get Jason and Eric, seated on either side of me, to open up about tensions within their team and possibly implicate one of their own.

With a tinge of jealousy, I watched Craig chatting with Cherie. Her big brown eyes sparkled as they laughed. Talking to strangers came so easily for him.

Perhaps sensing my discomfort, Craig glanced at me and gave me a reassuring wink with a slight nod as if he was sending me a message: "You've got this!"

Grandma Kilpatrick, a champion of etiquette, taught me from a young age the importance of proper conversation at formal dinners. She stressed that during the first half of the meal, the woman must always speak to the gentleman seated to their right. Following her guidance, I turned to Jason. "So, how long have you been training with Coach Wyatt?"

Jason flashed a grin, but his piercing blue eyes narrowed. "Naomi and I have been with Coach for three years," he said, then quickly dropped his gaze back to his plate.

I pushed my green beans around, trying to shake off the awkwardness. "How do you like Petersburg? Have you had any time to explore the area?" I tried to keep my voice upbeat, hoping to draw him into a conversation.

He took a sip of water. "We haven't had much time outside of the rink since we got here." With a shrug, eyes returning to his plate, he added, "But from what I've seen, it seems nice enough."

The sign of a good conversation is the back and forth, like a dance of words between the participants. Jason was playing it safe, more interested in eating than in conversing, or was he avoiding me?

Usually, I wouldn't mind and might even feel relieved to not have the pressure to engage. But tonight was different. I needed him to open up so I could get information about his teammates.

When he brushed a stray blond hair from his forehead with his wrapped hand, I saw an opportunity.

"What happened to your hand?" I asked, gently nudging his arm.

Startled, Jason sat upright, looking between his hand and me and back at his hand. "Oh, it's no big deal. Naomi and I were practicing a lift, and her blade got me." He gave a light chuckle, dropping his eyes again. "All in a day's work, I guess."

"Lucky it wasn't worse," I said. "I understand you're hoping to make the Olympic team next year."

"That's the game plan. That is if Coach gives us a chance."

I leaned in. "What do you mean? Doesn't he want all his teams to qualify?"

Jason hesitated, his eyes darting briefly to Danny, who sat across from us, his gaze fixed intently on Jason. Perhaps it was my imagination, but the air in the room seemed to thicken as they exchanged silent glances charged with unspoken tension.

Katie nudged Eric's shoulder and gave him a questioning look.

For a moment, the mood lightened ever so slightly as Jason cleared his throat and said, "Of course."

However, the lull did not last long. Danny and Jason's eyes locked again, and the heaviness in the air grew more intense. They shifted in their seats before turning away from each other and returning to their plates, the clinking of cutlery breaking the silence.

Trying to dispel the tension between Danny and Jason, I took a sip of water and thought of a new topic. "I heard some skaters had their equipment stolen at your old rink. That's awful. Do you have any idea who might've done it?"

A troubled expression crossed Jason's face as he dabbed his lips with his napkin. "Sorry," he said. "I'm not feeling well. I think I'll go lie down. I'm sure I'll see you later."

As Jason gathered his plate and silverware, I sighed. The coach hadn't yet indicated it was time to turn to our partners on the left, but with Jason's departure, my gaze drifted to Eric. With Olga, his other dinner partner, also gone, I figured it was as good a time as any to make my move."

Channeling my inner *professional journalist* thanks to Professor Ladd's tips, I knew I had to ask something engaging that wouldn't elicit a simple "yes" or "no" answer. If I wanted Eric to give me the inside scoop about the skating team, I needed to get him comfortable giving me more than one-word answers.

So, I started with something safe—the same question I had asked Jason. "How are you liking Petersburg?"

He lifted his glass to his lips and took a sip. Silence.

Undeterred, I tried again, "Do you like—."

"It's fine," he cut in and shrugged. "A little cold for April, but I spend most of my time in the rink anyway, so it doesn't really matter."

Okay, not the riveting response I was hoping for, but it was a start. I smiled, determined to steer the conversation back on track. Time to dig a little deeper. "How many hours do you practice a day?"

"Four to six on the ice and another one or two doing off-ice training like ballet or working out." He reached for the breadbasket, grabbing a roll before offering the basket to me.

Shaking my head, I asked, "Every day?" As soon as the words left my mouth, I mentally kicked myself for breaking my own rule against asking questions with one-word answers.

Eric paused for a moment as he meticulously spread butter on his dinner roll. "No. Coach insists we take Sundays off. He's a big believer in that whole *day of rest* thing," he replied, glancing up.

"That's not all bad. I'm sure everyone appreciates a break," I chuckled.

Eric's expression shifted, his voice dropping to a whisper. "You'd think so, but a few around here might prefer *his* day of rest to be more…permanent."

"So much for one big, happy family, huh?"

His eyes locked onto mine, intense and unyielding. "Every family has skeletons in their closet," he stated with no emotion.

His gaze drifted to Danny, who was sharing a laugh with Cherie. "Take that dude. Ever since he waltzed into our lives, things have gotten weird. Now, I'm not saying it's his fault, but is it a coincidence that equipment and tapes started going missing when he showed up? I don't think so."

I glanced back and forth between Danny and Eric as it occurred to me that neither Jason nor Eric had tried to hide their animosity for Danny. Everything in me wanted to dive deeper into whatever drama was happening.

Still, my instincts warned me now was not the time.

Instead, I played innocent, and even though I already knew the answer to my question,I asked, "Do you skate singles or pairs?"

"Singles. Definitely single in every sense of the word," he countered with a smirk. "I certainly don't need the complications that come with pairs skating. Talk about tearing a family apart…"

Just then, Eric stopped mid-sentence, acknowledging Olga sliding back into her seat.

"Now, Eric. Let's not stir up trouble," she said, giving him a side-eye that warned him to be quiet.

She then leaned over the table, addressing me directly. "Every family has squabbles, but in the end, we're a family, and families stick together." She paused; her brown eyes flickered toward Eric. "And when they don't, bad things happen. I don't think any of us want that, do we?"

Everything seemed to freeze at that moment. The carefree sound of chatter that had filled the room just seconds before disappeared. All eyes were on Eric and me. I glanced at Eric, shifting in his chair, pulling back as if he wanted to escape. Even Coach's warm smile vanished.

As if getting into character, Coach took a deep breath, regained his smile, and said, "Craig and Michelle. Why don't you go out to the patio while Olga and her crew clear the table and set up for dessert? I'll be right out."

Relieved, Craig and I made our way through the kitchen. The strains of Elton John's new release, "Philadelphia Freedom," and the clatter of dishes faded as Craig slid the patio door shut behind us. The fresh air was what I needed, dispelling the heavy weight of the awkward tension I had just experienced in the dining room.

As the two of us gathered on the cement pad, I inhaled the cool evening breeze and caught the faint aroma of wood smoke drifting from a neighbor's outdoor fireplace. The scent, mingled with the crisp breeze, eased my nerves as I waited for Coach to join us and begin what I assumed would be a serious conversation about his death threats.

I glanced up at the slim crescent moon, one of the few phases I remembered from my Astronomy 101 class last year, and an unsettling feeling swept over me despite the beauty of the evening sky. After talking to Jason and Eric, I knew all was not well with Coach Wyatt's team, but how was I supposed to tell him that his "big, happy family" was more an illusion than reality?

As much as I wanted to lose myself in the stillness of the night, the threatening notes and the incidents of sabotage kept creeping back into my thoughts. Before I could quiet my concerns, I heard the creak of the patio door opening.

Coach stepped outside wearing a cardigan sweater, replacing his blazer from earlier. He motioned for Craig and me to take a seat.

As the coach settled into a green and white webbed

folding lawn chair that had seen better days, he loosened his tie. But despite giving the appearance of a man ready to relax, there was an urgency in his voice. Leaning forward, he asked, "Did you learn anythin'? Do you have any leads on who might've sent the notes?"

Craig shook his head, his brow furrowed in frustration. "No, sir. Cherie and Naomi were very positive. Neither one had anything negative to say about anyone on the team, including you and Olga."

Coach Wyatt turned his attention toward me, his intense gaze locking onto my eyes. "And what about you, Miss Michelle? What did you find out?"

I hesitated for a moment, trying to choose my words wisely. "Well, sir, I got the distinct impression Jason thinks you're showing favoritism to Cherie and Ethan. And, Eric hinted at a lot of drama between the two pairs teams."

Coach Wyatt sat up straight and crossed his arms. His jaw clenched as he absorbed what I had said. "Jason ought to know better than that. Cherie and Ethan have been skatin' together longer and, naturally, have more difficult moves in their arsenal. It only makes sense they'd get higher scores than Naomi and Jason. Sure, Cherie and Ethan are favored to make the Olympic team, but I'm no fool. One stumble, one injury, and bam! Just like that, they're outta the runnin'." He snapped his fingers, the sound echoing in the quiet night. "That's why I always want my backup team, if I dare call them that, primed and ready. I *never* put all my eggs in one basket."

"Are Jason and Danny good friends?" I asked, leaning back in my chair.

Coach Wyatt took a moment as thoughts crossed his mind. "Danny's a likable young man. I reckon everyone 'round here thinks of him as a friend. Why do you ask?"

I shrugged, trying to hide my uneasiness with his assessment. "It's probably nothing, but I noticed when Jason started complaining, Danny shot him a look, and then Jason clammed up."

"Ah, Danny's a peacemaker. He's always been the one to patch things up. My guess is Jason was feelin' slighted, and Danny was just makin' sure he knew there was no cause for concern. That's just his way of tryin' to keep everybody happy."

Despite my reluctance to raise doubts about Danny's sincerity in Coach Wyatt's mind, I voiced my reservations. "Well, I'm not sure everyone would call Danny a peacemaker. Eric mentioned things have been weird since Danny came into their lives. Is there any truth to that?"

Coach Wyatt leaned back, the creases in his forehead growing more pronounced the longer he thought. "I can see why Eric might say that. All those incidents with the missin' tapes and skate guards happened after Danny started workin' at the rink. But I can't bring myself to suspect him of bein' up to no good. He's a dedicated worker with a reputation for doin' things the right way."

The coach turned toward Craig. "You're related to him, aren't you? You must know that he's of good character. It's amazin' when you think about his parents and all the trouble they caused."

Craig's shoulders dropped. "The fact is, I never met him until yesterday."

A puzzled look came across Coach's face.

Craig took a breath before continuing. "I didn't grow up in Petersburg, so our paths never crossed."

"That's a shame," the coach replied, shaking his head. "But trust me, once you get to know him, I'm sure you'll agree that he is incapable of committing these awful things plaguing me and my team."

I considered the coach's words. "While that may appear to

be true, we can't ignore the timing. The death threats started when Danny returned to Petersburg. It feels like more than a mere coincidence. We can't dismiss that he's possibly behind it." My eyes narrowed as I gazed at the coach, waiting for his reaction.

After a few moments of contemplation, Coach Wyatt nodded, understanding but not pleased. "I follow your reasonin', but truth be told, accordin' to your logic, any of my skaters could be a suspect or…all of them. Every one of them had the same opportunity and accessibility as Danny."

He shook his head as he slammed his fist on the arm of his chair. "Despite the evidence pointin' to someone on my team writin' the notes and stealin' equipment, there's got to be another explanation! I need you to find it."

A heavy silence followed the coach's outburst, and I couldn't shake the image of Olga stepping in to quiet Eric's complaints.

Despite the risk of further infuriating Coach Wyatt, I had to know more about her. I took a deep breath. "What about Olga? She seemed bothered by what Eric was telling me about the trouble between the pairs teams. What do you make of that?"

Coach furrowed his brows, and I could almost hear the gears turning in his brain. "Olga understands a house divided cannot stand. She's like the mama bear 'round here, always there for her cubs," he said, with a hint of admiration in his voice. "Everyone goes to her with their troubles, and she does a mighty fine job keepin' them all focused on their goals and learnin' the value of supportin' each other. Olga's an asset around here in more ways than one. I don't know what I would do without her."

The patio door swung open, bringing a halt to our conversation. Katie popped her head through the opening and said, "Coach, you've got a phone call."

Coach Wyatt glanced at his watch and frowned. "Now, who would be callin' me at this hour?" Rising from his chair, he shot Craig and me a quick glance and added, "Excuse me, y'all. I'll be back. If you need anythin', just ask Naomi. She's in the kitchen. She'll take good care of ya."

As Coach Wyatt attended to his call, Craig pulled his chair closer to mine. "Okay, so what did you *really* think about dinner?" he asked, his green eyes glinting with curiosity.

I shared my deeper concerns about Danny, Eric, and Jason. The latter two clearly did not trust Danny, and there was trouble brewing between the two pairs teams, whether or not Coach wanted to admit it. My guess was Olga was well aware of the drama but intent on Eric not cluing me in on the details.

I added, "I didn't get to talk to Katie. Did you?"

Craig shook his head. "No, she spent most of the evening talking to Danny or the coach. But, before Coach gets back, I want to tell you what Naomi said—I'd rather not say it in front of him...at least not yet."

I leaned in, eager to hear what he had to say.

He lowered his voice. "Naomi thinks Coach Wyatt and Olga have more than just a business relationship. She assured me nothing scandalous was happening—said it was more about the vibe between them when they're together. But she feels Olga is more invested in the relationship than Coach."

I raised my eyebrows, trying to wrap my head around it. "Really? I wonder how long that's been going on?" I took a deep breath and thought about the interactions at dinner tonight. I had noticed nothing between the coach and Olga, but then again, I wasn't looking for anything. When my thoughts drifted to Eric and Jason, another question came to me. "Did she mention anything about Jason's hand getting cut?"

Craig nodded. "Naomi said Coach Wyatt pushed them to

try a lift that was beyond their ability. That's what led to Jason's injury. She said if her blade had hit Jason in the head or had the cut been more severe, they might've been unable to compete in their next competition or, worse, the entire season. Naomi was still shaken up about it."

I took a moment to process it all: team dynamics on the rocks, a possible romance in the shadows, and a coach whose decision-making was putting a pairs team's future at risk. It was a lot to take in.

Perhaps sensing my unease, Craig placed his hand on top of mine. When the warmth of his skin touched my cold fingers, I sighed with relief.

"You're freezing," he said with that bright smile of his as he sandwiched my hands between his. "Here, is this better?"

"That does help," I admitted, trying to hide the blush I felt crawling up my face.

"Would you like my coat?" he offered.

I couldn't help but smile back. "Thanks, but I don't want you to get cold too. Do you think Coach would mind if we waited for him inside?" I replied, shivering. "I guess I should have grabbed my jacket before coming out here," I added with a little laugh.

Before Craig could respond, a dog's loud barking echoed through the night air.

Instinctively, I jumped up from my seat, squinting into the shadows.

"What's wrong?" Craig asked.

"I thought I saw something, but I guess not," I admitted, trying to shake off my nervousness.

Craig stood and peered into the darkness. "No. I don't see anything either, but I think it's safe to say we're not the only ones cold outside tonight. I bet that dog wants to go inside where it's warm." He extended his hand toward me. "Come on. Let's go see what's happening in the house. Maybe we can find someone willing to talk while we thaw out."

He slid the patio door open, letting me pass first. Naomi was heading from the kitchen to the dining room, balancing a slice of cherry-covered cheesecake in each hand, her head bopping to Earth, Wind & Fire's "Shining Star."

On the counter beside an empty pie dish, four more plates of my favorite dessert waited.

She glanced over her shoulder with a warm grin. "Can I get you something?"

I shook my head. "No thanks. Just came in to warm up. It's getting chilly out there."

My gaze drifted to a row of skates lined neatly along the wall, their silver blades catching the light. "Wow, that's a lot of skates!" I said, counting eight pairs.

Naomi chuckled. "They're not usually here. Mr. Hansen sharpens our blades. We usually grab them before practice, but he wanted to talk to Coach, so he dropped our skates off tonight to save us time in the morning."

"Mr. Hansen was here?" I inquired.

"You just missed him. Coach was on the phone, and you guys were here, so he didn't stay long—said it could wait."

A piercing scream tore through the house.

Naomi jumped, the plates crashing to the floor. Without hesitation, she bolted down the hallway. Craig and I followed on her heels.

Naomi flung open the office door, and the scene inside sent chills down my spine.

Cherie stood like a statue, pale and wide-eyed beside Coach Wyatt's motionless body.

Craig dropped to his knees and pressed two fingers to the man's throat, searching for a pulse. He looked up at me, and the grim expression on his face said what I already knew.

I stood in the doorway, paralyzed, as Cherie collapsed into Naomi's arms. Olga and Ethan barreled past me. Ethan wrapped his arms around Cherie and Naomi, while Olga dropped to the floor, sobbing as she flung herself over Coach's body.

Katie joined the shocked trio of skaters as I hurried to Olga, kneeling and putting my arms around her. After a few moments, Craig and I lifted her gently and guided her to an office chair, her body trembling.

Once Olga was seated, I yelled, "Someone call 911!"

"I'll do it," Ethan said, stepping forward. He reached for the phone on Coach's desk, but Craig stopped him.

"Use the one in the kitchen! Don't touch anything—the police might be able to get prints."

Police? Why would we need —

Then I saw it.

The scarf. White. Silk. Wrapped around Coach Wyatt's neck.

He had been strangled, and, as if matters couldn't get any worse, I had seen that scarf before.

But where?

The curtain fluttered. The door was ajar.

I stepped toward it, but Craig called out, "Don't touch it. Fingerprints, remember?"

He was right. This was now a crime scene. The police would want to preserve every bit of evidence and dust for prints. The less any of us touched, the better.

Ethan rejoined Cherie, Katie, and Naomi. The four huddled together, silent and lost in their grief. They looked at me with pleading eyes. Eyes that begged for answers I didn't have.

With an urgency to find clues, I scanned the room—two bookcases on either side of the oil painting of Charles Hathaway were behind the desk, and a few random plants by the windows. At that moment, I realized I had not seen Danny, Eric, and Jason since we discovered Coach's body. Where were they? My mind raced with the implications of their absence as I gazed at the scarf—the one that ended Coach Wyatt's life.

And then it hit me.

That scarf—

It was Danny's.

chapter six

The presence of death in a room is hard to explain. It's almost like an icy sensation creeps in, sucking the air out of everyone who experiences it. I had to escape its suffocating grip if there was any hope of clearing my head so I could think straight. I didn't hesitate. I bolted to the door.

"Are you okay?" Craig called behind me.

"I need to step outside for some fresh air. I'll wait for the EMTs," I replied.

Craig nodded, concern written on his face.

As I headed for the front door, memories of Coach Wyatt, Craig, and our conversation on the back porch flooded my mind. Not long ago, he was alive; now he was gone. Death had slipped into our lives like an unwelcome intruder, violently snatching away Coach's life.

Why did it feel like death was always right behind me, nipping at my heels?

Just last October, I discovered Professor Ladd dead in her office. Then, just before Christmas, Shelly passed away at the Petersburg Health and Fitness Center's open house. Unlike the movie *Death Takes a Holiday*, in real life, death never takes a break.

I replayed the last thirty minutes of the evening in my

head, a relentless loop of fragmented moments. If only the coach hadn't taken that phone call, or if Craig and I had come inside sooner, perhaps we could have done something to save him. A hundred *what-ifs* ran through my mind, but in the end, I knew such thoughts were pointless. Coach Wyatt was dead, three skaters were unaccounted for, and Danny's scarf was tied around the coach's neck.

Suddenly, the hallway erupted with heavy pounding. For a moment, I was confused—trying to figure out what was happening and where the noise was coming from. As the sound grew louder, I came to my senses. Someone was at the door. I raced to it and threw it open. The EMTs rushed in.

"Down the hall," I said, pointing toward the office.

As they hurried past, I was taken aback to see Detective Douglas and Lt. Grogan behind them. The detective didn't bother to conceal his exasperation as our eyes locked.

"Ms. Kilpatrick," he started, each syllable laced with a biting edge. "What are you doing here? No. Let me guess. You're working on another story."

The sarcasm underscoring his words was undeniable. How many times had I used *writing a story* to justify my sleuthing over the past several months?

I had lost track.

Unfortunately, he had not.

I didn't flinch but stood tall with my chin up and arms crossed, fully prepared to face the man in front of me. "Actually, Detective, I'm writing an article for the university paper on Coach Wyatt and his team."

I took a breath, realizing the focus for my story had changed drastically. "At least, I was…until this. Coach Wyatt invited Craig and me over for dinner tonight."

He nodded, his gaze probing as if he expected more details, but he stayed quiet, so I didn't elaborate further.

"Mr. Miller is here as well?" he grumbled. "Great, just

what I needed—the two of you tangled up in my murder investigation…again."

"Excuse me!" I stepped back. "It wasn't exactly my idea to be here when someone killed Coach."

He grunted. "Can you tell me who left in the limo?"

"What limo? The only person I know who left was Mr. Hansen. He's the rink manager. He dropped off some skates he had sharpened."

My stomach turned. "Not that same limo again?"

Detective Douglas frowned as he turned to Lt. Grogan. "Go back to the car and request patrols to watch for a black limo. I want that license plate. Got it?"

As he gave further instructions to Lt. Grogan, my mind raced with memories—how a limo seemed to appear every time something terrible happened: the cemetery when I was held at gunpoint, the parking lot at the fitness center, the guy putting the threatening note on my car, and now this—Coach Wyatt's neighborhood on the night someone strangled him.

Coincidence?

I didn't think so.

Detective Douglas's voice snapped me back to reality. "Hansen, you say? What time did he leave?"

"I don't know. Check with Naomi. She's the one who told me he was here."

He scribbled something down, then shot me a glance, barking orders. "Tell everyone to meet me in the living room, and no one, and I mean no one, is to leave the house until I say so. Understand?"

"Yes, sir," I said, trying to keep my voice steady while pretending to be in control of the situation.

I led the detective to the office, where he immediately summoned Olga and Craig. I left and made my way to the kitchen, where I found Naomi, Katie, and Cherie seated around the table, mascara leaving a trail down their cheeks.

The upbeat music from earlier now replaced by their soft sobs.

"Ummm…" I said, wanting to relay the info without intruding on their grief. "Detective Douglas wants us all in the living room. He'll be there in a few minutes."

I pulled open the patio door, stepping into a scene that was no less somber. Jason and Danny stood slouched against the railing while Eric and Ethan sat at the table, both looking lost in their thoughts.

All eyes shifted to me as I stepped onto the cement pad. "Sorry to interrupt, but the detective wants us all in the living room."

Danny straightened, concern flickering across his face. "Any idea what he wants?"

I shook my head. "Probably just to ask some questions, and…he said no one is supposed to leave."

Danny took a deep breath and walked past me into the house. The others followed like a line of little ducklings, leaving me to follow behind.

Craig intercepted me in the hallway. "Are you okay?" he asked, putting his arm around me and pulling me close.

"No. I can't believe he's dead." I replied, my voice barely above a whisper. "I should call my dad and let him know I'm going to be late. He's going to love this," I added, rolling my eyes to hide my anxiety. "Tell Detective Douglas I'll only be a couple of minutes."

The urgency to call my father was real, but it wasn't the only reason I wanted to delay entering the living room. With everyone there, the kitchen was my last hope for a few moments of solitude—a space where I could gather my thoughts and process the surreal events of the evening before facing the detective's relentless questions.

After stealing some precious alone time, I dialed my home number. The phone rang—five, six, seven, eight, nine times.

No answer.

That's strange. My father always answers the phone, and the answering machine is off.

I called again, my worry increasing with each unanswered ring. I couldn't shake the feeling that something was wrong.

Frowning, I peeked down at my wrist, tugging my sleeve to glimpse my watch. Almost 9:00 p.m.

"Michelle, are you coming?" Craig poked his head into the kitchen. "Douglas is asking for you."

"Tell him I'll be there in a minute. I'm trying to get a hold of my dad," I replied, the knot in my stomach tightening.

"Okay." He nodded. "But make it fast. He's getting impatient."

The dark stone in my mood ring caught the kitchen light as I redialed the number, my fingers crossed, in a silent prayer that my dad would pick up.

After it rang several times with no answer, I tried my sister Crystal's number, rubbing the charm on my neck-lace. *Please, please answer.* I was about to hang up when someone picked up, but it wasn't Crystal. It was her husband, Mel.

"Michelle, where are you? Are you home?" He sounded panicky.

"No, I'm at Coach Wyatt's house. He's been—"

"Listen, don't freak out, but your dad had to take your mom to the hospital. We had no idea how to get in touch with you."

My heart skipped, a fresh surge of fear washing over me. I pressed my back against the wall, trying to grasp what was happening. "What? What's going on? Is she okay?"

Mel's voice crackled over the line. "The doctor says she has some kind of pneumococcal bacteria in her bloodstream."

"She has pneumonia?"

"Yeah, uh, n…no. Not exactly." He paused. "I'm not sure. You'll have to talk to Crystal. She spoke with the doctor… something about having the same bacteria that causes pneumonia, but when it gets into the bloodstream, it creates a whole new set of problems."

I closed my eyes and let out a deep breath. "What hospital is she at?

"Petersburg General, but I doubt you'll be able to see her tonight. Visiting hours are almost over."

"Listen. I'm in a bit of a mess. Someone killed Coach Wyatt, and the police aren't letting any of us leave. I'll ask Detective Douglas if he'll let Craig drive me to the hospital. My car is at home." I paused, my heart racing. "Can you call the nurses' station and have them tell Crystal or my dad what's going on here? Tell them I'll be there as soon as I can."

I explained to Detective Douglas that my father had taken my mom to the hospital and that I needed to get there right away.

After taking a long breath, he frowned and said, "Fine. You and Craig can go, but you better stop by the station tomorrow to give your statements. Understand? No excuses. Tomorrow."

Craig and I nodded obediently, and the detective added, "And do not talk to any of Coach Wyatt's team or Mr. Hansen before I see you."

***

As Craig and I pushed through the hospital doors, each step fueled my determination to see my mother. But my resolve crumbled when I spotted the empty reception desk and the cardboard clock with its hands frozen. The sign "Will return" at 8 a.m. taunted me like a cruel joke. How was I supposed to plead my case if there was no one to listen?

Perhaps sensing my spirit wilting, Craig took my arm with a gentle grip. "Let's try this," he said, leading me to the elevator. He pressed the button for the second floor, and as the door slid open, my determination returned. I scanned the area for the nurses' station. Although no nurse was in sight, a lone candy striper sat perched on a stool at the corner of the counter, meticulously sorting through a stack of files.

"Excuse me. Can you help me?" I asked, my voice breaking the silence.

The girl, taken aback by my sudden intrusion, spun around. Her pink and white striped nurse's cap bobbed as her dark brown ponytail swung behind her.

"Sorry," I said. "I didn't mean to startle you."

Her laughter echoed softly in the empty corridor. "No, that's okay," she reassured me, a smile crossing her face. "I just didn't hear you come to the desk." She paused, wrinkling her nose. "I'm sorry but visiting hours ended half an hour ago."

I let out a heavy sigh. "Yeah, I know, but it's my mom. I just found out my dad brought her to the hospital tonight. I think he might still be here, but I don't know what room she's in. Is there any way you can find out for me? Her name is Nancy Kilpatrick."

She stood up, her pink and white uniform slightly crumpled from sitting. "I wish I could help, but I can't give you permission to see a patient after visiting hours—rules and all that."

There was no way I was going to back down, not when I was this close. "I know it's late, but I really need to see her. I just want to tell her I love her. I'll be quick. I promise. Please."

Out of nowhere, a voice boomed behind me. "Paula. When you finish those files, you can go home. I'll help these people."

Craig and I whipped around, finding ourselves face-to-face with the imposing figure of a stocky nurse, her stern expression like that of a drill sergeant ready to bark orders to "Drop and give me twenty!"

"Ma'am, I need to find my mother," I said, launching into

an abbreviated account of the night's chaotic events, hoping to appeal to her sense of compassion.

Her expression softened. "Sounds like you've had quite the evening. Tell me, what's your name, child?"

"Michelle…Michelle Kilpatrick. My mother is Nancy Kil—"

"Kilpatrick. Yes. I know. It's against policy, but your father has been worried about you."

"He has?"

"Yes, both he and your sister," she confirmed. "Now, why don't you and—" Her gaze shifted to Craig, assessing him like an overprotective lioness. "Is this young man family?"

"No, this is Craig," I replied with a smile. "He's not technically family, but he might as well be. I think my mom has adopted him."

"I see. Well, for tonight, the doctor is only allowing *immediate* family members in your mother's room. When she's stronger, that will change. Until then, Craig, you can wait for Michelle in the waiting room at the end of this hall. Michelle, follow me. Your mother's room is just around the corner. Your sister left a few minutes ago, but your father is still with your mom."

As I entered the dimly lit hospital room, my father straightened in his chair.

"We didn't know how to get in touch with you." His words were drenched with frustration despite his hushed tone.

"I know. I'm sorry. Craig and I were at Coach Wyatt's house. I didn't have a number to leave with you. Did the nurses tell you what happened?"

"Something about that coach being murdered and you being held for questioning," he said. "What in the world have you gotten yourself mixed up in this time?"

"First of all, we weren't being held for questioning. Detective Douglas was just trying to account for everyone's whereabouts and see if anyone had heard or seen something strange. He let Craig and me go so we could come here. We'll stop by the police station tomorrow and give our statements. We're not in trouble or anything."

"Well, that's a first," he retorted sarcastically.

I took a deep breath and shifted the focus to my mother. "How is Mom? What happened?"

"Her temperature kept going up, and then she started having trouble breathing. I called the doctor, and he said to get her to ER. With a high fever and her blood work showing an infection, they admitted her. The nurses have been trying all night to get her temperature down. Finally, someone suggested an ice bath," he said, shaking his head. "Your mother hated it, but it did the trick."

"Is her fever under control now? Is she going to be okay?"

"I don't know, Michelle. I just don't know," he said, rubbing his forehead. "One of her lungs has collapsed, and her white blood cell count is high. The doctor said it might be a couple of days before we know if she can fight this."

"Why? What else is going on?" My voice trembled.

"The doctor is concerned that the infection may have spread to her kidneys, heart, or spleen. They've got her on several IVs and will run tests tomorrow. After that, we'll have a better idea of how she's doing. Just pray she doesn't develop sepsis. That's the last thing she needs right now."

My father leaned back in his chair, looking at me with eyes heavy and worried. "Why don't you go home? There's nothing you can do tonight. I'll stay with her. I'll call if something changes." He sternly added, "You will be home, won't you?"

"Of course, I will," I said, biting my lip. "Should I skip class tomorrow and come to the hospital?"

He shook his head. "No. Go to school. We won't have the test results back until tomorrow afternoon, anyway. Maybe you can find time in your busy schedule to come to the hospital and check on your mother after school."

Holding back any defensive remarks, I nodded. "I'll stop by after class. Call me if you need anything tonight."

As I closed the door, I spotted Craig pacing in the hallway. Our eyes met, and he rushed to meet me. "How is she? What do the doctors say?"

I pressed my fingers to my temples, inhaled deeply, and exhaled slowly. "She's stable, but it's too soon to tell. We'll know more after they run some tests tomorrow."

Craig's arms encircled my shoulders, and he gently pulled me close. "It's going to be okay. The doctors will take care of her."

When I entered the hospital, I felt brave...strong even. I managed to keep my emotions under control while talking with my dad. Had I cried in front of him, he would have blown up. His tolerance for tears was nonexistent. But now, wrapped in the warmth of Craig's hug, the floodgates opened, and the tears I had held back streamed down my cheeks—every ounce of composure gone.

"How 'bout I take you home?" Craig asked, resting his head on mine.

"Yeah, that'd be great," I replied. "Dad's staying with Mom, but he told me to go home. What am I going to do? First, someone kills Coach Wyatt, then I find out that crazy limo was in the neighborhood, and now my mom's in the hospital. It's almost too much."

"I know. I know, but it'll be okay," Craig whispered. "We'll get through it together." He pushed the elevator door button and reached for my hand.

The dark stone in my ring was a beautiful shade of teal.

For the first time tonight, I felt safe.

chapter seven

Wednesday, April 16th

Ring. Ring. Ring. The sound sliced through the quiet of the night that had turned into morning. Groaning, I buried my head under my pillow, hoping the ringing would stop. Beside me, Gidget, my furry feline companion, pawed at my cheek, demanding that I take care of the annoying sound.

I rolled over, ignoring her pleas. The ringing stopped—briefly—then started again. Still half-asleep, I blinked.

Was I dreaming?

What was that awful noise?

With a start, I jolted upright—*the phone!*

I stumbled into the hallway and down the stairs, but by the time I reached the living room, the ringing stopped—again. I collapsed into my father's recliner by the phone, telling myself they'd call back if it was important and hoping it wasn't the hospital.

Clutching my mother's afghan, I cuddled underneath it—warm and cozy.

As my eyes closed, the phone rang, jarring me into the here and now.

"Hello?" I croaked, my voice thick with sleep.

"Michelle. Sorry to call so early." Craig's familiar voice came through the line.

"Craig?" The word came out scratchy, despite trying to sound wide awake. "What's up?"

"The police arrested Danny for the murder of Coach Wyatt."

"Huh? "I paused, his words sinking into my consciousness. "Danny? They think he killed the coach?"

"Yeah. Danny's scarf was around the coach's neck. After talking to the skaters and Hansen, the police think they have a solid case against him."

"Why? What did they tell the police?"

"Someone said they overheard Danny arguing with Coach Wyatt shortly before Cherie found his body."

Despite my suspicions that Danny was involved, it was hard to wrap my mind around him killing Coach Wyatt. He seemed like a decent enough guy. Why would he want the coach dead? It didn't make sense. I racked my sleep-deprived brain for possible explanations.

Sinking further into the recliner, I asked, "Are they positive it was Danny they heard and not someone else arguing with the coach? Did anyone see Danny leave the office?"

"Whoever told the police about the argument was certain it was Danny, and no, no one saw him come out, but remember the other door in the office?" Craig continued. "The one you wanted to close because of the draft? Well, it opens to a small porch, and the police found Danny's prints on the doorknob."

I rubbed my neck. "That doesn't sound good, but he doesn't strike me as someone who'd commit murder."

"Neither did his parents nor Sarah, if you think about it," Craig said. "Look, I know you're dealing with a lot right now with your mom in the hospital, but my mother wants us to help Danny. She's already been to see him at the jail this morning, and he claims he's innocent, that someone set him up."

"How does he explain that it was his scarf around the coach's neck?" I asked.

"Danny says he doesn't know how it ended up in the coach's office. He said he left it at the rink and planned to pick it up later."

"And what about the argument with Coach Wyatt?"

Craig sighed deeply. "Danny said he went to the office to talk to the coach. The door was open, but when he saw the coach was on the phone, he turned to leave. Coach told him to wait outside on the porch, that he'd only be a few minutes."

"Then what happened?"

"Danny claims that while waiting for the coach, he heard a noise in the bushes, so he went to investigate. When he was out by the fence, he heard someone scream and ran back to the office. Danny said he freaked out when he saw the coach lying on the floor with his scarf around his neck. He panicked and hid in the backyard."

I bit my bottom lip, troubled with doubt.

"Michelle?" Craig pressed. "Are you still there?"

"Yeah. I was thinking…Did he say when he got to the patio? He was with the other guys when I told them Detective Douglas wanted everyone in the living room."

"Danny said that after the EMTs arrived, he snuck into the house while you were talking to Detective Douglas and then went to the porch."

"Did he say if Cherie saw him by the door outside the office when she found the body? I don't remember her mentioning Danny at all."

Craig didn't hesitate to answer. "I asked him about that. He said she was so hysterical she probably didn't even notice him."

Danny's alibi was a little too perfect, with every detail accounted for. Yet, with no witnesses to substantiate his story, how could anyone prove he was telling the truth? In my opinion, the police had plenty of reasons to doubt his story—the evidence pointed to his guilt.

Still, I was curious about what Craig thought. "Do you believe him?"

"I think he's guilty, but my mother's hired a lawyer to represent him. The thing is, she wants us to prove Danny didn't kill Coach Wyatt. She doesn't want his case to go to trial."

I toyed with the afghan, rubbing my mother's handiwork between my fingers. "I...I...don't know. I want to help. I really do, but until my mom is home from the hospital, my father's going to need me to do extra stuff at home. I just don't see how I can swing it. Can't his sister help, or your mom hire a private investigator?"

"Linda's somewhere in Europe...her aunt wasn't forthcoming on her whereabouts. And you're right. Mom could hire a P.I., but she's convinced we can find the answers...fast. Like it or not, we've got a reputation for uncovering the truth."

"But what if the police have gotten to the truth? I'm sure they did a thorough investigation before arresting Danny. All the evidence points to him."

Craig let out an exasperated sigh. "Seriously? Even though I think the police are right about this one, you know as well as I do that once Detective Douglas sets his sights on someone, he stops looking for other clues. He's like a horse with blinders. He looks straight ahead and doesn't see anything off to the side."

"Yeah, you're right," I admitted, my shoulders slumping. "But I just don't know how I can help."

"I understand, but don't let *no* be your final answer. What's your schedule like today?"

"I'm on campus from 10 a.m. to 2 p.m. Then I need to run

by the hospital to visit my mom before I start work at 5:00 p.m."

"Any breaks between classes?"

"I'm free from noon till one."

"How 'bout I meet you at the Commuter Lounge at noon? We can talk more then," he suggested.

"Okay. I'm not sure my answer will be any different, but you can stop by."

"And don't forget, Douglas wants us to swing by the police station to give our statements today."

"Shoot! I forgot about that." I sighed, suddenly feeling the walls caving in around me. "Great. Now I have to figure out when to go to the police station."

"Don't worry about that now. We can talk about it at noon."

After I hung up, the stone in my mood ring was black—no surprise there. I was tired and getting more stressed by the minute. The day wasn't off to a great start, and it didn't look like it would get better soon, especially since I had to deal with Detective Douglas later.

Glancing at the clock, I had just enough time to get dressed for school, brush my teeth, and apply some makeup that would hopefully mask the dark bags under my eyes before T.J. pulled into the driveway.

***

As the grandfather clock chimed the half-hour, T.J. arrived —right on time. I hastily closed my bedroom window while the thumping bass of The Rolling Stones' "It's Only Rock 'n Roll" reverberated from his speakers through the crisp morning air.

I descended the porch steps and marched toward T.J.'s car. My determined stride syncing with the beat of the music. However, when I pulled on the passenger door handle, it didn't open. It was locked. I knocked on the window, but T.J. was lost in his own world, singing with his favorite lead vocalist, Mick Jagger, and oblivious to my plight.

Walking to the driver's side, I leaned over his window, which was rolled down, and shouted, "Little loud, isn't it?"

Startled, T.J. tore his gaze from the road and adjusted his aviator sunglasses.

"The door." I pointed to the other side and yelled, "It's locked. Can't. Open. The. Door."

T.J. nodded, reaching over to hit the door-lock button, popping it up. I crawled inside and buckled my seatbelt.

With the music still blaring, he was obviously not concerned in the least about either of us going deaf. So, I took it upon myself to turn down the volume ensuring I would be able to hear my professor's lecture this morning.

T.J. jerked his head toward me. "What'd you do that for?"

"Because I value my hearing." I shrugged. "What's up? Everything okay?"

T.J. fell silent, waiting for two cars to pass before pulling out of the driveway. It wasn't until we reached the stop sign that he finally spoke.

"It's Meg. We had another big fight last night," he confessed.

"But I thought you were going to work things out with Meg," I said, puzzled.

"Yeah, I thought I could, but we got into it again." T.J. sighed. "Do you realize I still haven't met her father? I don't understand why she won't introduce me to him. When I brought it up, she blew a gasket."

"I'm sorry."

"It's not your fault. I just don't get it," he mused, furrowing his brow in confusion. After a moment, he turned to me with a forced smile. "How was your night? Hopefully better than mine."

"Not exactly. My mom's in the hospital."

"Why? What happened?" T.J.'s voice shifted to concern.

"She's got pneumonia, and the bacteria got into her bloodstream."

"Is she going to be okay?"

"She should be. It's going to take some time for the antibiotics to work. I called the nurses' station this morning, and they said she had a good night. Dad stayed with her. I'll visit her tonight."

"Wow. I had no idea." T.J. murmured, placing a comforting hand on mine.

"That's not all." I paused and took a deep breath. "Someone murdered Coach Wyatt last night."

"Murdered? What happened?" T.J. asked, his eyes wide with disbelief. "How'd you find out? Was it on the news?"

"I'm sure it was, but—"

"Wait. Don't tell me you were there when it happened. You and Craig went to his house for dinner last night, didn't you?"

"Yeah. We were there when he was killed." A shiver ran down my spine, recalling the events of the previous evening. "One minute, he was talking to us on the back porch, and the next, he was lying dead on the floor in his office."

"I'm sorry, Michelle, but man, how many times have I told you that Craig is bad news? Trouble follows that dude wherever he goes." He paused. "Do the police know who snuffed the coach?"

"Danny Goodright. At least, that's what they think. His scarf was around Coach Wyatt's neck, and someone overheard them arguing."

"Sounds like the apple didn't fall far from the tree," T.J. said, referring to Danny's parents. "What is it with that family? Do they kill anyone who gets in their way?"

I shrugged and leaned back against my seat. "It's not fair

to judge Danny just because of his parents. He said he didn't do it, and after thinking about it, I'm starting to believe him."

T.J. glanced in my direction. "But you said his scarf was the murder weapon and that he and the coach had an argument?"

"Yeah, but Danny said he didn't have the scarf at the house. He left it at the rink that day and denies that he and Coach had an argument," I countered, my mind racing. "Weird things have been happening with Coach Wyatt and the skaters—missing equipment, threatening notes. I don't think it's out of the realm of possibility that Danny was framed."

T.J.'s knuckles tightened around the steering wheel. "You're not thinking about getting involved, are you?"

I let out a deep sigh and grasped the Eiffel Tower charm around my neck. "Part of me would like to. I wanted to write an article about Coach Wyatt and his skaters and, well, that's toast now, but the investigation would give me a whole 'nother angle for a story—"

"You've got to be kidding, right? It sounds like the police have a solid case against Danny."

"But if he's innocent, I'd like to help."

T.J. raised his eyebrows, his voice rising. "That is *if* he's innocent."

"No need to get into such a tizzy," I sighed. "No matter how much I'd like to get involved, I can't...not with my mom in the hospital. My family needs me."

T.J. relaxed his grip on the steering wheel, a re-lieved smile creeping across his face. "Music to my ears. I'm glad you're going to stay out of it."

"Yeah," I said, gazing out the window. Despite my logical reasoning for not investigating Coach Wyatt's murder, I felt the nagging urge to uncover the truth. What if Danny was in-nocent? If so, it meant the real killer was still out there.

Restless, I shifted in my seat, knowing that for my own

peace of mind, I needed assurance that Detective Douglas had the right person in custody. But how could I make that happen?

I glanced at T.J., his eyes focused on the road and, as usual, not a hair out of place. He'd never understand it if I got involved in the investigation.

Yet, I knew if an opening came my way, I was going to take it.

***

After my first class, I descended the stairs to the Commuter Lounge. The aroma of coffee grew stronger as I moved closer to my friends sitting at our tables.

The coffeemaker was pushed next to the wall, and I instinctively scanned the room for any sign of Alice. As expected—since brewing our black-market liquid depended upon her absence—she was nowhere in sight.

I placed my books on the table, glancing at Tasha, Billy, Jimmy, T.J., Lawrence, and Amy, who was shuffling a deck of cards. A coffee cup sat in front of each one.

I pulled out the chair opposite T.J. "Looks like this coffee thing is going well."

T.J. grinned, his eyes sparkling as he took a sip of coffee. "This is such a good idea. I can't believe we didn't think of this sooner. I'm going to save so much money!"

I leaned in slightly. "Any trouble with Alice?"

T.J.'s smile grew wider. "So far, everything's cool. We lucked out. She's gone for the rest of the week at some conference…won't be back until next Monday."

"Wow! That makes life easier!"

"It sure does," Jimmy chimed in with a gleam in his eye. "In fact, this entire enterprise has me thinking. Why don't we turn it into some kind of club like the Commuter Lounge Coffee Crew? Who knows? Maybe we'll start a movement on campuses nationwide. I can't believe we're the only ones who hate getting gouged by The Man."

I cocked my head. "What do you mean? A club?"

Ever the voice of reason, Lawrence placed his arm on Jimmy's shoulder and explained, "Jimmy, my man, wants to write a constitution and elect officers. You know, the whole nine yards."

"Why am I not surprised, coming from the future president of the United States?" Amy teased, winking at Jimmy.

"So, when do we start with your great idea?" I asked.

Jimmy beamed. "Rick said we could meet at his place Saturday night. Does that sound good to everybody?" He scanned the table as nods of agreement rippled through the group. "Then it's settled. This weekend, a new adventure awaits!"

As chatter resumed at our table, I felt a flicker of excitement amid my concerns for Danny and my mom. Perhaps this new *adventure* would be just the distraction I needed.

But then again, what if it wasn't?

chapter eight

"Did someone say my name?" Rick asked with a chuckle, dropping his books on the table and sliding into the seat next to mine.

"Yeah, dude," Jimmy said with a grin. "I was telling them about the plans for Saturday night at your house. We're still on, right?"

"Definitely," Rick said, rolling up the sleeves of his green paisley shirt as he leaned back and turned to me. "You gonna make it?" he asked as he deposited some coins into the jar and poured himself a cup of coffee. "Or," he paused, his eyes darting to the cup in his hand, "do you work that night?"

"I do, but Mae closes the shop early on Saturdays, so I should be able to come as long as my mom is doing better."

Rick's brown eyes narrowed. "What's wrong with your mom?"

I explained, "She's in the hospital with pneumonia, but I'm hoping she'll come home in a few days."

"Sorry, she's sick. That's a real bummer." He took a sip of coffee. "I don't suppose you've seen *Tommy* yet with every-thing going on?"

"No, but the reviews I read said it was good. I'd like to see it. I just haven't had the time. Have you?"

A high-pitched screeching noise cut through the air.

We both jumped, then laughed when we spotted the source of the screeching—a metal chair scraping across the tile.

"Oops," Craig sheepishly said as he pulled his chair beside T. J.

He draped his blazer over the back of his seat and asked Rick, "How's your mother doing these days? Things shaping up at the fitness center?"

"Business is booming. She couldn't be happier. Well, for the most part." Rick straightened. "She's still grappling with all that stuff surrounding Sarah. Man, I can't believe Sara fooled us. She only pretended to be Mom's friend so she could destroy the fitness center and get rid of her boyfriend's competition."

"She was quite the con artist, wasn't she?"

Rick nodded and, with a sad edge to his voice, added, "Sarah dying in jail has really upset my mom too. She thinks the mystery man who told Sarah to kill Shelly was behind it. And she worries that if the police don't catch him, he'll strike again."

"Speaking of Sarah..." Craig scanned the table until he spotted Lawrence, absorbed in a card game with Jimmy, Tasha, and Amy. "Lawrence, any updates on Sarah's case?"

With his poker cards fanned out in front of him, Lawrence peered over his glasses. "A few. Let me finish this hand first, then we can talk."

While Lawrence focused on his cards, Craig took the opportunity to launch into his pitch, outlining why I should join forces with him in uncovering the truth regarding Coach Wyatt's untimely demise.

"As I said," Craig stated, "I am skeptical about Danny's innocence, but my opinion may be influenced because he is Steve's and Barb's son. On the other hand, my mother has known him for years and thinks highly of him. She says he is nothing like his father. But then again, her judgment might not be the most reliable. She trusted Steve until he pulled the gun on her. But all that aside, she wants us to dig deeper into the coach's murder and get to the truth about what happened that night."

I sighed. "I get it, Craig, and I want to help, really, I do. But with my mom in the hospital and not knowing when she'll be back on her feet, I can't commit right now. I wish I could. If Danny is innocent, I don't want him taking the fall for something he didn't do, but I don't see how I can help." Shrugging, I shook my head. "My family's got to come first this time."

Craig started to speak, but T.J. cut him off. "Hey man, give her some space. She can't do it. Got it?"

Craig shot T.J. a look but stayed silent, reaching across the table to gently rest his hand on mine. "I understand. But promise me you'll think about it. You never know. Maybe you'll hear that your mom is going home today, and everything's all right. Will you at least consider helping?"

I glanced at T.J., his ears turning red in anger, then back to Craig, who was waiting for me to respond. I nodded, torn between my desire to delve into the mystery surrounding the coach's death—which could result in another investigative piece for the newspaper—and my responsibility to my family while my mom recovered. As much as I hated to turn down this opportunity, I had to act responsibly.

As I shifted in my chair, Ringo Starr's "It Don't Come Easy" echoed in my mind, and my shoulders sagged under the weight of my thoughts. Doing what was right sometimes came with its own complications.

Lawrence left the card game and settled into the seat next to me. "What's the deal with you guys? So serious this early in the day?"

"Just trying to recruit Michelle for a little project, that's all," Craig said, his eyes sparkling with mischief as he clasped his hands behind his head.

Lawrence reached across the table for the coffee pot. "By project, do you mean looking into Coach Wyatt's murder?"

"Yeah, can you believe this guy?" T.J. shook his head in frustration. "Her mom is in the hospital, and he wants to drag her into another one of his investigations."

"It isn't an investigation," Craig responded, a smirk on his lips. "We're not going to interfere with Detective Douglas's case. I just want to examine all the facts myself, and I could use Michelle's help.

T.J. protested. "She said she's—"

"Enough already," I blurted. "I already said I wasn't going to do it. Can we let it drop?"

"I agree," Lawrence chimed in, his brows slightly furrowed. "Now, if you'll all be quiet, I'd like to tell you what I learned regarding the Sarah mystery."

"We're all ears," I said, leaning forward slightly, hoping for news of a breakthrough in the case.

Lawrence took a deep breath and said nothing for a few moments. A wry grin crossed his face as he allowed the tension to swell before speaking. "Detective Douglas connected with one of the transferred guards. According to him, he and his partner were patrolling the section of the prison that housed Sarah's cell when they received orders to report to the warden's office. The guard who brought the message said he'd cover their post until they returned. But when they got to the warden's office, it was empty. They returned to their post, and, surprise, surprise, the dude was nowhere to be found. And when they did their rounds, guess who they found dead? Sarah."

"Who was this guard?" I asked, leaning on the table and cupping my chin.

"Not a clue." Lawrence shrugged. "The dude told Douglas

neither one of them had ever seen him. They assumed he was one of the new hires."

I thought for a moment, twisting my Eiffel Tower charm between my fingers. "So, how do we find out who he was?"

Before answering, Lawrence surveyed the room and lowered his voice. "Douglas called in a favor from a guy he knows who works in the prison records department and asked him for the tapes from that night."

"I thought the video of Sarah's cell was missing?" I asked.

"It is, but Douglas hopes there's a recording of the guy telling the guards to go to the office—they weren't by her cell at the time. If there's a tape, hopefully, we'll be able to read the name on the mystery guard's badge."

"But," I said, my eyes squinting, "there's no guarantee the name on the badge will be his." I shrugged. "He might have swiped someone's uniform."

"We thought of that, but it will give us a starting point," Lawrence said, his steel-gray eyes peering over the round, wire-rimmed glasses perched on his nose as he shifted in his chair.

"I know you're waiting on the tapes, but could the guard describe the guy?" I asked.

"He wasn't a lot of help—said he was a younger man, maybe early twenties, and had a slender build. Not much else."

Craig shook his head. "It's sounding more and more like part of a master plan, doesn't it?"

I twisted my neck from side to side, trying to relieve the tension knotting up in it. "Do you think the mystery guard could be the guy who told Sarah what to do?"

"That's the million-dollar question," Lawrence said.

"Speaking of million-dollar questions," Craig said, crossing his arms, "how strong is the case against Danny Goodright?"

Lawrence sat up. "Man, what is it with that Goodright

family? First, his mom and dad do away with Professor Ladd and embezzle money from the lumber company, and now their son kills the skating coach."

"As inclined as I am to agree with you, his guilt is yet to be determined," Craig said matter-of-factly.

"Yeah, man, I get you're related to the dude, but I'll tell ya, it doesn't look good. The coach ended up with Danny's scarf around his neck. A witness overheard Danny arguing with him, and Danny's fingerprints were on the doorknob leading outside. In my book, that's case closed."

Craig nodded. "Even so, I wonder why Danny would want to murder Coach Wyatt? What would he have to gain?"

Lawrence shrugged. "I have no idea. Why do people kill? Sometimes it doesn't make sense, but it happens."

He was right. Just because it didn't make sense that Danny would murder the coach didn't mean that he didn't do it. Perhaps things got out of control during the heat of their argument. Or maybe it was an accident. Of course, I'm not sure how you accidentally tie your scarf around someone's neck and choke them until they die. There has to be more to the story.

"Any idea what they were fighting about?" Rick asked.

"Yeah," I added. "I thought he and Coach Wyatt got along pretty well."

"Apparently not. According to a witness, Danny and the coach were shouting at each other. They couldn't make out what they were saying except for hearing Olga's name.

"That's weird," I said, furrowing my brows.

"Not really," Lawrence explained. "The rumor among the skaters is that Danny had a thing for Olga, their choreographer. But she was all about Coach Wyatt and wouldn't give Danny the time of day—there is a bit of an age difference between them. But, regardless, maybe he was jealous and decided to eliminate the competition."

I leaned back, processing Lawrence's theory. The idea that

Danny was infatuated with Olga didn't seem right. Granted, she looked exotic—long, wavy dark hair, delicate features, and olive complexion. But, as Lawrence said, she was quite a bit older than Danny. Despite her youthful energy, I guessed her to be in her mid-30s, younger than my mom but older than my sister. And more to the point, I never saw Danny paying much attention to Olga during last night's dinner. If he was so madly in love with her, wouldn't he have tried to get her attention or, at least, kept an eye on her? No. I didn't buy the idea that he had a crush on Olga. If anything struck me odd about Danny, it was the tension between him and Jason.

If I was going to accept the *jilted lover* motive, I needed more information. "So, you're telling me Danny killed Coach Wyatt over Olga? I don't see it," I said, scrunching my eyebrows.

"People have done some messed up stuff for way less than a shot at love," Lawrence shrugged. "Plus, it seems that Danny Boy was a bit of a power broker. I'm not sure what his game was, but the skaters were, for lack of a better word, scared of him. Some even thought he was behind the missing equipment and the notes Coach Wyatt was receiving."

I shook my head. "Sorry, but I just don't buy that Olga was the reason Danny would have killed Coach Wyatt. But I do agree there was tension between Danny and the skaters. I saw it between him and Jason and Eric. Which reminds me, do you know if Detective Douglas talked to Mr. Hansen yet? I suppose there's an off chance he heard the coach arguing with someone. Maybe he could identify the other voice."

"Douglas spoke with Hansen last night. He's supposed to come in later today to give his written statement, but with all the evidence, though, I'm not sure it'll make any difference what he did or did not hear," said Lawrence. "After all, we have a witness who saw Danny go into the office, and we have his scarf and fingerprints."

"I still think the police are overlooking something," I replied. "Think about it. Why would someone go to all the trouble of grabbing their scarf, most likely from their room, to strangle the coach in his office? I don't care what you or Detective Douglas say. The evidence might seem to point to Danny, but I can't believe he'd be dumb enough to use his own scarf, especially if the murder was premeditated like you're suggesting. I think he would have thought that through."

Craig nodded. "I agree. Although I can easily believe in Danny's guilt, the police may have stopped looking for clues too soon. Face it. We all know that when Douglas is convinced he's got his man, he stops looking."

I glanced at Lawrence. "Has Detective Douglas asked the team to stay in town? I mean, does he still need them available for questioning?"

"I wouldn't think so. He seems confident he has the evidence he needs, but then again, I can't say for sure," Lawrence replied. "But I do know that Douglas mentioned the team will be in Petersburg until after the memorial service the university is planning for next week."

"How will they keep up their training without a coach? That's got to be hard," I said.

"You got me there, but I suppose Olga will keep things going," Lawrence answered. "Who knows what will happen after the service? I have no idea how the skating world works. How long does it even take to get a new coach?"

Rehashing the events of last night, I remembered something, "Sorry to change the subject, but did Douglas mention if the police found the limo he saw?"

"No," Lawrence shook his head. "It's like it just vanished."

"That's too bad," said Rick. "I remember Michelle saying there was a limo at my mom's fitness center around the time Sarah murdered Shelly."

"Ah, yes. The mysterious limo," Craig sighed as his green eyes locked onto mine. "I wish they could have found it. Whoever was inside might be involved with the murder. Regardless, if Danny is not the killer, it will be up to us to clear his name. The police aren't going to do it. I wouldn't ask if it wasn't important."

Craig's voice dropped, each word underscored with urgency. "If you won't do it for Danny, do it for my mom. She deserves to know that if Danny stands trial for murder, it's because he's guilty, not because someone framed him."

He leaned over the table. "I know you're worried about your mom and dad, but I can help with that—" he glanced at T.J. "I'll do whatever your family or you need me to do. Plant crops. Clean. Cook. I'm at your service. Just think about it."

The image of Craig, famous NYC mystery writer, covered in dirt, sweaty and exhausted after planting vegetables with my dad made me almost want to take him up on it.

With his eyes fixed on mine, Craig added, "We're in this together. If Danny is innocent, we owe it to him to find out the truth. I need your help." He paused. "So, what do you say? Will you help?

Lawrence leaned over the table. "I don't want to influence your decision, but I've been thinking about what you just said…there may be more to this murder than what Douglas sees. You have a valid point about the scarf. I think if you—"

Lawrence stopped mid-sentence as someone stood behind me and tapped my shoulder.

Startled, I spun around and saw Melinda, one of the students who fills in for Alice when she's gone. As I opened my mouth to say "Hi," the words stalled in my throat. One look at her face and I knew something was wrong—really wrong.

"Michelle, there's a call for you in the office," she said, her tone serious.

It took a moment for her words to sink in. Who would be

trying to reach me at the Commuter Lounge? Who even knew I was here? My family—they were the only ones I could think of. As I stood, my hands trembling, Rick steadied me with a reassuring hand on my arm.

Once inside Alice's office, I approached her desk and picked up the receiver. "Hello? This is Michelle," I said, attempting to disguise my nerves.

After listening to the voice on the other end, I stumbled back to our table, my mind in a complete haze.

T.J. was the first to speak. "Everything okay?"

I paused, mustering my self-control as I gathered my books. "No." I shook my head. "It was my sister, Crystal. Mom's in ICU. Someone tried to kill her with an overdose of insulin in her IV. She's in a coma."

chapter nine

I spotted my family in the back corner when Craig and I arrived in the ICU waiting room. My sister Crystal, her long brown hair pulled into a tight bun, was hunched over with her husband Mel's arms wrapped around her. Suzie, my brother Mike's wife, sat on his other side, her hands twisting a gold chain around her wrist. Half-opened bags of chips, empty bottles of soft drinks, and a magazine flipped open to the latest spring fashions cluttered the coffee table in front of them.

The waiting room, decorated in muted shades of green and brown, gave off impersonal vibes. The green vinyl chairs, stark white walls, and faded floral prints on the walls did nothing to create the homey atmosphere I think someone was hoping to achieve. Instead, the area felt outdated and sterile. There was no doubt I was in a hospital.

Crystal leaped from her chair and threw her arms around me, holding me close as tears streamed down her face and dampened my shoulder. "I'm so glad you got here," she whispered. "Mike remembered you saying you went to the Commuter Lounge between classes, so I thought I'd try reaching you there." She turned to Craig and gave him a warm hug. "Thank you for coming with Michelle. I was worried about her driving—being upset and everything."

I glanced around the room and down the hallway as Crystal spoke with Craig. "Where are Dad and Mike? Are they here?"

"Only two people can be in Mom's room at a time," Crystal explained, her shoulders slumping as she collapsed back into her chair. "When Mike comes out, you can go in. Just...don't freak out. Mom's got a lot of wires and gadgets attached to her."

Craig and I slid into the seats next to her, while I asked, "How'd this happen? Why did someone give Mom insulin? She's not diabetic." My voice trembled.

Crystal heaved a deep sigh. "They think someone tried to kill her. There's no other explanation."

My eyes grew wide. "Why would anyone want to kill Mom?"

Crystal shook her head. "I have no idea, but Dad told me about the threatening note you received while you were investigating that girl's death at the fitness center. Maybe this is in retaliation for you not stopping your sleuthing?"

I leaned back, aghast. "You think I'm responsible for someone trying to kill Mom?"

"I didn't say that," she countered. "But what other explanation could there be? Mom's done nothing to hurt anyone, but it seems you've taken it upon yourself to upset some dangerous people."

"I can't believe you're blaming me. I would never do anything that would put Mom or Dad in harm's way."

"Yet, after you got the note, you kept looking into the whole treadmill thing, didn't you?"

I opened my mouth to defend myself but stopped when Craig placed his arm around me. "What's important is that your mother gets better," he said, his voice steady and reassuring. "Knowing why this happened is not as important right now as finding out who did it. We don't want them to try again."

The possibility of another attempt on my mom's life hadn't crossed my mind. What a horrible thought! My jaw tightened, and I clutched my charm. "You don't seriously think someone would try again, do you?"

Craig shrugged. "Until the authorities catch the person, anything is possible."

He leaned forward and glanced at Crystal, Mel, and Suzie. "Do you know if anyone saw a nurse or doctor who shouldn't have been on this floor go near your mom's room?"

Mel put his magazine down. "When Detective Douglas was here, he mentioned that one of the candy stripers noticed a young man dressed in scrubs coming out of Mom's room. She didn't think anything of it until she checked on Mom later and found her unresponsive. I guess the detective shares your concerns that the guy might try again. He posted an officer outside Mom's door to be on the safe side."

"Detective Douglas was here?" I inquired.

Crystal stiffened and, wearing her *I'm the big sister and you're in so much trouble look*, said, "Yeah, and when he learned the victim was your mother, he said something about not being surprised. Now, why would he say that?"

"How should I know? It's probably because I was at Coach Wyatt's house when he got murdered."

"How do you always end up around all these dead bodies?" Suzie asked.

"I don't know. Bad timing, I guess," I replied, shaking my head. "But I suppose it makes sense Detective Douglas is on Mom's case since it sounds like an attempted homicide." A chilling realization struck me. "Shoot! I almost forgot." I glanced at Craig. "We still need to go to the station and give him our statements. I thought maybe we could go between classes today."

With a calming smile, Craig said, "I think the good detective will understand why we haven't been there. But I'll tell you what—after we leave here, if there's time before your next class, we'll swing by and see if Douglas is around. If not, we'll go after your last class, and I can take you home, so T.J. doesn't have to wait."

"Okay," I nodded, glancing at my watch. "My next class starts in ten minutes, so depending on when we leave here, I might make part of it. But you know what? I think I'll skip it. I wouldn't be paying attention anyway."

"Whatever you're comfortable with," Craig said, his eyes peering over my shoulder.

I turned as Mike leaned over and hugged me. "How's my favorite co-ed?" He turned to Craig, extending his hand. "And Craig, glad you're here. How have you been, man?"

Mike plopped into the vacant chair next to Craig. As they exchanged pleasantries, I marveled at how well they got along. In many ways, they were complete opposites. My brother, three years older than me, embodied a rugged charm in his well-worn jeans, tennis shoes, and faded t-shirt. Meanwhile, with his crisp chinos, leather loafers, and blazer, Craig —a year younger than Mike—radiated a world of Ivy League polish and privilege.

The way they dressed was only one of their differences. Mike was a man of the land. Despite having no formal college education, he was well-learned in the science of agriculture. He taught himself about crop rotation, planting schedules, companion planting, and natural pest control. His calloused and stained hands were his badge of courage, which he proudly wore. I doubted there was a man alive who was more content with his chosen path.

At the opposite end of the spectrum was Craig, who had a prestigious education and a successful writing career. Yet, despite everything he had, he always seemed to be searching for something. He never seemed content. I sometimes wondered why Craig thrived on solving the crimes that came our way. The murders, of course, brought him no joy, but the challenge of uncovering clues and piecing them together certainly did. Perhaps that was why he was a mystery writer —he could solve the puzzles he created.

Mike thought highly of Craig, and even though Craig and I had ended our engagement, he still hoped we'd get back together. It was tough watching him bond with Craig, knowing that what Mike wished for was most likely not in the realm of possibilities.

"Hey, anybody home?" Mike pressed, reaching behind Craig and tapping my shoulder.

"What? Oh, I'm sorry. Did you say something?"

"Yeah, you can go in and see Mom. She's still in a coma, but the doctor said she might be able to hear you. Ignore Dad if he says anything cantankerous. He's just worried, okay?"

"Sure," I sighed. "I won't be long."

The hospital's fluorescent lights flickered overhead as I approached my mother's room. I wasn't prepared for what I saw—my mom lying in bed, her eyes closed, knowing she wasn't sleeping. I froze in the doorway, struggling to keep my tears in check. My mom looked so frail, so helpless.

Crystal's words replayed in my mind. What if she was right, and I was to blame?

As a lone tear escaped and trailed down my cheek, I bit my bottom lip and reminded myself *if* Mom could hear me, my sobs would upset her. I didn't want that.

I passed my father as I gingerly walked to the far side of her bed. He sat attentively, holding her hand through the railing.

"How's she doing?" I asked.

He glanced up, his brown eyes tired with worry, and sighed. "I don't know, Michelle. The doctor says she's stable. All we can do is wait." His focus returned to my mother, her eyes still closed, a white sheet tucked under her arms.

"Did they say how long—"

"I said, I don't know." The gruffness of his tone cut through me like a knife.

"I'm sorry, I was wondering—"

My father shook his head again and growled, "Like I said, I don't know."

Abandoning further attempts to talk to my father, I bent over the railing and kissed my mom's cheek. "I love you. Get better soon. We need you!" I swiftly looked away and stared at the wall, fighting back tears.

After a few moments, I returned my gaze to my mother. Had it not been for the tubes in her nose and her arms and the large observation window, I might have been able to convince myself she was resting and taking a much-needed nap. But such was not the case. Mom was sick—very sick.

I desperately longed to pull up a chair and stay by her side, but the tension between my father and me overshadowed any such desire. I realized my presence might be making him even more irritable. After all, if Crystal was right that my father blamed me for the attempt on my mother's life, I was most definitely the last person he wanted around.

With that thought in mind, I whispered, "I guess I better go so someone else can come in."

My father grunted in agreement, never moving his focus away from my mother's face.

"Well, okay…I'll see you later." I paused for a moment. "If you need anything, let me know."

Dad looked over his shoulder as I made my way to the door. "I'm sure you've got better things to do. Crystal and Mike will be here to help if I need something."

His words were the proverbial straw that broke the camel's back. As soon as the door slid shut behind me, I hurriedly walked past the guard and threw myself against the wall. A waterfall of tears trailed down my face.

Craig appeared by my side within a matter of seconds. "What's wrong? Is it your mom?"

"No…my dad…he blames me…" I managed through sobs.

"I'm sure he doesn't," protested Craig.

"Oh, no, I'm quite sure he does…everyone does." I looked into Craig's eyes and pleaded, "Can we go? I want to go now."

He wrapped his arms around me and held me close, stroking my hair. "It's going to be all right." Lifting my chin, he stared into my eyes. "Everything's going to be okay. Come on. Let's go."

As I wiped the tears from my cheeks, I told Crystal, Mel, Mike, and Suzie we were leaving. They tried their best to comfort me, assuring me Mom would be up and about soon, but I could feel the weight of Crystal's judgment as she said, "There's nothing *you* can do now but pray."

Mike rolled his eyes and hugged me. "Don't let her get to you," he whispered. "Crystal's just being a pain."

Craig and I walked in silence toward his silver Jaguar. The sunlight bouncing off it starkly contrasted with the drab hospital building behind us. As he held the passenger door open, I slid into my seat, jerked the seatbelt across my lap, snapped it closed with trembling fingers, and stared out the window.

"Campus or the police station?" Craig asked, turning to me as he started the engine.

I glanced at my watch. "Let's swing by campus. I need to leave a note on T.J.'s car, so he doesn't wait for me. Then we can go see Detective Douglas. I really want to get it over with."

"Mind if we listen to some music? It might clear our heads?"

"Sure. I don't care," I muttered, returning my gaze to the horizon.

Craig shuffled through his cassette tape collection, then the unmistakable click of a case opening, followed by the sounds of America's "Sister Golden Hair." As I hummed along and listened to the words, I wondered if he picked the song randomly or was subtly asking me to meet him halfway and help him determine Danny's guilt or innocence.

My mind wandered to the limo by Coach Wyatt's house that deadly night. Was it the same limo I saw at the cemetery when the Goodrights tried to kill Mae and me, or the one at the fitness center that fateful night? Could the vehicle be the very one that delivered the threatening note to my house?

The possibilities raced through my mind, and my head throbbed as I considered the implications. If there was a connection between Coach Wyatt's murder and the limo, then his death might tie back to the man who ordered Sarah to kill Shelly. What if the same man targeted my mother? The thought jolted me upright in my seat.

I knew my father needed me to pick up my mother's responsibilities while she recovered, and I didn't want to let him down. Yet, reflecting on the events of the past few months, I could only arrive at one conclusion.

Turning toward Craig, I blurted, "I'll do it. I'll help investigate Coach Wyatt's death, and if Danny didn't do it, we'll find out who did."

Craig's eyes widened. "Why this sudden change of heart? Don't get me wrong. I'm thrilled you're on board, but I'm a little taken aback, especially after the hard time Crystal gave you."

"That's exactly why. What if it was my fault that someone tried to kill my mother?"

"No. Don't say that. It's not your—"

"No," I interrupted. "You don't know that. I don't know that. The thing is, I'll never know unless I look into Coach Wyatt's death. My gut instinct tells me the limo at his house that night was not coincidental. I think the deaths of Professor Ladd, Shelly, Sarah, and Coach Wyatt—and now the attempt on my mom—are all connected. Don't ask me how, but I intend to find out, and no one is going to stop me."

chapter ten

As luck would have it…or not…Detective Douglas was the first person I saw when Craig and I entered the police station. The detective stood in front of Lawrence. One look at Lawrence's scowl told me their conversation was not going well.

His eyes flickered in our direction, revealing a hint of surprise mingled with frustration. But before he could respond, Detective Douglas turned his head and caught sight of us.

"Ms. Kilpatrick and Mr. Miller, how nice of you to find the time in your busy schedules to stop by. I assume you're here to give your statements," he said with an air of sarcasm.

"We said we'd come by," I shot back, my voice sharper than I intended. "But you can appreciate that my mother took precedence today. After all, someone did try to kill her," I added, narrowing my eyes. My patience was wearing thin.

Craig placed his hand on my arm. "Detective, I'm sure you understand our delay," he said, with an air of professionalism. "But we're here now. Where would you like us?"

A wry smile crept across Lawrence's face as he shuffled through papers. He kept his head down, undoubtedly eavesdropping and enjoying every word of the showdown.

"Lawrence," Detective Douglas barked over his shoulder, "escort these two *fine citizens* to the interrogation room. There's no need for you to stay with them. I trust they won't leave before I get there." He turned his gaze back to us, his brown eyes narrowing as they darted between Craig and me. "I'll be with you in a few minutes. Lawrence will show you the way. Try to stay out of trouble."

Lawrence set his papers on the counter with a soft thud and gestured for us to follow. "Right this way," he said, leading us down the stark white corridor. As Craig and I trailed behind him, I couldn't shake the memory of the last time Lawrence guided me through these fluorescent-lit halls when I was a murder suspect in Professor Anne Ladd's murder just a couple of months ago.

Although I wasn't under suspicion this time, thinking about the questions Detective Douglas might hurl my way filled me with dread. A tight knot formed in my stomach as I prepared myself for the possible conversation about someone trying to kill my mother. I could hear Douglas saying, "I told you so." And why wouldn't he? He had warned me to back off from investigating Shelly's death, but I had ignored his advice. Now, according to my father and sister, my mother was paying the price for my recklessness. I could only imagine Detective Douglas would echo their sentiments.

Absorbed in my thoughts, I almost missed Lawrence asking me, "So, what do you think? A blizzard this weekend?"

"What?" I turned my head, startled. "A blizzard. Are you kidding me?"

"Welcome back to the real world. Thought we lost you for a moment," he grinned.

"Yeah, sorry 'bout that. I was thinking about the first time Detective Douglas called me into his office."

"It's been a crazy ride the last few months, hasn't it? With that professor's murder, Shelly's death at the fitness center, and now this," he said, shaking his head as though he still couldn't quite believe the series of events. "You're practically a regular fixture around here."

"Great. Exactly what I always wanted," I remarked, half-jokingly.

"At least this time, you're not a suspect," Lawrence said, removing his wire-rimmed glasses. He breathed on the lenses before wiping them on his shirt sleeve and adjusting them on the bridge of his nose.

He gave a satisfied nod. "Things are definitely looking up."

Meanwhile, Craig leaned in, nudging me. "Look on the bright side. Perhaps we can learn something from Douglas to help with our investigation."

Lawrence froze. "Investigation? No, no, don't say another word. What was it Schultz used to say on *Hogan's Heroes*? 'I hear nothing'. Whatever you're up to, I don't want to know about it...at least not right now."

"Fair enough," I said before taking a deep breath. "Changing subjects. Has Detective Douglas made any progress on the identity of the mystery guard?"

Lawrence's posture grew rigid as he glanced over his shoulder. He took a cautious step closer, lowering his voice to a whisper. "Not now," he said, glancing toward the door. "There's too much going on, and if anyone thinks I'm feeding you information, they'll have me out of here in no time flat."

"Gotcha. I didn't mean to cause you any trouble."

"You didn't," he said as his eyes darted about the hallway before stopping in front of the Interrogation Room. "It's just that things have been tense around here the last few days. Everyone's on edge, but no one's talking. I have no idea what's going on."

We both flinched as a metal box clattered to the floor behind us. Lawrence leaned in closer, his voice barely above a whisper. "For now, I just want to keep my head down, stay alert, and focus on my job."

He pulled the door open. "Go ahead and take a seat. Douglas will be here in a couple of minutes. We'll talk later."

As Lawrence closed the door with a decisive click, Craig and I slid into the chairs on one side of the table. I glanced at the oversized mirror hanging on the wall and wondered if it was like the ones the police used on TV to observe suspects while they were waiting to be questioned. Of course, that also meant someone could be listening to our every word. My heart raced as I felt under the table for any hidden devices, the mere thought sending a wave of paranoia over me.

I nudged Craig. "Do you think they're watching us?"

Craig studied the mirror. "Most likely," he agreed, a glint of mischief sparking in his eyes. "Should we give them something to talk about?" With a wink, he flashed a playful smile into the mirror and made a funny face.

"That'll make them take us seriously," I chuckled, then sighed deeply. "I wonder what's taking Detective Douglas so long. I really just want to go home."

Craig smiled. "We've only been here a few minutes. Aren't you enjoying my company?"

"No offense, but it feels like an eternity since Lawrence shut that door."

Craig shrugged. "I would think Douglas would be here soon. But, then again, he might be trying to let us stew for a bit. I can't imagine why, though. We have nothing to hide. We're just here to give our statements."

I twisted my Eiffel Tower charm. "Be honest. Do you think someone tried to kill my mom because I didn't back off from investigating Shelly's death?"

Craig didn't answer.

"Do you?" I pressed, unable to conceal my desperation for his answer.

"I think you're asking me two different questions. First: Did the person who threatened you follow through and attack your mother?" He paused, his eyes darkening. "Possibly…probably."

My shoulders slumped as the weight of guilt engulfed me.

"But," Craig continued, "if you're asking me whether you bear any blame in this situation, the answer is unequivocally no. *You* did not try to kill your mother. *You* did not force anyone to inject insulin into her IV. The person responsible for that heinous act is to blame. He and he alone." He reached over, squeezing my hand. "Got that? He is the one at fault—not you. Don't let anyone convince you otherwise."

I nodded. His words, while comforting, unfortunately, did not erase my guilt, and for the next few minutes, we sat in silence. I leaned back in my chair, surveying the room from one side to the other, while Craig, still holding my hand, maintained a stoic demeanor, sitting straight and focused ahead. Only the tightness of his grip betrayed the tension simmering just below the surface.

I had almost convinced myself that Detective Douglas had forgotten about us when the door creaked open. He stepped in, followed by Lt. Grogan. Neither said a word as they sat across from us.

"Let's get right to the point, shall we?" Detective Douglas said, looking at Craig. "What can you tell me about last night when Coach Wyatt was murdered?"

"Coach Wyatt," Craig responded, his posture growing even more rigid, "invited Michelle and me to the Meet-and-Greet at the ice rink and dinner afterward at his house."

"And why did he invite both of you? Were you both friends of his?" the detective pressed.

Craig leaned forward, resting his elbows on the table. "Coach Wyatt and I have…or had…the same literary agent. He was writing a memoir and had recently signed with

Suzette. When she learned he was relocating to Petersburg, she suggested the two of us meet up, which we did at the ice rink on Monday. Since the school paper had asked Michelle to write a story about the coach, I thought it would also be a good opportunity for her to meet him. It was after our meeting that he invited us to dinner."

Lt. Grogan's pen flew across his notepad as he recorded Craig's answers, intermittently glancing up.

"So, to clarify, your dinner with Coach Wyatt was strictly social, nothing more?"

"Not exactly," I said. "When Craig and I met with Coach at the rink before the Meet-and-Greet, he told us about some problems he was having at his former rink, which led to his decision to train his team here."

"And those problems were?"

"Missing equipment and rumors that he was giving his skaters performance-enhancing drugs and... bribing judges," I said.

"I see," the detective continued, "So, Coach Wyatt brought his team here because of the trouble at his home rink?"

Craig and I nodded in agreement.

"Is that a yes?"

"Yes," we answered together.

"Did he discuss anything else with you?"

"Well...he was receiving some rather threatening notes while at the other rink, and he thought they would stop when he came here, but they didn't. He found one in his locker just the other day."

"And these threatening notes prompted him to seek your help?"

"I...I...guess so," I stammered.

The detective's eyes darted between Craig and me. "If he was so concerned about the threats, why didn't he go to the police? Or did you two tell him you could handle it better?"

The heat climbed up my face. "We did no such thing. He asked us to help and—"

"And what, Ms. Kilpatrick? You agreed because you are an experienced investigator?"

I jumped out of my chair. "No, it wasn't like that."

"And what was it like, Ms. Kilpatrick? Tell me why a college student would take on a case when the last one she got involved with put her family's life in danger?"

I sank into my seat. "He asked us to help. He thought if we talked to his skaters, they might tell us what was happening. That's all."

Lt. Grogan paused, his pen momentarily still, as he glanced at Detective Douglas, who remained focused on me.

Craig placed his arm around my shoulder. "Detective, our intentions were to help the coach by talking to his team. Had we discovered anything significant, we would have come to you with the information."

The detective's expression was skeptical. "Whether that would have been the case remains uncertain. Let's move on. Describe everyone's movements that night."

We recounted everything we could remember about the whereabouts of the skating team and Danny during and after dinner when Cherie found the coach's body and about Mr. Hansen dropping the skates off at the house. Lt. Grogan jotted down every word, occasionally asking us to repeat something.

Mentally and physically drained from reliving all the moments of that dreadful night, I wilted in my chair as the detective continued, "Let me get this straight. Danny's scarf was present at the crime scene when you discovered the coach's body. No one brought it in later?"

I addressed his obvious omission. "The scarf was around the coach's neck when we went into the office," I replied. "But that doesn't mean Danny strangled him. Someone else could have been out to frame him."

"And why would anyone want to frame Danny Goodright?" the detective asked, condescension ringing loud and clear.

"I have no idea," I shrugged, exasperated. "Maybe he was getting on someone's nerves, or...perhaps his scarf was easy to grab." I paused. "What if Coach Wyatt brought the scarf home from the rink? Danny said he left it there. If the scarf was in the office, anyone could have used it."

I watched Lt. Grogan jot my words on his paper, and when he finished, I continued. "Have you talked to Mr. Hansen? Did he see or hear anything?"

The detective stood abruptly, leaning over the table. "Ms. Kilpatrick, I think I can conduct an investigation without your help." He glanced at Craig and then back at me. "You're both free to go, but I must ask you...no, I'm ordering the two of you to stay out of this investigation. Now, if you'll excuse us, Lt. Grogan and I have other cases to work on. We'll be in touch if we have more questions. Good day."

He strode toward the door as Lt. Grogan slammed his notepad shut and put his pen back in his pocket, scrambling to follow the detective into the hallway. After the door clicked shut, Craig and I sat in silence, exchanging stunned glances as we assessed the situation.

Finally, Craig spoke. "Well, that was interesting. I think it's safe to say he doesn't buy the idea that someone might be trying to frame Danny."

I stood and pushed my chair under the table. "No surprise there. He's got his mind made up."

After taking a few steps toward the door, I stopped. "You know, it's funny, but the more I answered his questions, the more convinced I became that Danny is innocent. The evidence against him looks bad, but would he really strangle Coach Wyatt and then leave his own scarf wrapped around Coach's neck? No. It feels too much like a setup, and my money's on Eric. He didn't even try to hide his dislike for Danny at dinner, not for one moment."

Craig held the door open, lowering his voice, "We'll talk more in the car. They might still be listening."

I nodded and whispered, "You're right. Considering what happened to Sarah, we can't be too careful."

chapter eleven

Craig swung open the car door, and I slid into the red leather seat. My hands trembled as I fumbled with my seatbelt—a leftover case of nerves from dealing with Detective Douglas. But when I glanced at my watch, a fresh wave of anxiety washed over me.

"Oh, no," I gasped, "Your mom is going to hit the roof! I didn't realize it was so late. I'll never make it to work on time."

"Relax," Craig replied with a reassuring smile. "What time are you supposed to start?"

"At five."

"It'll be okay. I'll handle my mother," Craig chuckled, still holding the door. "By the time I tell her you've agreed to look into Coach Wyatt's murder to prove Danny's innocence, she'll be so thrilled she won't care what time you get there."

"But what if we end up proving Danny killed the coach? What then?" I slumped back in my seat, imagining how devastated Mae would be.

I'd only met Danny recently at the rink, but Mae had always spoken fondly of him. Now, with her cousin in prison and her sister dead, the only family Mae had left was Danny, his sister Linda, and Craig. If Danny was guilty, it might be more than she could bear.

Craig leaned against the door, considering my words. After a moment, he straightened. "We'll handle that when the time comes. One step at a time," he said with a self-satisfied grin like he believed he'd just imparted some great words of wisdom that would make all my problems disappear.

As he settled behind the wheel, I asked, "What if the store gets swamped with customers and your mom can't handle it? Mae gets flustered when more than two people are in line! Stopping by the hospital will make me even later, but I need to know how my mom's doing. I suppose I could call the nurses' station, but even that will take time I just don't have."

"Would you relax?" Craig said, checking for traffic before pulling out of the parking lot. "I can cover your shift until you get there. I'm getting pretty good at this manual labor stuff," he teased. "Seriously, it's no big deal. Trust me. I got this."

"Are you sure?" I asked.

He nodded.

"Tell Mae I'll be there as soon as I can," I said, mentally listing everything I had to do when I got home—change clothes, grab a bite to eat, call the hospital. Just thinking about my mom conjured unwelcome images of her lying helplessly in bed, tethered to beeping machines.

Craig had argued I wasn't to blame, but the guilt lingered. If I'd taken the threatening note seriously and backed off investigating Shelly's death, maybe Mom wouldn't be fighting for her life now.

"What if my mom doesn't recover? What if he tries again? What if—"

Craig's hand settled on my shoulder. "One thing at a time. She's in good hands, and Detective Douglas has an officer stationed outside her room to prevent another attempt. But remember, no matter what, I'm here for you. I'll even cover your whole shift tonight if you want me to. It'll be mother and son bonding time," he chuckled.

My heart softened as he spoke. "That's sweet, but I'll be there tonight. After all, you've got things you should do, like finish your book."

"Don't worry about that," he dismissed with a wave. "I do my best work late at night, anyway." He grinned. "There's nothing like being in an old creaky house in the middle of nowhere to get those creative juices flowing."

"How is your book coming?"

"It's almost finished," he replied, his voice taking on a thoughtful tone. "I'm on the last two chapters but can't decide how to wrap it up. I've added a romance subplot to this one, and Suzette thinks the couple should end up together. I'm not so sure. Life and love don't always work out the way we want. So…should I follow Suzette's advice and go the romantic route or end with a dose of reality?"

"I'd go with romance." I shrugged. "I don't read to be reminded that life doesn't always have a happy ending. Reality does that often enough."

"True, but don't you think happy endings can feel a bit contrived?" he countered.

"I suppose, but I don't mind. Give me a hopeful ending with the *possibility* of love any day—even if it's not guaranteed, it's better than not having any hope at all."

"You might be on to something," he mused, glancing at me.

"What? You're agreeing with me?" I laughed.

"Sure. An ending that doesn't tie up all the loose ends but leaves the reader thinking about, as you said, the possibility that love might prevail. After all, not all relationships are clear-cut. People don't always know where they stand with each other. It takes time to figure things out, and sometimes, people don't always get the answers they were hoping for."

I turned and stared at Craig for a moment, scrunching my brows. "I don't think that's what I said at all."

"Perhaps, but you can't deny it's true."

"No, I can't," I murmured, shaking my head. "But I want to believe things will work out in the end."

Craig's expression turned pensive. "Yes, but with *whom* will it work out?"

As I unbuckled my seatbelt, I mulled over Craig's words as thoughts of our fake engagement and my unresolved feelings for T.J. raced through my mind. Was I romantically attracted to T.J. or tired of being alone? Perhaps what I felt was nothing more than feeling safe with a kindred spirit.

I wrapped my fingers around the door handle and glanced over my shoulder. Craig was watching me closely, his eyes searching mine. At that moment, I wondered if my feelings for T.J. would become clear if Craig expressed a desire for more than a working relationship with me. What if he just had?

****

When I stepped into the house, Gidget was perched on the bottom step, her large green eyes tracking me as I kicked off my shoes. With a soft thud, she hopped down and followed me into the kitchen.

Moving with the elegance of a ballerina, she studied me with wide eyes as I checked for any notes Crystal might have left when she stopped by the house to pick up clothes for Dad.

Nothing.

I opened the refrigerator and stared at its empty shelves. Two dozen brown eggs, a container of cottage cheese, a half-empty glass bottle of milk, and a random assortment of condiments. That was it.

Gidget sniffed around the empty refrigerator and let out a

worried meow. To ease her distress, I poured a saucer of milk and sat beside her, gently stroking her soft fur. "We'll get through this," I whispered, unsure whether I was trying to comfort her or myself.

The empty fridge shouldn't have caught me off guard, but it did. With Mom in the hospital, neither Dad nor I had gone grocery shopping, and chances were, she hadn't felt up to it for days. Who knows how long she'd been pushing through, pretending she felt fine?

I started to blame myself for the empty shelves but then remembered why I hadn't noticed sooner. I'd been living off the muffins Crystal dropped off. Not exactly the most balanced meal plan, but it had satisfied my hunger—until now.

At least having no food was one problem I could fix. I needed a grocery list. While Gidget lapped up her milk, I rummaged through the pantry: canned vegetables, apple jelly, peanut butter, and a sad, half-empty bag of marshmallows.

Gidget weaved between my legs, meowing again. I scooped her up. "Oh, what are we going to do?" I sighed, holding her close. Helping Craig investigate Coach Wyatt's death felt like the right thing to do—but at what cost this time?

I stroked Gidget's head, and she began to purr, her tiny motor revving hard.

"As long as you feel loved, have a roof over your head, and food to eat, all is well in your world," I murmured. "If only it were that simple for me."

My stomach growled loudly. Gidget stared at me, eyes wide, as if she was scared I might explode.

"It's okay. It's just me," I chuckled, setting her down. "Nothing to worry about."

I made a peanut butter and jelly sandwich and took a bite. The sweet and salty combination hit me like a revelation—I had not eaten since breakfast.

No wonder I was so hungry.

I savored each bite while listening to the messages on the answering machine. The first ten were from family and friends checking on Mom. The last one was from Crystal, about an hour ago. Mom was stable, but still in a coma. Dad planned to spend the night at the hospital.

Guess I don't have to call the hospital. If anything changes, Crystal will let me know. One less thing to do.

I wandered into the living room and stared out the picture window. Pink blossoms swayed on the trees, and yellow daffodils danced along the driveway. I tried to take comfort in Crystal's update—Mom was stable, Dad was by her side, and a police officer stood guard.

Surely, whoever tried to harm her wouldn't dare try again. Right?

I twisted the charm around my neck, thoughts drifting to Coach Wyatt's murder and Sarah's death. *Was it crazy to think they were connected? Or was I seeing shadows where there were none? Why had a limo been by the coach's house? Why—*

The chime of the grandfather clock snapped me from my spiraling thoughts. Finding answers would have to wait. Work was calling. Despite Craig's willingness to cover for me, I couldn't stop worrying about how Mae would react to my tardiness. I didn't want to lose my job.

I ran upstairs, Gidget close behind. *Of all days to wear jeans to class!* Mae never allowed casual clothes at work—no jeans, no T-shirts, not even when unloading boxes. I had to change.

In record time, I was dressed in a navy plaid skirt, crisp white blouse, and navy cardigan. Loafers on, I dashed to the door. But just as I stepped onto the porch, the phone rang. I hesitated, debating if I should go back and answer it or continue to my car.

If it was Crystal or Dad, I couldn't risk missing it. I darted back inside.

"Michelle? How is your Mom?"

T.J.

I smiled. "Hey. Thanks for calling. She's still in a coma, but she's stable. The doctors think she'll pull through, but they'll know more once she wakes up."

"That's crazy. I thought she had pneumonia or something. Why were they giving her insulin? I didn't know she was diabetic."

"She's not." I took a deep breath. "Someone tried to kill her."

"For real?" T.J. gasped. "Are you sure? I mean, I know that's what you said at the Commuter Lounge, but I thought maybe you were in shock or something. Why would anyone want to kill your mother?"

I twisted the phone cord around my hand as I paced behind the sofa. "Oh, T.J., I've made such a mess of things. Do you remember the note I got when I was looking into Shelly's death and the malfunctioning treadmill?"

"The one warning you to back off?"

"Yeah, that's the one. My family thinks my mom is in a coma because I didn't stop investigating."

"I'm sure they didn't mean it. They're just upset, that's all."

Crystal's and my father's words echoed in my mind. "No. You didn't see their faces. Crystal, my dad, and even Suzie think I'm to blame. What am I going to do? I have to make this right."

Silence traveled across the line.

"T.J.? Are you still there?"

"Yeah, I'm here. I was just thinking. How 'bout I come over, and maybe we can think of something?"

"I'd love that, but I have to work tonight. In fact, I was just heading out the door when you called." I took a breath. "Could you come by when I get home tonight? About 9:30? Or...do you and Meg have plans?"

"No. We're taking a break. I need some time to clear my

head, but yeah, I can come over," he said. "Will your dad be chill about that?"

"Actually, he's spending the night at the hospital, so it's no problem."

"Okay, I'll let you get to work, and I'll see you tonight. And try not to worry. Everything will be fine."

Everyone keeps saying that, but they *don't know for sure. It's going to take more than comforting words for everything to work out.*

As I unwound the tangled telephone cord from my hand, thoughts tumbled through my mind—Coach's murder, Sarah's death, the reappearing limousine, and the mysterious man giving deadly orders. What if he was behind Mom's attack? Would he strike again? What was his endgame?

The weight of it all only fueled my resolve.

It was time to end this madness, and I knew exactly where to begin.

chapter twelve

After a long evening at work, I pulled into my driveway and felt a renewed surge of energy when I spotted T.J.'s car parked beneath the basketball hoop. The low, rhythmic bass from his speakers pulsed through the cool night air. In classic T.J. fashion, the windows were rolled down, and the radio cranked to a deafening volume.

I walked toward him, grinning as I watched his head bob in time to "Black Water" by The Doobie Brothers. Lost in his own world, he didn't notice me sneaking up to the passenger side. Just as I was about to slip in undetected, he turned, startled, and then broke into a sheepish grin. Without missing a beat, he resumed his off-key singing, undeterred by my laughter.

Soon, we were both laughing until tears streamed down my face. It felt so good!

I leaned back, a mischievous idea taking shape. "Let's go raid the freezer! I'm pretty sure Mom hid some leftover Christmas cookies in there."

T.J.'s eyebrows shot up. "Christmas cookies in April? Bold move, Kilpatrick!"

"Can't think of a better time to break into the stash. A

minute in the microwave, and they'll be oven-fresh—or close enough to it," I grinned.

We threw open the car doors and headed for the house, the porch light casting a warm glow over us, welcoming us home.

Inside, T.J. draped his jacket over a kitchen chair while I popped the cookies onto a plate. As I set them in the microwave, he grabbed two glasses from the cupboard and filled them with milk—perfect for dunking.

I was having so much fun hanging out with T.J. that I almost forgot why he'd come over in the first place. Then the phone rang. My heart stopped. Judging from the panic in T.J.'s eyes, his might have too. I froze, terrified of what news might be waiting on the other end.

"Do you want me to answer that?" he asked.

"No." I sighed. "I'll get it."

T.J. followed me into the living room, pausing at the edge of the couch. I took a deep breath before picking up the phone. When I heard Crystal's cheerful voice, I mouthed to him that it was my sister—everything was all right.

He smiled and headed back to the kitchen, leaving me alone to finish the conversation. Crystal apologized for blaming me for the attempt on Mom's life. Her words hit the right notes, but her tone left me questioning her sincerity.

I bit my tongue, trying to be the bigger person. "It's okay," I said, although it really wasn't. Not in the least.

Back in the kitchen, T.J. and I rehashed the night the limo pulled into my driveway—the shadowy figure placing a note on my car, warning me to back off investigating the treadmill accident and Shelly's death.

T.J. launched into his usual tirade about how working with Craig always leads to trouble. "I hope you've learned your lesson. Stay away from that dude. And whatever you do, do not investigate that coach's murder with him."

"But I have to," I said, my voice steady and sure.

He stared at me like I'd lost my mind. "What do you mean? After everything that's happened, you're going to go snooping again?"

"I'm not crazy." I set my chocolate chip cookie down. "But I need answers."

"You could start by letting the police do their job. They're trained to handle this kind of stuff!"

"Oh, come on. Detective Douglas is convinced Danny killed Coach Wyatt. He's not looking for anyone else."

T.J. leaned forward. "Maybe that's because he *found* the killer."

I crossed my arms. "He might have a case against Danny, but I can't shake the feeling someone set him up. And remember I told you about the limo by Coach Wyatt's house that night? Whenever it shows up, people die. I have to find out why."

"And I suppose Craig will be with you every step of the way?"

I cradled my chin in my hands. "I think *every step of the way* is an exaggeration, but, yeah, he wants to be involved. Danny's family."

"And you? What's your motivation—getting to the truth or working with the great mystery writer, Craig Miller?"

I shook my head at his sarcasm. "Don't be ridiculous. If someone hadn't tried to kill my mom, I wouldn't have given it a second thought."

T.J. narrowed his eyes. "Get real. Every time Craig snaps his fingers, you jump."

"That's not true, and you know it," I clutched the Eiffel Tower charm on the chain around my neck.

"Do I?"

How had we gone from cookies and laughter to accusations and hurtful comments?

"You're wrong. Craig is a friend." I paused. "Sure, we've gotten into a few scrapes, but he's helped me so much with my writing. I've learned so much from him."

"I bet."

"What's that supposed to mean?"

"I just don't trust him. Trouble seems to follow the guy, and I don't want you getting caught up in it."

"I appreciate your concern, but I can take care of myself."

T.J. slumped in his chair. "I don't suppose there's any way I can talk you out of this?"

I shook my head. "Nope."

After a moment of silence, he reached over, placing his hand over mine. His expression softened. "Then let me help. Tell me what to do."

My heart lifted. "Really? You're in?"

T.J. grinned, dunking a cookie. "I'm probably gonna regret this—but yeah, count me in."

A smile spread across my face as I fiddled with my charm. "You're the best!"

"That's what they say," he chuckled. "So, where do we begin?"

"I haven't figured everything out yet—"

"Now, that's a real surprise," he teased, biting into his soggy cookie.

"Oh, come on. Give me a break." I nudged him. "I only started thinking of a plan this afternoon."

"And what have you got so far?"

"We know Coach Wyatt was found with Danny's scarf. If Danny's telling the truth and left it at the rink, anyone could've grabbed it, including the coach."

"And motive?"

"Danny doesn't seem to have one. But that doesn't mean he doesn't. We need to dig deeper."

"What about the others? Anyone holding a grudge against Coach Wyatt?"

"Jason, one of the pairs skaters. He was quite vocal at dinner—accused Coach Wyatt of showing favoritism to the other pairs team. And Olga, the choreographer. There's a rumor she had feelings for Coach, but he didn't feel the same."

T.J. reached for another cookie. "Anyone else?"

"Eric. He's a singles skater. He didn't say anything against the coach, but I got the distinct feeling he didn't like Danny. He hinted that all the trouble at their old rink started when Danny came into their lives."

"Like the missing equipment?"

"Yeah. I can't remember if I told you, but after things began disappearing at the rink, Coach Wyatt told his skaters to take everything home with them after practice. Then, someone broke into a few of their apartments. Then there was this other coach that Wyatt suspected was out to get him."

"What's the story with that guy?"

"Jealousy. Coach Wyatt's skaters kept beating his for spots on the podium, possibly ruining their chances of going to the Olympics. Coach believed this guy was behind the rumors that he was giving his skaters performance-enhancing drugs."

T.J. frowned. "We need to find out who this dude is— sounds like a real contender as a murder suspect. What do the police know about him?"

"I'm not sure. I'll ask Lawrence."

T.J. refilled his glass. "So, right now, we've got Danny, Jason, Olga, Eric, and this mystery coach as possible suspects. Sounds like a good starting point."

"Yeah, it does, doesn't it?" I stopped. "You know what? I've got an idea. I think my mom has an old bulletin board in the basement. Would you mind checking Mom's junk drawer for some 3x5s and thumbtacks? "

"If you can't find any, straight pins will work too," I added with a laugh. "We should invent note paper that's sticky. Wouldn't that be great? We could move it around on the board and never worry about finding thumbtacks again."

I ran downstairs and came back to find T.J. sitting at the oak kitchen table, smiling as he organized the stack of notecards into a neat pile with a pen and several silver thumbtacks nearby.

"Whatcha thinkin'?" I asked, placing the bulletin board on the table.

T.J., beaming, balanced the pen on his finger. "Nothin' in particular. I'm just glad you're letting me help. Ever since Craig came into the picture, things have been…"

"Complicated? I get it." I shrugged. "Speaking of complicated, what's up with you and Meg?"

T.J.'s smile faded. "I like her. I really do, but…I can't get over that she doesn't trust me."

"Why not?"

"She thinks I'm hiding something from her."

"And are you?"

T.J. looked down. "I know I should have, but I still haven't told her about your fake engagement. I feel bad breaking my promise to you."

"But I said you could tell her."

"I know, but if I tell her the truth, I think she'll go ballistic. Worse yet, if I ask her to keep your secret, I don't think she will."

"Sounds to me like you both don't trust each other."

T.J. stared at the cookie in his hand as he swirled it in his glass of milk. "You might be right, but there's another problem. Her father. Why won't she introduce me to him? I think she's ashamed of me."

"Don't be ridiculous. Why in the world would she be ashamed of you? You're a fantastic person. Doggone close to perfect." I smiled before leaning closer. "Did you ever ask her why?"

"She says he's always out of town, but he's got to come home sometime, doesn't he?"

"Not necessarily. Maybe he moved out, and she's too embarrassed to tell you?"

T.J. shuffled the 3x5s. "That's crazy. Her dad's living situation would never affect how I feel about her."

"But does she know that?"

Taking a deep breath, I set aside my hope that T.J. and Meg would break up, focusing instead on his happiness. "No excuses. You have to tell her my engagement to Craig was not real. Be honest with her. If she tells the entire world, so be it. If you're serious about her, you have to know if you can trust her."

"And what about her father?"

"That might take more time, but maybe if you guys work through the trust thing, she'll tell you what's going on."

The heaviness in the air felt suffocating. My chest tightened.

Tonight was not going as I had hoped.

It had been a complete emotional roller coaster.

Looking down, I noticed my mood ring had turned dark brown—not surprising since I may have just thrown T.J. and Meg back together…again.

I turned away from T.J., unable to look into his brown eyes any longer, and glanced around the room. My eyes landed on the rooster clock—11:30 p.m.

"I didn't realize it was so late. We, dear sir, have class in the morning. Guess we better call it a night. "

T.J. pushed up the cuff on his striped shirt and nodded as he looked at his watch.

I scooted my chair away from the table and said, "I'll bring the cards with me, and we can work on this tomorrow in the Commuter Lounge. I can put them on the board when I get home. Sound like a plan?"

T.J. grabbed two cookies from the platter as he rose from

his seat. "Sounds good. Just curious, though. If you had to arrest someone for the coach's murder right this minute, who would it be?"

I sighed. "At first, I was thinking Eric, but now I'm leaning toward Jason. He had a motive and the opportunity. If Danny left his scarf at the rink, Jason could have easily picked it up. Which reminds me, do we know anyone who works at the rink?"

"Yeah, Yash. That's where he's doing his work-study this semester."

"Perfect! We need to see if he knows anything about Danny's scarf. If we're lucky, he saw someone with it that afternoon. And, come to think of it, Yash could ask Mr. Hansen if he witnessed anything suspicious that night. He likes Danny, so I bet he'd be happy to help."

"I can ask Yash in the morning. We've got a computer class together."

"Really? I thought he was a business major. What's he doing in one of your computer classes?"

"You know Yash. He's always looking for ways to edge out the competition in the job market. He figures having more than a working knowledge of computers will make him a more desirable candidate."

"Smart thinking! Maybe I should add a few computer classes."

T.J. wrinkled his nose.

"What?"

"If I remember correctly, you and computers didn't get along too well when you took that Intro to Computers class."

I cocked my head to the side and smirked. "I was much younger then."

"Right, it was just last year," he chuckled.

"Oh, shut up." I grinned. "And besides, I said *maybe* I should take a class. But for now, I've got to figure out how to narrow down our list of suspects."

A smile crept across my face.

"What are you thinking?" he asked.

"You know that house the coach was renting?"

T.J. uttered a drawn-out "Yeah?"

"I need to get back inside while the skating team is still renting it. Wanna help?"

chapter thirteen

Thursday, April 17th

Despite knowing I should pay attention to Dr. Andrews' lecture on feature writing, I instead concentrated on finding a link between Sarah and Coach Wyatt's deaths. The professor's husky voice faded into the distance as I drew a Venn Diagram, labeling one circle for the coach and the other for Sarah.

In Coach Wyatt's circle, I jotted down *scarf, strangled, threatening notes, disgruntled skaters, jealous coach*, and *enamored assistant*. In Sarah's circle, I had little information to add: a mysterious man ordering her to kill Shelly, her readiness to tell the police his identity, and death by strangulation. It was at that moment I realized they died in the same manner, although Sarah's was self-inflicted, so they said. Drawing a line through the word "strangled" in the two circles, I rewrote it in the area they shared in the diagram.

One connection made, but were there more? And if so, how many?

Cupping my chin with one hand, I drummed on my desk with the other, trying to fit all the pieces together.

Think. Think. Think.

Mae, my boss, had ties with both Sarah and the coach. Sarah and Mae were friends in Boston—they often socialized as their husbands were friends and colleagues. The link between Mae and the coach was pretty thin, but it was there, thanks to her son, Craig. He and Coach Wyatt had the same literary agent.

Then there was Danny, the son of Mae's cousin, Steve Goodright. He floated back into my mind. Could he be the link I was looking for? How ironic that when Danny left town, he ended up working at Coach Wyatt's rink.

What else? Ah, yes, Sarah and her warning to Mae—something along the lines of Mae having to pay for the sins of her husband. But which one? She has been married three times.

I wrote their names down:

- Tony Romano—Craig's father, died in a car accident
- Johnathan Miller—adopted Craig and worked with Sarah's husband in Boston
- Nathan Emerson—passed away after he and Mae moved to Petersburg

I looked up from my paper and glanced toward the front of the classroom. My inner monologue quieted as Professor Andrews said, "During my internship at *Rolling Stone*, I interviewed legends like Bob Dylan on releasing his album, *The Times, They Are a-Changin'*..."

His story would have had me spellbound any other day, but I was too restless to enjoy his walk down memory lane. I had a murder...or two...to solve. Refocusing my energy on my Venn Diagram, I drew another circle and wrote my mom's name in it—the victim of an attempted homicide. A wave of guilt washed over me as I again realized that whoever warned me to stop looking into Shelly's fatal accident might be responsible for my mother's condition.

My mind drifted to the limo spotted near the coach's house the night someone killed him. It was uncanny the way a limo showed up when murder was afoot—but one was always there.

But the big question remained unanswered: was it the same limo? I had no idea. Chances were it could be some strange coincidence, but then again, limousines in Petersburg were not an everyday occurrence. Despite no proof they were the same vehicle, I wrote "limo" in the space where Coach Wyatt's and Sarah's circles overlapped.

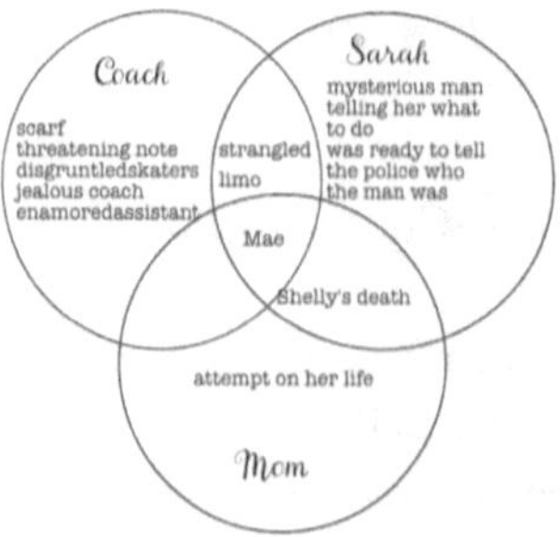

The snap of a book closing jolted me back to reality. I glanced around the room and saw classmates gathering their books. I stuffed my notebook into my bag and fell in the line, shuffling toward the door, doing my best to avoid eye contact with my professor as I passed his desk.

"Ms. Kilpatrick. Did you enjoy today's class?" he asked.

I muttered an automatic, "Yeah. Very informative," and scurried out the door, nearly colliding with the person in front of me.

Busted! So much for hiding that I wasn't listening. *Note to self: borrow someone's notes from class.* I had a hunch the midterm would include some questions from today's lecture.

The scent of freshly cut grass wafted through the air as I

stepped out of the hallowed halls of Sheffield Hall and into the outdoors. As I glanced across the green, the stately trio of old brick buildings—Whitley, Spencer, and Overman Halls—caught my attention. They reminded me of pictures I had seen of Harvard's campus, and soon my mind drifted to the Kennedy Compound in Cape Cod and landed on Boston, the city that tied Sarah, Mae, and their husbands together.

I quickened my pace to the Commuter Lounge as thoughts of Mae's second husband, Johnathan Miller, raced through my mind. Not only did he work with Sarah's husband, but he was related to Shelly, the girl Sarah had murdered. *What if the connection I'm looking for is between Miller and Coach Wyatt?*

A seemingly never-ending line of students exited Whitley Hall as I bounded up the stairs toward its massive double doors. As I stood off to the side, waiting for a break in the mass exodus, I debated the chances of Mae telling me anything about her second husband. She rarely talked about her family, but perhaps Craig could help. Although Johnathan Miller adopted Craig, he died when Craig was only six years old. I wasn't sure how much Craig remembered, but maybe he could get his mom to open up about her second husband. *It's worth a shot.*

Inside the walls of the Commuter Lounge, I made my way through the maze of tables and chairs as I observed the flurry of activity at our table. Todd was stashing the coffee maker under the table while Billy and Jimmy piled their backpacks around it. Glancing at the other end of the room, Amy and Tasha had Alice cornered outside her office.

I slid into a chair opposite Todd as he sighed deeply and nodded in Amy's direction. "Wow, that was close."

I leaned over the table and asked, in a hushed tone, "What's Alice doing here? I thought she was gone until next week."

Todd beamed like a kid who snuck a cookie without his

mother knowing. "Yeah, that's what we thought, too, until she popped out of her office a couple of minutes ago. Quick-thinking Tasha grabbed Amy, and they distracted Alice while we hid everything."

"And you're welcome," Amy said as she stood behind him and gave him a playful kiss on the head. "You owe Tasha and me a free cup of coffee—maybe two." She laughed, pulling out the seat beside Todd. A red blush, almost the same color as his Beatles t-shirt, crept up his face.

"Man, Alice is a real talker." Tasha plopped into the empty chair next to me and leaned back, crossing her arms. "I had no idea she could talk so much. I didn't think she was ever going to stop."

"What were you guys talking about?" I asked.

"We told her we were glad she was back and wondered if everything was okay since she was supposed to be at the conference for the rest of the week."

"And was it?"

"Yes and no," Amy interjected. "The conference went well, but it turned out her nephew is on that skating team that's training here. You know, the one whose coach got murdered," explained Amy as she adjusted her books on the table. "She said his parents were worried that their son's life might be in danger with a murderer on the loose and not knowing what else might happen. I mean, even my mother is concerned—"

I chimed in before Amy diverted the conversation further. "So, his parents got in touch with Alice?"

"No," uttered Tasha as she untangled a few strands of fringe on her suede vest. "They left messages on her answering machine at her house, but when she didn't call them back, they ended up calling her daughter, who told them the police had arrested someone but—"

"That didn't make them feel any better," said Amy, smiling as she regained control of the story. "So when her daughter got a hold of her, Alice came straight home, and now her nephew is staying with her."

"Do you know what his name is?" I asked.

Amy shook her head while Tasha wrinkled her forehead, trying to remember.

"I'm not sure. Sorry." Tasha said. "Maybe Jack...Jerod..."

"Jason?" I asked.

Tasha nodded, her brow furrowing. "Yeah, that sounds like it." She bit her bottom lip and scanned the room as if searching for answers. "I think it was Jason."

Just then, T.J. slid into the chair on my other side, grinning. "What I'd miss?"

"Oh, not much...just Alice coming home early, Todd having a stroke trying to hide the coffeemaker, and get this—one of the pairs skaters, Jason, is Alice's nephew and is staying with her."

T.J. laughed. "Glad I didn't miss much."

"Just another slow news day," I replied, smirking.

Out of the corner of my eye, I spotted Todd's eyes growing wide, fixated on something or someone behind me. I turned to see Alice strolling toward the back exit, briefcase in hand. The door clicked shut, and Todd sprang into action, retrieving the coffee maker from its hiding spot under the table. "Looks like our under-the-table coffee enterprise is back in business, boys and girls."

"Are you sure it's safe?" I asked, casting a wary glance at the door, half-expecting Alice to return.

Todd shrugged and plugged the coffee machine into the wall. "Yeah. We're cool. Alice only takes her briefcase with her when she's done for the day." He chuckled. "That's one thing about Alice—she's as predictable as clockwork."

T.J. slid two shiny dimes across the table toward Todd. "One cup for me."

Within moments, T.J. was sipping his coffee and, with a satisfied look, asked me, "So, what's the game plan?"

I pulled out my notebook and fished a bundled stack of 3x5s from my purse. Staring at my Venn Diagram, I twisted the charm around my neck. "I think there's definitely a link between Coach Wyatt's murder, Sarah's death, and the attempt on my mom's life. It all comes back to Mae, which makes me think that whoever's in that limo is part of this too."

Todd's eyes grew wide. "Wait, you were serious yesterday when you said someone tried to kill your mom?"

I filled Todd, Amy, and Tasha in on what had happened to my mom while T.J. sipped his coffee, his gaze glued to my diagram.

"How are you going to find out who did it? If you need any help, let me know," Amy blurted out.

"Thanks. Will do. The police are looking into it, but I'm going to focus on finding Coach Wyatt's murderer. I have a hunch that'll lead me to whoever messed with my mom."

Todd poured himself some coffee and added a heap of powdered creamer. "You don't think the police got the right guy behind bars?"

"I have my doubts, but I intend to find out for sure."

I removed the rubber band from the stack of cards, grabbed a pen, and neatly noted *MOTIVE*, *MEANS*, and *OPPORTUNITY* on individual cards. Then, I wrote each suspect's name on three cards.

"I don't know if I remember exactly how they did this on that detective show I saw on T.V., but, hey, it's worth a try. Maybe it will help us," I said as I spread the *MOTIVE*, *MEANS*, and *OPPORTUNITY* cards across the table. I added Danny's name under *MEANS* and *OPPORTUNITY* right away. After all, it was his scarf around the coach's neck, and he was at the house when the murder occurred.

Todd, Amy, and Tasha leaned in as I placed the cards with Olga, Eric, and Jason beneath *MEANS* and *OPPORTUNITY*.

They, too, were in the house and had access to Danny's scarf that night.

Thinking through what I knew, I also put their names under *MOTIVE*.

- The rumor mill said Olga was in love with Coach Wyatt but that he didn't reciprocate her feelings.
- Jason resented the coach's favoritism towards the other pairs team.
- Although Eric didn't seem to have a motive to kill the coach, he did not hide his dislike for Danny. Perhaps he wanted to frame him for murder—not my best idea, but it was one to consider.

Then there was the Unknown Coach, who had a motive, but did he have the means or the opportunity? I made a note to look into that as well.

And finally, there was Sarah's mystery man. My gut feeling told me he was involved. I penned *Mystery Man* on three cards, setting them aside, uncertain where they fit.

T.J. studied the cards. "Wouldn't the other skaters also have means and opportunity?"

I shrugged. "You're right. I've been so focused on Olga, Jason, and Eric that I totally forgot about the rest of them."

I jotted Cherie, Katie, Naomi, and Ethan on the 3x5s and placed them under *MEANS* and *OPPORTUNITY*.

"Oh, and I should probably add Mr. Hansen's name to the mix since he was also at the house that night."

I shifted in my seat as I focused on the three lengthy columns spanning the table's width. "Looks a little daunting, doesn't it?" I said to no one in particular.

"It certainly does," boomed a voice from behind me. I could see T.J.'s expression darkening, his jaw tightening.

I spun around to see Craig pulling the chair next to me, which Tasha had just vacated.

"We have quite the array of suspects, don't we?" he asked with a smirk.

"Yes, we do, but fortunately, we don't have to narrow our list down alone. T.J.'s agreed to help us," I beamed, glancing back at T.J. "Did you get to ask Yash about Danny's scarf?"

"Yeah. He didn't remember seeing a scarf in the locker room when he cleaned it after Wyatt's skaters left that day. He promised to ask around and see if anyone knew anything," T.J. replied.

"Fingers crossed he'll come through with something," I sighed.

"But," T.J. added. "All is not lost. He did have some news. Apparently, some of the skaters will be giving private lessons this week and next to help cover their training expenses."

Intrigued, I leaned closer. "Really?"

"Excellent." Craig tipped his chair back. "That might be just the opening we need."

"Huh?" T.J. and I both asked in unison, eyebrows raised.

"What better way to gather intel than by spending one-on-one time with the suspects? Maybe we each could take private lessons from a different skater?"

T.J. scoffed. "Count me out. Skating's not my thing."

Craig shrugged. "No loss if you sit this one out," he said, nudging my arm. "What about you? Are you in?"

"I'd love to, but…"

"But what?"

I sank back into my chair, feeling a bit conflicted. "I'm not sure I have the time, and then there's the—"

"Hey, if money's an issue, no problem. I'll cover it," Craig offered.

I wrinkled my nose. "That's sweet of you, but I couldn't let you do that. I don't know when I'd be able to pay you back."

"Like I said, it's no big deal. Besides, I can always send the bill to my mother. Think of it as a business expense for our investigative work. After all, we're doing this for her, right?" He grinned.

"I'm not sure it's fair to make your mother pay for my skating lessons," I chuckled.

"Tell you what, if it makes you feel better, I'll find out what they charge. It might not be that much."

"Okay. We can at least look into it," I relented.

"Glad we got that settled. By the way, do you have time to swing by the rink and talk to Mr. Henson?"

"I suppose, but T.J. and I were planning to work on some theories about Coach Wyatt's murder."

"You won't mind if we go, right?" Craig looked past me to T.J.

"Yeah, sure, go ahead. We can discuss our theories later… maybe at your house...tonight," T.J. said as he gathered the 3x5s into a neat stack. "I need to go find Meg anyway and tell her, well, you know."

"Good luck. Hopefully, you can figure out what's going on with her dad, and you can get past all this stuff," I said, trying to encourage him.

Craig raised an eyebrow. "What's up with Meg's dad?"

"Oh, nothing," I casually replied. "He just works a lot."

Craig shrugged. "That's good. The last thing we need is another mystery to solve."

His words sent an icy chill down my spine.

chapter fourteen

After a long day of classes, I wanted nothing more than to unwind on the way home, but I had barely crawled into T.J.'s car when he launched into a barrage of questions. "What did Craig find out about the skating lessons? Did you guys sign up? Is Mr. Money Bags going to cover the cost?"

"Wow! One question at a time," I replied as I fastened my seatbelt. "Yes, we signed up for lessons. I'm with Eric, and Craig is with Naomi. What else did you want to know? Oh yeah, payment." I sighed and looked out my window to avoid seeing T.J.'s reaction, which I could already guarantee would be one of disapproval. "And he's going to pay for my lessons. He thinks we can get information about Coach Wyatt and the rest of his team by working one-on-one with a couple of the skaters. I'm willing to try, but it makes me uncomfortable owing him money."

"Why didn't you tell him *no*? Honestly, Michelle, you need to stand up to the guy."

My eyebrows shot up. "Not this again. Like I told you before, I don't jump every time Craig speaks. The thing is, I'm running out of ideas about how to narrow down our suspect list, and Danny can't afford for me to botch this investigation.

His life literally depends on it." I shrugged. "I may as well try Craig's plan."

T.J. exhaled sharply. "I get that, but seeing Craig pull you into one of his investigations makes me nervous." He reached over and rested his hand on top of mine. "What if, instead of eliminating names, you just focus on the most likely suspects, like that Jason dude and Olga?"

I leaned back in my seat. "That makes sense. I should have thought of that. Guess I've got too much on my mind right now to think straight."

T.J. hesitated. "How's your mom?"

"I called Crystal this afternoon from school. She said Mom squeezed her hand and opened her eyes for a few seconds. That's a good sign, right?" I forced a smile.

"I would think so." T.J. slowed to a stop as the light turned red. "Do you have to work tonight?"

"Nope. Got the night off. I'm going to run by the hospital and stay with my mom for a while."

"What time were you thinking about going? If you want to go now, I can go with you. I've got nothing happening until later tonight."

"Sure. That'd be great. So....are you meeting with Meg later?"

"Yeah."

"How'd it go when you talked to her earlier? Did you guys straighten things out?"

"I told her the entire story behind your fake engagement, and, as I expected, she freaked. But by the time I left, she had cooled down. She's still miffed, no doubt about that, but at least I got that off my conscience." T.J. patted my hand. "She promised not to tell anyone, so fingers crossed—we'll see what happens."

"I'm sure it'll be okay," I said, though doubt gnawed at me. After all, I was the reason T.J. had kept a secret from her. I could only hope her fear of making him mad outweighed her desire for revenge against me.

Pushing aside all the *what-ifs* of Meg's reactions, I said, "It's good that you're getting together tonight. I mean, that's what you want, right?"

Once again, I was caught in the all too familiar struggle—wanting T.J. and Meg to break up while also wanting what was best for him. This internal conflict was wearing me down. I needed to move on, but how?

T. J. shrugged. "I'm not sure what I want anymore. I'm so confused."

I smiled softly. "I know exactly how you feel."

When T.J. turned the corner, I was relieved to see the hospital. The thought of seeing my mother, despite the risk of my father still being mad at me, provided a much-needed reprieve from discussing T.J.'s relationship with Meg.

Inside, we took the elevator to the fourth floor. The ICU waiting room was empty. I dashed ahead of T.J. and hurried to the nurse's station.

A blonde candy striper was filing papers in the corner. She glanced over her shoulder and flashed a warm smile. "Hi! Can I help you?"

"Yeah, can I go into my mom's room? Her name is Nancy Kilpatrick. I didn't see any of my family in the waiting room, so I didn't know if they were with her. "

"Just a minute, and I'll go see." She placed the paper on the desk and then headed down the hall. The young volunteer stopped and chatted with the police officer outside my mom's room. After their brief interchange, she opened the door and peeked inside. Sporting a broad smile, she made her way back to the nurse's station.

"You can go on in. A nurse is checking your mom's vitals. She said your dad had gone for supper." The teenager's gaze flickered to T.J. at my side and said with a sly smile, "Still only family allowed, but your boyfriend can take a seat in the waiting room."

"Oh, no," I interjected. "He's not my boyfriend. I mean, he's a boy…and he's a friend, but not—"

The candy striper's cheeks turned as pink as the stripes on her uniform. "I'm..I'm sorry," she stammered. "You two just seemed so…"

My face went hot. "Oh no," I said with a nervous laugh. "We've been friends forever. Sometimes it's like we're an old —" I caught myself just in time. Clearing my throat, I hurried on. "Anyway, how's my mom doing? My sister said she opened her eyes earlier today."

The girl's calm smile returned. "Why don't you go and see for yourself?"

When I opened the door to Mom's room, I couldn't believe my eyes. She was propped up in bed with a bowl of soup in front of her.

After jotting something on Mom's chart, the nurse looked up and smiled. "You must be Michelle. Your mom was hoping you'd stop by after school." She clipped the chart to the foot of the bed. "You two have a nice visit. Just don't tire her out. She's been one sick lady, but I think she's on the road to recovery now. I'll be down the hall if you need me."

Tears ran down my cheeks as I reached for my mom's hand. "I'm so glad you're doing better. I'm sorry. I never meant—"

Mom's voice trembled, barely above a whisper. "I know. It'll be all right.

"But what if—"

She squeezed my hand. I leaned forward and hugged her, careful to avoid the IVs, monitors, and oxygen tubes connected to her.

As I perched on the edge of her bed, she reached for the spoon, her fingers trembling as she tried to guide it from the bowl to her mouth. After a few failed attempts, she sighed, letting it clatter back into the soup.

"Here, let me help," I said gently, lifting the spoon to her lips.

She smiled weakly after swallowing. "That tastes so ood."

She managed to eat almost half of her soup before her eyelids drooped. Sinking into the pillow, she fought to stay awake.

"I'm going to let you rest. I'm glad you're doing better. I'll be back tomorrow." I kissed her cheek. "Love you!"

As I reached for the door handle, I glanced over my shoulder. She was fast asleep.

Despite my talent for crafting words into meaningful sentences, I was speechless as T.J. and I walked to his car. I had no words to explain what I was feeling. Worry for my mother's life, guilt over my actions, and the need to find Coach Wyatt's killer without further damaging my relationship with my family completely overwhelmed me.

Once seated inside T.J.'s car, I leaned against the passenger door, cradling my head as a wave of despair came over me. The names of suspects rolled through my mind like the closing credits of a movie. Only this time, I couldn't just get up and walk away. I was stuck in this mystery, and the story just wouldn't end.

T.J. tapped my shoulder, his voice soft. "I'm here if you want to talk. If not, I understand."

I exhaled. "Thanks. "I just…I don't even know where to start."

"I know, but with everything that's been going on with your mom, do you think it's smart to be working with Craig on this murder thing? I mean, I'm sure he can handle this on his own. He's a big boy."

I nodded.

He had a point.

"I know he can investigate this without me. But I…oh, I

don't know how to explain it...I can't help but believe that finding the coach's killer is the only way I can protect my family. I owe them that."

T.J. frowned. "But couldn't you be putting them in even more danger? Suppose you're right that Wyatt's death is connected to the other murders. Won't poking around make this mastermind even angrier?"

I let out a deep sigh. "But if I don't find the answers, do you honestly think he'll just stop? I don't think so. If revenge is what he's after, at what point does he decide it's enough? When he thinks justice has been served? What if he's on some kind of power trip?" I paused. "He has to be stopped, and the only way to do that is to figure out who he is, and I want to be part of that."

T.J. gripped the steering wheel. "I think you're playing a very dangerous game, and if you don't stop, I'm afraid more bad things will happen—to you or your family."

I slumped in my seat as he pulled into my driveway and stopped under the basketball hoop. "So, you think I'm responsible for what happened to my mother?"

He looked away for a moment and then back to me. "It's not like you meant for someone to hurt your mom. It's that, well, when you play with fire, you're gonna get burned."

I blinked back the sting in my eyes, his words hitting me hard."Wow. Thanks. That makes me feel so much better. Maybe you need to reconsider your offer to help me. I wouldn't want you to get burned."

And with that, I threw open the car door and marched to my front door.

"Michelle!" T.J. called after me.

I didn't look back.

Inside the house, I tossed my books and purse onto the couch and collapsed into the cushions.

I can't believe T.J. thinks I'm responsible for the attack on my mother!

But no matter how hard I tried to dismiss his words, in my heart, I feared he was right. My involvement in proving Danny's innocence could carry high stakes for me and my family. Yet, I was convinced that if I chose not to take any action, there was no guarantee this mastermind, as T.J. called him, would stop killing people. The only way to end the madness was to get to the truth, wherever it was, no matter how long it took.

I buried my head in Mom's orange and brown afghan as I sat in the corner of the couch and fought back the urge to have a massive meltdown. Releasing the stress and crying might've felt good for a few minutes, but I knew how that story ended—red eyes, a pounding headache, and zero progress.

Gidget jumped on top of the crocheted blanket covering me. Before lying down, she pawed the loops of yarn until she approved the cushy surface she had created. I gently removed a lone fiber from the afghan wrapped around one of her nails. She inspected my work and closed her eyes, satisfied that I had done a satisfactory job.

Not wanting to disturb the slumbering ball of fur, I reached for the notebook in my purse next to me, mindful of keeping my movements to a minimum.

Although Craig's idea of us taking private skating lessons was interesting, I wasn't convinced it was the best way to gather all the intel we needed. No, there had to be another way.

Grabbing the pen on the end table by the telephone, I jotted Lawrence's name with a notation to see if he could find the identity of the person Coach Wyatt suspected of spreading the rumors about performance-enhancing drugs. Also, maybe he could find out if any of the skaters had dirt in their backgrounds.

I tapped the pen on my notebook, ran through my list of names, and added Olga to Lawrence's to-do list. After that, I needed to talk to Danny. Since he was still in jail, having had bail denied because he was considered a flight risk, I needed to speak with him and hear his thoughts on why someone would want to frame him.

Next, I wanted to go inside the Hathaway House, where the skaters lived. Who knew what I might find there? Plus, I was eager to go through the coach's office. Although I had no idea what I was looking for, I was sure I would know when I saw it.

Inadvertently, I moved my leg, upsetting Gidget, who had to go to great lengths to reposition herself and get comfortable again on the blanket. She glared at me as she settled in, making it clear she would not be happy with any more disruptions. Her displeasure, for some reason, reminded me of the limo.

I wonder if the police ever tracked it down.

I jotted *limo* under Lawrence's name.

My deep sigh in the otherwise silent room caused Gidget's ear to twitch. I was still missing something. Craig and I needed more information about Coach Wyatt's former rink—the coaches he worked with, the skaters training there...those sorts of things. Perhaps Mr. Hansen could help. After all, he was the one who got Danny the job there. He must know someone. Maybe Yash could find out. It was worth a try.

I closed my notebook. Even without a clear game plan, I felt better knowing I had the beginning of one. Talking to Danny and asking Lawrence for his help would be easy. The tricky part was getting into the Hathaway House, but I had to find a way.

chapter fifteen

From the moment I picked T.J. up for our morning commute to school, things were awkward between us. He attempted to apologize several times, but I shut him down. I knew he didn't want me to be mad at him, but his words from the previous night still stung, especially since I knew he truly believed them.

To make it clear that I had no desire to talk, I cranked up the volume on the radio as Olivia Newton-John sang "Have You Never Been Mellow." I quietly hummed along until a cloud of melancholy enveloped me. That's when it hit me why I was so angry with him. I wanted T.J.'s unwavering support, no matter what I did, but I also needed his honesty. The truth was, he couldn't always give me both.

I glanced at T.J., who was staring out the passenger window. His words had hurt me, and my silence had wounded him. It was time to clear the air.

"I know you didn't mean to upset me last night and that you think I should stay out of investigating Coach Wyatt's murder, but I'm going to do it, and I'm not changing my mind. If you still want to help me, I'd like that. But if not, that's okay. I promise not to be mad. I just ask that you do the same and understand that there are some things I have to do."

I had hardly finished my sentence before T.J. chimed in. "Of course, I'm going to help you. That's the only way I can make sure you're safe. Craig certainly won't keep you out of trouble."

"Are you sure?"

"What? That Craig puts you in dangerous situations or that I will help?"

"That you'll help, silly. And it's not Craig's fault that I sometimes find myself in a predicament. I do a pretty good job of that all by myself." I grinned.

"No argument from me," he chuckled, leaning back. "So, where do we begin?"

"I know you're not going to like this, but I need to get inside the Hathaway House when everyone is gone."

"You're not going to break in, are you? I'm all for helping, but I draw the line at getting arrested." His eyes widened with worry.

"No, nothing that drastic. But I've got an idea."

"Now I'm scared," T.J. sighed.

***

Mid-morning, T.J. and I met up at the Commuter Lounge. He reviewed his notes for his next class as I flipped through the school newspaper. My eyes landed on an advertisement for a skating exhibition that evening at the university's ice rink.

Coach Wyatt's team was scheduled to perform their programs from the World Figure Skating Championships last month in Colorado Springs. Members of the Petersburg Ice Skating Club would also be featured. Proceeds from the evening's ticket sales would go toward expanding the club's programs and creating a scholarship in Coach Wyatt's name.

I nudged T.J.'s arm and pointed to the ad. "This is our chance. Everyone will be at the rink. The house will be empty."

"Are you sure?" T.J. replied. "Olga might not have to be at the exhibition."

"I'll ask Eric during my lesson this afternoon," I said. "If she's going to be at the rink tonight, it'll be the perfect time to check out the house."

T.J. leaned back in his chair, crossing his arms. "I don't suppose you've figured out how we're going to get inside without breaking down a door or crawling through a window, have you?"

"Funny you should ask," I grinned. "I thought about that last night, and then I remembered Mae said she was going to the police station to see if they would let her take Danny's personal items. She's scared they'll lose them. If his keys were in that stash, I'm sure she'll let me borrow them if I explain that I need them for our investigation."

"And if she doesn't have the house key?" T.J. narrowed his eyes.

"I haven't quite figured that out yet," I admitted. "First, I'll see if Mae has the keys. If not, I'll come up with another plan."

"Plan? What are you up to now, Michelle?" Lawrence asked, sliding into the chair across from T.J. with a grin. He shot a knowing glance at Billy, then snatched a playing card from his hand and slapped it onto the table. "Boom." Lawrence smirked as Todd groaned and shook his head in defeat.

"Now, where were we?" Lawrence asked, turning his attention back to me. "Ah, yes. What is Michelle up to?"

"Nothing," I shrugged. "I was just telling T.J. about the ice exhibition tonight. It should be fun. Everyone will be at the rink!"

Lawrence's gaze shifted between T.J. and me. "Why do I think there's more to this story than what you're telling me?"

Rick pulled out the chair next to me and chuckled. "If I know Michelle, it's probably because there is."

Lawrence rolled his eyes and flicked two dimes across the table to Amy, who caught them with a grin and dropped them into a canvas money bag. Without missing a beat, she poured him a steaming cup of coffee. He reached over, lifted the mug, and gave it a slow swirl, watching the dark liquid ripple inside.

After a long sip, Lawrence peered at me over his glasses. "So," he said with a slight furrow in his brow, "tell me, what's really up?"

I scanned the faces around the table. "You all promise you won't tell anyone?"

Everyone—Lawrence, Billy, Amy, Tasha, Yash, Rick, and Todd—nodded in agreement. But naturally, Lawrence couldn't resist adding his two cents.

"As long as you're not breaking the law," he said, arching an eyebrow. "Because if you are, I fully reserve the right to rat you out. Just saying."

"No worries," I shook my head. "I'm not breaking the law. It's just that Mae might have Danny's keys to the Hathaway House. If she does, I'll use them to get in. There's no harm in that, especially if I'm picking something up for Danny, like maybe a book."

"What do you hope to find?" Rick asked.

"I don't know," I replied with a shrug. "But there's bound to be something that will point me to the killer."

"What makes you think the police overlooked something? I mean, I wouldn't doubt it, but why do you think so?" Tasha asked.

"Because as far as Detective Douglas is concerned, Danny is guilty," I said, resting my chin on my hand. "Between Danny's *supposed* argument with Coach Wyatt and his scarf being used as the murder weapon, Douglas has quit looking."

"I don't think you give Douglas enough credit. It's not like he has it in for Danny," Lawrence countered.

"Are you sure? I mean, it was only a few months ago he arrested Danny's parents for murder and attempted murder. Why wouldn't he think Danny is guilty by association?"

Lawrence's expression darkened. "Let me put it this way," he said, his tone serious. "You're playing a dangerous game. You need to leave the investigation to the police."

"That's what I keep telling her," T.J. grunted.

"Come on, guys," I said. "Trust me. I know what I'm doing."

"Do you?" Lawrence asked with a shrug.

Needing an escape from his judgment, I changed the subject. "Anything new on the Sarah investigation?"

"Douglas and I reviewed the security footage from the night Sarah died—when that dude pulled the guards away from their post," Lawrence said.

"Any idea who he was?" I asked.

"We found him on the tape, and, just like we suspected, he *borrowed* a uniform. The name on his badge doesn't match the actual officer."

"So, now what?" I leaned forward.

"We've got a still frame of him…it's pretty grainy since we pulled it straight off the video, but Douglas has the forensic artist working on a composite sketch." He took a sip of his coffee.

"How long will that take?" I asked, pressing him.

"We should have it today."

"I hope you can figure out who he is. He's got to be Sarah's mystery man or tied to him somehow." I leaned back, my thoughts racing. "What about the limo Detective Douglas saw near Coach's house?"

Lawrence set his cup down. "He's contacted all the local limo services, but no one has a record of their vehicles being in that neighborhood that night."

"Yeah, but if I were committing a murder, I wouldn't report being near the scene of the crime, so how reliable are their records?" I argued.

"Douglas thought the same thing, so he got copies of their mileage logs. He's got some rookie officer checking for gaps between reported routes and actual miles driven," Lawrence replied.

I crossed my arms. "Sounds like a tangled mess."

"Maybe." Lawrence conceded, slipping his camo jacket on. "But we'll get to the truth. It'll just take time. We need to be careful not to ruffle too many feathers or alert those responsible that we're closing in on them. That's the tricky part, especially since we have no idea who's behind all of this."

As Lawrence's words hung in the air, a sharp gasp from Billy made me jump. A second later, he lunged for the coffee pot from Amy's hands. Then it clicked—Alice, the ruler of the Commuter Lounge, had to be nearby. Just as I was processing what that meant, Billy flinched as hot coffee splashed over his hand.

"Ouch! That hurts!" he muttered, shoving the coffee maker under the table and kicking his backpack in front of it.

Amy grabbed his hand, inspecting the burn.

Alice marched over, eyes locked on Billy. "Are you okay?" she asked, leaning in to examine his hand.

"I just spilled some coffee on it." Billy shrugged, brushing a stray curl from his face. "It's fine. No big deal." He quickly covered the burn with his other hand.

Alice raised an eyebrow, surveying the table. "Funny. You don't have any coffee."

Amy jumped in. "It was mine. I accidentally spilled it on him."

Alice shook her head. "Hmm...and not a drop on the table."

"I guess it all ended up on his hand," Tasha added without looking up from her book.

Alice smirked. "Interesting. You know, there's a rumor going around that you guys have started a coffee business." Her eyes landed on the backpack near Billy's feet. "Any truth to that?"

Rick chimed in with feigned innocence. "Who would start a rumor like that?"

I reached for the charm around my neck and my heart skipped.

It wasn't there.

After a second of panic, I remembered that in my rush this morning, I'd left it on my vanity.

Meanwhile, Alice straightened and folded her arms. "If a rumor like that were *true*," she said slowly, "it might cause me some trouble. Especially if someone got hurt—say, like a burn or something." She glanced at each one of us, one by one. "Now, you wouldn't want to cause me any trouble, would you?"

Like naughty children who had been caught, we lowered our eyes and shook our heads.

"Good. I'm glad we all understand." She smiled, satisfied. "Billy, come with me, and we'll get some medicine on that burn."

As Billy scooted his chair back, Alice turned to leave, then paused."Of course," she added over her shoulder, "if you were to submit a written proposal for setting up a coffee maker in a permanent spot in the Commuter Lounge with a list of your responsibilities for buying supplies and cleaning up, that might be something I could consider."

Once Alice and Billy disappeared into her office, we burst into laughter.

"I thought we were toast," Rick grinned.

"Yeah, me too," I agreed. "I thought for sure she was going to kick us all out."

"That was crazy," T.J. added. "But did I hear her right? She's open to the idea of our coffee business if we submit a business plan?"

"That's what it sounded like to me," Lawrence said with a mischievous grin.

"Guess I know what we're doing tomorrow night at my house," Rick said, grinning. "Instead of a club constitution, we need a business plan. I'll find the one my mom used for her fitness center. Yash, if I get it to you, could you adapt it to what we need? Man, we're about to go legit."

Todd's face fell. "I'm not sure how I feel about all this pandering to The Man's rules. I like being a rebel."

"Yeah, me too," Rick sighed.

Yash scooted into Billy's vacant chair. "Who says it has to end?"

Todd frowned. "You heard what she said. If we want to continue, she needs a business plan."

"True," Yash nodded, with a playful glint in his eyes. "But no one said the plan we give her has to be the one we actually follow."

"What do you mean?" I asked.

"We can write a nice corporate kind of business plan for Alice to keep her happy, but we can run our committees how we want," Yash explained.

"Why do we need committees?" Amy asked, tossing her light brown hair behind her back.

Yash grinned. "Business plans outline how the business will be managed. We might include a team-building committee to keep us all on the same page and build camaraderie. But who says that committee can't plan parties and field trips to places like Daytona Beach for spring break? Or the committee in charge of inventory could be a group of us renting a house together next year." Yash's grin widened. "Don't you see? We can still have fun with this and outsmart The Man."

Heads nodded around the table.

Amy squeezed Todd's arm, winking. "Cool! I wanna be on the party committee!"

"Duly noted." Todd grinned. "Okay, tomorrow night we play by the rules and…bend a few others."

After checking the clock on the wall, I gathered my books and noticed T.J. glancing at his watch.

"Where are you off to?" he asked. "I thought your next class wasn't until later this afternoon."

"Yeah, but I'm meeting Eric for my skating lesson at the rink." I glanced at Yash, engrossed in conversation with Todd. Not wanting to disturb him, I turned to T.J. "That reminds me —did you ask Yash about Danny's scarf? Did he check to see if Mr. Hansen noticed anything unusual at the house while he was there?"

"Yash said he was on it," T.J. replied with a grin.

I narrowed my eyes. "What are you grinning about?"

"Just that, judging by how eager Yash was to help, I think he enjoys being a snoop. Who knew?"

***

When I stepped onto the ice for my lesson with Eric, it quickly became clear that ice skating wasn't in my DNA, or at the very least not in my ankles. I fell several times just trying to make it halfway around the rink.

Naomi took pity on me and asked me what size shoe I wore. After determining we wore the same size, she suggested I try a pair of her backup skates. They fit like a dream, snugly supporting my ankles and giving me stability on the ice—something I had never had before.

Eric then asked me to skate around the rink so he could assess my ability—or lack thereof.

As I carefully maneuvered forward, I caught sight of Katie skating into a jump. She soared into the air, but when she went for the landing, she fell off the edge of her blade and hit the ice with a loud thud. To my bewilderment, she sat there crying instead of getting up. Olga, standing behind the boards, shook her head and turned away.

I barely had time to process the moment before my attention snapped back to the ice just in time to see Jason and Naomi speeding through their footwork sequence, heading straight for me. Unable to skate fast enough to get out of their way, I grabbed the boards and yanked myself tightly against them, just in time to avoid a collision.

Eric skated over to me, laughing. "And they say hockey is dangerous."

"Man, they go way faster than I ever imagined," I sighed, relieved to be out of everyone's way. I glanced at Katie, still crying on the ice. "Is she okay? Did she get hurt?"

"Only her ego," Eric said. "Happens all the time."

From the boards, Olga called out, "Katie. Do it again."

Eric smirked. "Olga doesn't do meltdowns. It's work, work, work. I remember once, I had a lesson on my birthday, and she told me we would celebrate by working very, very hard. Lucky me!"

I raised a brow. "Do people like working with Olga?"

"*Like* is such a vague word." He chuckled. "Do we like her bedside manner? No way… but we do like the results we get with her choreography. You bet we do. Don't get me wrong, that's not to say we don't butt heads with her from time to time. I think we've all had more than a few disagreements with Olga, but in the end, we do it her way. After all, she's one of the best."

I shook my head, watching Jason and Naomi locked in what looked like a tense discussion with Olga. Her scowl only deepened the longer they talked.

"And here I thought figure skating was all about elegance and having fun," I mused. Who knew there was so much drama?

By the time my lesson with Eric ended, I had not only gotten a glimpse into the world of competitive figure skating, but I could now execute a T-Stop. No more relying on my less-than-graceful method of slamming into the boards.

As I unlaced my borrowed skates in the locker room, I asked Eric, "Are you skating in the show tonight?"

"Yeah, I'm doing my long and short programs from Worlds, plus my exhibition number. We also have a group finale with the skating club," he replied.

"I bet it's challenging to put together a routine with so many different levels of skaters," I mused.

"It can be, but we've done group numbers before. We just pieced together elements from previous shows to create something new. The tough part was adding all the skaters from the figure skating club. Olga nearly pulled her hair out with the youngest ones," he chuckled. "She's not used to working with beginners, but she figured it out. And she'll be right by the boards in case they get turned around during their routines."

"Sounds like you've all got a busy day between practicing, teaching, and the show tonight. Will you have any time to rest?"

He laughed. "Not today. Olga arranged to have dinner delivered here so we wouldn't have to go back to the house. That way, we can chill and unwind instead of spending our downtime running back and forth."

I nodded. "That was smart thinking." I handed Naomi's

skates to him. "I can't imagine being back at the house after what happened."

Eric's expression darkened. "Yeah. It's a little creepy sometimes. I try not to think about it, but it's unsettling being in a house where someone was murdered." He opened Naomi's locker and placed her skates on the bottom shelf. Pivoting back, he added, "We're all glad the police arrested Danny. As long as he's behind bars, we're all better off."

"Do you really believe Danny killed Coach Wyatt?"

A flicker of anger crossed Eric's face. "Of course he did. Danny's been nothing but a troublemaker since he came into our lives. He wormed his way into Coach's life only to try to profit from it. When that didn't work, he took matters into his own hands—literally."

I leaned against the lockers. "What do you mean *profit*? How could Danny make money off Coach Wyatt?"

Eric shook his head. "Look. I don't want to speak ill of the dead, but Coach was involved in some things that weren't exactly on the up-and-up."

I frowned. "What do you mean?"

"Never mind." He shrugged. "It doesn't matter. What's done is in the past. There's no going back, but the dude was right—Danny was trouble."

"The dude?"

Eric's attention shifted as the door to the coach's room creaked open. A woman's voice called, "Eric. Can you come here?"

Olga stood in the doorway.

"Be right there," Eric replied, turning back to me. "See you next week for your lesson?"

"Sure. Sounds good."

He took a few steps toward the office, then paused. "Don't forget about tonight. Should be a lot of fun."

I nodded. "I'm sure it will be."

chapter sixteen

T.J. pulled into my driveway at 5:45 p.m. We had planned to arrive at the skaters' house by 6:00 p.m. By then, anyone who had forgotten something for the show would have already come and gone. The last thing we needed was a surprise visitor while we searched the house for evidence.

As I climbed into his car, I gave T.J. a once-over from head to toe. He, in turn, did the same to me. We burst into laughter. Although we never talked about what to wear on our secret mission, we were twins in our all-black get-ups.

"I guess great minds think alike," I chuckled, shaking my head.

T.J. glanced down at his shirt, a mischievous grin spreading across his face. "Isn't this how all cat burglars dress?"

Raising my chin, I countered, "I prefer to think of us as detectives working undercover to ensure justice is served."

"Yeah, yeah, whatever you want to call it," T.J. teased, his smirk widening. "All I know is I had to borrow this shirt from my dad. He thinks I'm trying out a new look, you know, something other than striped shirts. Man, if only he knew."

Jefferson Starship's "Miracles" played in the background

as he drove. I hummed along, gazing out the window at the trees and the lilac bushes dotting the landscape.

"Speaking of miracles," T.J. said, his tone suddenly serious, "we're gonna need one to pull this off tonight."

I turned to him, puzzled. "Why makes you say that? We've got a key to let us in, and we'll have the house all to ourselves."

T.J. furrowed his brows, keeping his eyes on the road. "Did Mae want to know why you needed Danny's house key?"

I wrinkled my nose. "Actually, she didn't have it."

He jerked his head in surprise. "Then how'd you get the key? Wasn't it with Danny's stuff from the police station?"

I twirled a strand of hair, buying time before I answered. "No. Turns out they wouldn't let Mae take any of his stuff."

T.J. flicked his gaze toward me, then back to the road. "So…how are we getting in?"

With a flourish, I dangled a key in the air. "With this."

"But I thought you said Mae didn't have Danny's keys."

"Correct." I nodded.

T.J. rubbed the back of his neck, the lines on his forehead deepening. "Dare I ask how you got it?"

I flashed a teasing smile. "Are you sure you want to know?"

"Michelle!"

"All right, all right." I sighed. "*Maybe* I asked Lawrence if I could go through Danny's belongings at the police station. And *maybe* he left the box on the counter when he answered the phone. And *maybe*, just *maybe*, I picked up a key to examine it and…*accidentally* dropped it into my purse."

T.J. gasped. "Oh, my word! You mean Lawrence let you steal evidence?"

"No. He has no idea I have it," I corrected. "And I didn't *steal* it. I borrowed it. I'll give it back. No big deal."

T.J. parked his car in front of the Hathaway House and

slumped back into his seat. "No big deal she said as they slapped the cuffs on her and her best friend and hauled them off to jail."

"Come on, T.J.," I said, nudging his shoulder. "It's not that bad."

He didn't say a word, just drummed his fingers on the steering wheel, each tap sounding duller than the one before.

"Look, you don't have to do this if you don't want to," I said. "I'm fine going in by myself."

T.J. shifted in his seat. "I still don't think this is a good idea, but I said I would help you."

"And I appreciate that. Really, I do," I assured him as I tried to read his expression. "But if you'd rather not—"

"I'm here, aren't I?" he snapped.

"Yeah, but—"

"I just hope you know what you're doing," he retorted, concern creeping into his eyes. "I don't want either of us ending up in jail."

"Neither do I," I said as I opened the car door. "But I don't see why we'd get in trouble. We're not breaking in. We're simply trying to find evidence that will point us to the person who killed Coach Wyatt."

"And what if the police already have the murderer behind bars?" He stopped on the sidewalk. "Be honest. If you find evidence that points to Danny, will you accept it and stop your investigation?"

"Of course I will," I said without any hesitation. "But I don't think that'll be the case."

T.J. exhaled sharply. "Okay, then. Let's do this." He walked up the porch steps and froze. "Wait—is that a light on in the front room? You don't think someone is at home, do you?"

I followed his gaze. "I wouldn't think so. Everyone's supposed to be at the Exhibition Skate. They probably left a light on so they wouldn't come home to a dark house." I paused before adding, "Eric mentioned the house has been kind of creepy since Coach died."

T.J. groaned. "Fantastic."

"Tell you what, I'll ring the doorbell first," I suggested as I stepped in front of him. "If someone's home, they'll come to the door."

T.J. nodded. "Sounds like a plan."

I pressed the doorbell, my hands shaking slightly. I thrust it to my side, hoping T.J. wouldn't notice my fear. If he did, he was either polite enough—or too nervous himself—to mention it.

Nothing.

I willed myself a steadier hand and pressed the button again.

We waited.

No movement inside.

T.J. and I exchanged glances and nodded. It was time to move forward with our plan.

I slid the key into the lock, twisting it until a faint click echoed in the quiet evening air. The door creaked open, and I stepped inside, scanning the dimly lit room.

T.J. stood motionless on the porch.

"All clear," I whispered, waving him in.

The house was empty. We were alone.

T.J. glanced down the hallway. "What do you want me to do?"

"I'll search Coach Wyatt's office. You can either go upstairs and start looking in the bedrooms, or, if you want, you can help me."

"Don't you think it'd be better if we stayed together?"

"Good idea. It might go faster that way," I said, motioning for him to follow me. "Come on. It's this way."

We moved down the hall, stopping at the office door.

"You sure this is a good idea?" T.J. asked.

"It'll be fine," I assured him, rolling my eyes with determination.

He didn't move. My partner in crime was having second thoughts.

"If it'll make you feel better, why don't you stand guard and keep an eye on things in case someone comes home early," I suggested as I pulled a mini flashlight from my pants' pocket.

"But I thought you said they'd all be at the rink," he protested, panicking.

"They *should* be," I said with a shrug. "But I guess you never know. With my luck, Detective Douglas will show up and catch me in the act."

T.J.'s eyes widened as his jaw tightened. An exasperated "Great!" slipped from his lips.

"It'll be fine," I promised, flickering on my flashlight and sweeping the beam across the office.

Dark wooden bookcases lined the walls, their shelves crammed with thick binders, framed photos, and a few dusty trophies. A large walnut desk anchored one end of the room, a leather chair tucked neatly beneath it as if waiting for its occupant to return. My stomach knotted as I took it all in. Was it really just the other night that Craig and I sat in those chairs, talking with Coach Wyatt? It felt like a lifetime ago. Almost as if that moment belonged to a different world.

At first glance, nothing seemed out of place, but my gut feeling told me to keep looking. I moved behind the desk, rifling through the drawers. The notes Coach Wyatt had shown us were gone, likely confiscated by the police. Other than their absence, nothing stood out.

I brushed my fingers against the smooth wood of the desk, and a memory surfaced—my grandfather's old oak desk.

Hmmm. I wonder…

I slid my hand under the narrow center drawer, fingers searching.

Then, I felt it.

A tiny metal pin.

Holding my breath, I pressed it, and the pin released. The drawer quickly pulled free.

"What'd you find?" T.J. asked.

"Give me a minute. I'm not sure." I replied as I sorted through the papers. "Nothing much. A bunch of old receipts from the 30s and 40s. Probably the previous owner put them there and forgot about them." I shrugged. "Oh, here's a small key, like the one my mom uses for the porcelain clock on her nightstand."

"How'd you know to look for that drawer?"

"My grandfather in Tennessee had a desk with secret drawers," I said, brushing dust from my hands. "He used to hide little pink mints and shiny half-dollars in them for Crystal, Mike, and me to find while Mom and Dad packed up the car for our trip home. Grandpa always made finding the hidden compartments our little game."

I returned everything to the drawer and pressed it shut, ensuring the pin clicked into place so it would stay hidden.

Next, I removed the bottom drawer on the right side of the desk, running my fingers along the part of the desk it had covered. My pulse quickened as I traced the outline of a lock, and I focused my flashlight on it. Just as I suspected—a false panel.

"There's something here, but I need a key," I said, my fingers following the faint edges of the hidden compartment.

"What about that key you just found?" T.J. asked excitedly.

"Good thinking!" I fished the tiny bronze key out of the drawer and inserted it into the lock. A soft click sounded, and *voila*, the false back swung open.

A cascade of papers tumbled out.

T.J.'s curiosity apparently got the best of him. When I

glanced up, he was walking toward me, his eyes locked on the scattered papers. "What'd you find?"

I sifted through the pages, studying the handwriting. I took in a deep breath.

"Well?" T.J. asked impatiently.

"They're love letters," I murmured. "From Olga."

T.J. blinked. "Olga? The one you said worked with the coach?"

"Yeah." I nodded. "Some of these are dated from five years ago." I held up a piece of deckled-edged stationery. "But this one? It's from last November. Since when do guys save love letters?"

"I don't know." T.J. shrugged. "Obviously, some guys do. Did Coach Wyatt seem like the romantic type to you?"

I shook my head. "Not really, but then again, I didn't know him that well."

T.J. peered at the papers. "Anything else interesting?"

I rummaged through the remaining contents. "No…wait." A chill ran down my spine as I angled the paper for a better look. "It's one of those threatening notes, but this one's different from the ones Coach showed Craig and me."

"What do you mean?"

"It's handwritten."

T.J. edged closer. "What are you doing?"

"What does it look like I'm doing? I'm putting them in my pocket."

"I know what you're doing, but *why*? You're not seriously taking those with you—that's tampering with evidence."

I locked eyes with T.J. "The police searched this room, and they didn't take them. So… since they didn't consider them as evidence—"

"I don't think that's how it works," T.J. argued. "Especially when you found them in a secret drawer—one they didn't know anything about."

"It's not my fault I figured it out, and they didn't."

T.J. groaned. "Michelle—"

"Don't worry. I just want to compare the handwriting." I pulled one of the threatening notes from my pocket and held it up against one of Olga's letters. "I'm no expert, but Olga might've written both. The handwriting looks *awfully* similar."

I folded the note and some of the love letters, tucking them in my pocket.

"You're taking the love letters too?" T.J. asked.

"I need a better look. Plus, I still need writing samples from the skaters so I can—"

T.J. interjected, "Are you sure you're not going to get into trouble for having those papers?"

"It'll be fine. I'll turn everything over to Detective Douglas when I'm done."

"Yeah," he sighed, running a hand through his hair. "And how do you plan to explain to him how you got those *writing samples?*"

"I'll worry about that later. Right now, let's go check the bedrooms upstairs and see what we can find."

T.J. hesitated. "Or, hear me out. We could leave."

"I'll only be a few minutes," I assured him as I headed to the hallway. "Stay here if you want. Just close the office door when you leave."

Without waiting for a response, I darted toward the staircase.

The thought of searching the bedrooms unnerved me. It felt *different,* more invasive than going through Coach Wyatt's office. I took a deep breath, dispelling my misgivings by rationalizing that in the name of finding the coach's killer, it had to be done.

The first room I entered was a disaster—dirty clothes piled on the floor, an unmade bed, open dresser drawers. It reminded me of my brother Mike's room at home when he still lived there.

When searching Coach Wyatt's office, I knew *exactly* where to look, but this room? I had no clue. *Under the bed? The closet? The dresser?*

With nine bedrooms to go through and no idea how long I could keep T.J. from leaving the house, I had no time to waste.

Kneeling, I lifted the bedspread and looked under the bed. Shoes. Mismatched socks. Dust bunnies. Nothing useful.

Stepping over the pile of dirty clothes, I reached for the nightstand drawers—pens, paper, letters addressed to Eric. As I searched through the mess, a book slipped out and landed with a thud on the floor: *The Death of a President* by William Manchester.

I stared at the title, remembering the paper I had written on the Kennedy assassination back in high school. Sure, I'd earned an A+, but that wasn't what came to my mind now. It was the realization that the truth often hides in plain sight— twisted, manipulated, and dangerous, just like now.

Then, something caught my eye—a notecard wedged between the nightstand and the bed. I leaned over and picked it up. I couldn't believe my eyes.

A phone number. An address.

Boston

Sarah was from Boston. My mind spun. What secrets might be uncovered with this information?

Suddenly, heavy footsteps thundered up the stairs, shattering my thoughts.

"Michelle," T.J. panted from the hallway outside the bedroom. "Someone just pulled into the driveway. What do we do?"

I slipped the notecard into my pocket and reached for the bedroom light, but froze as the footsteps thumped on the porch steps.

The screen door squeaked.

Panic surged through me.

"Quick," I whispered. "That room." I pointed to the one at the end of the hall, hoping it had a larger bed for us to hide under.

"Turn off the light!" T.J. said.

I shook my head. "No, they might have seen the light on from the street. If it suddenly goes dark, they'll think something is up. Come on!"

We bolted to the bedroom. My eyes swept over our surroundings— a razor, cologne, a wooden valet box on the nightstand. *A man's room.*

I motioned for T.J. to slide under the full-size bed as I did the same.

Once settled, T.J. scooted closer to me. I could feel his warm breath against my cheek.

Our eyes locked, and he protectively put his arm over me.

The footsteps creaked up the stairs.

Then silence.

A woman's voice drifted into the room. "Eric. Will he *never* learn to turn off the lights?"

Olga.

I clenched my jaw.

T.J.'s breath quickened. His arm tightened around me.

Then, as if things couldn't get any worse, the phone on the nightstand next to the bed we were hiding under rang.

I held my breath.

I watched a pair of heels click across the floor, stopping inches from my face.

Olga picked up the receiver.

"Hello?" A pause. "Yes, I will look for them. Give me one minute."

Her footsteps retreated, only to return a minute later.

"I found them. I'll meet you in the coaches' room in a few minutes."

A thud as she set the phone down.

Silence once again.

We waited. The front door closed.

"Man, that was close," T.J. muttered.

"Yeah, way too close." I nodded.

"Let's get out of here!" T.J. said as he hurried down the hallway.

"Wait. I want to search Olga's room."

He blinked at me in disbelief. "You've got to be *kidding*?"

"Five minutes." I held up a hand. "That's all."

T.J. groaned. "Why do I let you talk me into these things?"

"Because you know I'm right."

He muttered something under his breath and trudged downstairs.

Now, to find Olga's room.

Behind the first door I opened was a twin-sized bed with a blue bedspread, surrounded by a chaotic mess of clothes and scattered belongings. Probably not Olga's room. *If only I had more time.*

But I didn't.

The second door opened to a similarly small bed adorned with a floral bedspread, its walls plastered with movie posters. I closed it almost instantly, knowing it wasn't the right room.

Finally, behind the third door was a room that looked exactly as I imagined Olga's private retreat—tidy, a floral bedspread with meticulously arranged pillows. A black and white photograph of her sat on the dresser.

I yanked open the drawers, carefully shifting the contents. My hands brushed against something smooth—a ribbon.

A bundle of letters tied with a pink satin bow.

My curiosity swelled. I knew I *should* take the time to read them, but time was something I didn't have.

I grabbed two letters—one from the middle and one from the bottom—then shut the drawer.

My hands were shaking. Olga's surprise appearance had

unnerved me more than I thought. T.J. was right. We needed to go home.

I rushed down the stairs.

He stood by the door, arms crossed.

"I'm done!" I said, pushing past him onto the porch.

"Find anything?"

"A couple of letters. I'll read them in the car."

"What if Olga notices they're missing?"

"She won't. I'll put them back before she ever realizes they're gone."

I pulled open the car door. "Let's get out of here."

chapter seventeen

After running to T.J.'s car, I slid into the passenger seat, placing the letters on my lap as I buckled my seatbelt.

T.J. frowned. "Why'd you put 'em down? I thought you couldn't wait to read 'em."

"Yeah, but I can't read them in the dark, and I don't think it's a good idea to turn the light on while we're parked in front of the house. Someone might see us." I gestured toward the road. "Let's go someplace away from here."

T.J. nodded and drove to Yancy's, parking under the warm glow of a lamppost. I unfolded the first letter and began to read aloud: "To my dearest Olga," I stopped and flipped the letter over. "It's signed 'W.' For Wyatt?"

"That'd be my guess," T.J. replied.

I skimmed the letter. "It seems to be a love letter. Whoever wrote it says, 'I miss you. I am counting the days before we meet again'…yadda, yadda." I placed it on the console between us and reached for the second one.

"Ah…this one is more interesting." I looked at the signature on the bottom. "It's from Olga…I guess she never sent it."

"What's it say?"

"She asks Coach if he is seeing someone else and if that is

why he wants to reevaluate their relationship." I noticed the date. "It was written six months ago."

"Sounds like that rumor about Coach Wyatt and Olga might be true," T.J. said. "Do you suppose she offed him because he dumped her?"

"I don't know." I shrugged. "But I want a handwriting expert to compare this letter from Olga with the writing on the threatening notes."

"And how are you going to manage that?" T.J. asked, wrinkling his forehead.

I bit my bottom lip, mulling over my options. "Perhaps Craig could help. He's worked with a private detective before. He might know someone who can analyze the writing samples."

T.J. scoffed, "Yeah. Craig to the rescue."

"Oh, don't be like that. Craig has his good points, and his connections come in handy from time to time," I said.

"Lucky us," he murmured, turning away.

As I slumped back in my seat, I felt something in my back pocket. I pulled out a crumbled notecard.

"What's that?" he asked, squinting at the writing.

"Something I found in Eric's room."

T.J. leaned closer as I continued. "Someone wrote an address and a phone number on it.

I rested my elbow on the console. "Between finding evidence of a jilted lover and the notecard with a mysterious phone number and address, I'd say we had a pretty good tonight."

"I'd say by not getting caught, we had a very good night," said T.J.

"But you agree it was a good night?" I asked, grinning.

"Yeah…why?"

"Because it's nice to have you on board, and…we've got more work to do."

T.J. crossed his arms and rolled his eyes.

"Oh, don't worry. It's nothing too crazy," I reassured him.

T.J. shook his head. "And what's your definition of *not too crazy*?"

"No more breaking and entering—I mean, using a key—at least for now." I chuckled.

"I can live with that." He sighed. "So what's next on our to-do list?"

As T.J. drove me home, I shared my plan to have Lawrence see if he could find out who the phone number and address belonged to. I paused, then added, "I guess if he can't help….well, there's always Craig's private investigator."

"And how will you explain having the letters or the notecard?"

I took a deep breath. "I don't know. I'll deal with that later. For now, let's thing about what we know and how we can use it to get more information." I stared out the window for a few moments. "Naomi told Craig about her suspicions that something was going on between Olga and Coach Wyatt. So, I don't think anyone would find it strange if I asked about the rumors. I might be able to get some of the girls to talk."

"Any of them seem easier to talk to?" T.J. asked.

"Maybe Naomi. She let me borrow an old pair of her skates today for my lesson. Perhaps I could repay her by buying her lunch. Or wait, maybe Craig could help. He's taking lessons from her, and, you've got to admit, he has a way of getting people to open up to him. I'll call him tonight."

I twisted my Eiffel Tower charm and let out a deep sigh. "I hate to admit it, but you're right—the notecard is a bit trickier. That one's going to take some time."

T.J. smirked as he turned off the highway and started down the country roads toward home.

When he stopped at the intersection, he glanced over his shoulder. "Have you ever considered that all this might be for nothing? No matter how hard you try to pin this murder on someone other than Danny, he might be guilty. After all, his scarf was the murder weapon, and people overheard him arguing with the coach. And there is the possibility that he lied about leaving his scarf at the rink."

I shook my head. "I can't shake the feeling that Danny didn't strangle the coach. I could be wrong, but I don't think so. I'll ask Yash tomorrow if he found anything out about the scarf. And don't forget, there's that other coach who was causing trouble. Until we follow all the leads, I'm not giving up on Danny."

T.J. pulled into my driveway, and as I looked at the house, I gasped as panic gripped me.

"What's wrong?" he asked.

"My dad's home!" I exclaimed. "He was supposed to be spending the night at the hospital." My heart raced as an uneasy feeling came across me. "You don't suppose something happened to my mom, do you?"

"Or he just needed a decent night's sleep," T.J. said as he parked next to my car, placing his hand on mine.

"You're probably right. Mom was doing fine when I saw her this afternoon. The nurse even told me they might release her this weekend."

I opened my car door but whipped around when T.J. yelled, "What in the world?"

"What's wrong?" I asked, panic resuming.

"Your car!"

I dashed out of T.J.'s car and stood frozen in shock, staring at my shattered windshield.

"How on earth did that happen?" Confusion ran rampant in my thoughts as I scanned the area, looking for answers—no tree limbs had fallen, nothing seemed out of place.

I spotted a rock on the driver's seat through the cracked glass. Beneath it, a piece of paper. Using the sleeve of my turtleneck to grasp the door handle, I retrieved the note and read it out loud: "Decisions have consequences."

T.J. shook his head. "Not another warning."

He slowly walked around my car, scanning for more damage.

I reread the note as I leaned against the basketball hoop pole, anxiety tightening in my chest. "Do you think this is because we went to Coach Wyatt's house?"

T.J. scratched his head. "Could be, but how did they know we were there? That's just creepy."

"Yeah, that means someone's been following us. Oh, T.J., I'm so sorry for dragging you into this."

He exhaled and turned toward the house. "I wonder if your dad heard anything."

"Let's go inside and ask him," I suggested. Then, with a long breath, I added, "I guess I better call the police too. Detective Douglas is going to read me the riot act."

T.J. shrugged. "Let's talk to your dad first. I know you have to call the police, but unless your dad saw something, they won't have much to go on."

I dreaded the thought of filing a police report, but at least I hadn't touched anything with my bare hands. Hopefully, the police could lift some prints.

I glanced again at the shattered windshield. "What if the same guy who tried to kill my mom did this?"

"That's a possibility," T.J. agreed. "But it only means he leaves us no choice—he must be stopped."

"We?" I met T.J.'s gaze. "As much as I appreciate your help, I never should have involved you in this. It's my battle, not yours. For your safety, you need to stay out of it."

"No way! We're in this together. No one threatens my best friend and gets away with it."

***

Despite T.J. staying with me, my father flew into a rage as

I explained the damage to my car and the note that had been left behind.

"How many times do I have to tell you? Stay out of these murder cases, Michelle! Do you want to end up in a ditch somewhere?" he shouted, an undeniable shade of red creeping up his neck and face. "What will it take to get it through your thick skull that you're putting your life and everyone around you in danger? Why can't you just let the police do their job?"

My attempts to defend myself did nothing to dissuade my father and only infuriated him even more. I glanced at T.J. for moral support but realized I was on my own. Having never witnessed my father's anger before, T.J. stood frozen, his mouth open and eyes wide.

When my father finally paused for a breath, T.J. seized the opportunity to bolt toward the front door. Oh, how I wanted him to stay, but I couldn't blame him. If I could have left, I would have gone with him.

I locked the door behind T.J. and turned to face my father. But he was gone. The garage door rumbled open. I figured he was heading back to the hospital, which meant I had a reprieve from his wrath...at least for now.

Unfortunately, knowing I wouldn't have to face him until tomorrow didn't help me rest any better.

While lying in bed, I debated whether I should call the police at that moment or if it could wait until morning. There was no doubt in my mind that the *always-on-my-case* Detective Douglas would give me another verbal thrashing.

That thought alone almost convinced me to wait until the next day, but, against my better judgment or perhaps because of it, I called the station and reported the vandalism.

Detective Douglas was out, but the officer on duty sent a car out. They looked around, took the note, and said they'd be back tomorrow, which was fine by me. I was tired, and morning was coming way too soon.

chapter eighteen

Wearing my new daisy-print dress, white cardigan, and leather platforms, I climbed into my brother's car—thankful he let me borrow it to get to work. When I called Mike earlier and told him what had happened, he tried to be reassuring—unlike our father. "As soon as the police catch this guy, everything will be okay. Just hang in there," he told me.

Fortunately, the police said I didn't need to be home when they came back today, so at least I didn't have to upset Mae by calling off. I'm not sure I could have handled another person being mad at me.

Like always, I parked behind the row of shops and walked around to the front. But the moment I unlocked the door to Mae's Gift Shop, I froze. Craig was standing in the cash wrap, arms crossed, with a giant scowl.

"Craig! What's wrong? Is Mae okay?" I braced for the worst.

"She's fine," he replied, his tone as frosty as his expression. "The cash drawer is ready, and she'll bring it up, so you don't have to do that. But we need to talk."

"Wow, that sounds ominous. What's up?" I stepped closer, scanning his face for clues.

"What were you doing last night? And why didn't you tell me?" His gaze bore into mine.

I bit my bottom lip, grappling with my racing thoughts. "What do you mean?"

"Don't play coy with me. Lawrence called me this morning," Craig said, his voice sharp. "He said that you and T.J. were sleuthing last night and may have gotten in over your heads."

"Oh…that." I pulled my cardigan tighter and shifted my stance.

"Yeah, that. Out with it, Michelle," he pressed. "What were you guys doing?"

I set my white leather tote on the glass counter. "Well, T.J. and I…Wait. Why did Lawrence call you?"

Craig's jaw clenched as he continued, "A little thing called a police report caught his attention. Something about T.J. dropping you off at your house and discovering your windshield smashed and, oh, yeah, let's not forget, a threatening note left in your car. Lawrence said he suspected you had gone to the Hathaway House. What were you doing there?"

My heart sank. "I knew the skaters and Olga would be at the skating exhibition last night, and I wanted to look around the Hathaway House while they were gone."

"Wait. You broke into the house?" His voice rose, eyes widening in disbelief. "You could get arrested for that. What were you thinking?"

"I didn't break in," I protested. "I used a key I found in Danny's personal items at the police station."

"Lawrence let you take the key?"

I hesitated. "N..n…not exactly. I borrowed it, that's all. I'm going to give it back."

Craig exhaled sharply. "Michelle. If Lawrence finds out,

he'll have to turn you in. You can't go around stealing police property."

"Oh, don't look at me that way. I didn't know how else to get into the house without breaking in. It was the most *legal* illegal thing I could think of," I confessed.

Craig ran a hand through his hair and sighed. "Well, did you find anything?"

A smile crept across my face. "Yeah, we did—some love letters from Olga to Coach Wyatt and a threatening note hidden in a secret drawer in his desk. I'd like someone to compare the handwriting and see if the same person wrote them."

"Anything else?" he probed, narrowing his eyes.

"In one of the bedrooms, I found a notecard with a phone number and an address on it."

"And?" Craig tugged at the sleeve of his orange turtle-neck, peeking under his brown sports coat.

I reached for my Eiffel Tower charm and twisted it. "Nothing else. Olga scared us to death when she came home early. I think she was picking something up for someone. Anyway, when she left, we didn't stay too much longer. We wanted to get out of there."

"Please tell me you're not doing anything dangerous, are you, Michelle?" Mae's voice loomed behind me. "Craig thinks you might be in some kind of trouble."

I pivoted, meeting Mae's worried gaze. "Everything's fine. We're being careful, and I might have uncovered some infor-mation that will shift the focus of the police off Danny. I'll know more in a day or so."

"Just promise me you'll be careful. I appreciate what you and Craig are doing to help Danny, but I don't want either of you to get hurt or worse. Understand?" Mae said, concern etched on her face.

"Yes, we'll be careful," I said, crossing my fingers behind my back.

Mae glanced briefly around the shop, checking the surroundings before adding, "I think we're ready to open."

I looked at Craig as he leaned against the antique brass cash register. "Can you cover things while I run to the back room and drop off my purse?"

He nodded, saying nothing.

As Mae unlocked the front door, I hurried to the back. When I returned, Craig said, "I'm just worried about you. I don't want you getting hurt, and I don't want you to get arrested, okay."

"You're right. I was a little reckless, but don't you see, it's about more than Coach or Sarah—it's about my family, and I'll do what I have to do to protect them."

"I get that," he said with a reassuring smile.

With the tension melting between us, I shimmied past him and playfully booted him away from the register.

"I guess that's my cue to be on my way," Craig grinned. "Do you have the notecard with you?"

"Yeah. It's in my purse."

"Would it save you some time if I took the notecard to the police station to see if Lawrence could help?"

"That'd be great. My purse is on the table by the door. The notecard is in a small envelope." I paused. "Would you mind getting it so I don't have to leave the register? I don't want your mom to think I'm slacking off."

"Absolutely, I'd be glad to, and I'll keep you updated on what I find out. By the way, before I forget, do you have plans for this evening?" he asked.

"Rick is having a bunch of us from the Commuter Lounge over to his house this afternoon. We're putting together a business plan, so Alice will let us sell coffee in the Commuter Lounge."

"Huh?"

"It's kind of a long story, but the guys got tired of paying high prices for their coffee at the Student Union, so they decided to brew their own in the lounge. But when Alice found out, she threatened to shut it down unless they came up with a business plan that she could present to the administration. She doesn't want to get into any trouble with the powers that be in case someone ever gets hurt."

"Intriguing proposition." Craig paused. "How about you call me when you get home from your meeting? If I have any new information, I can come by…unless, of course, you have other plans."

The only person I might have done something with after work was T.J., but now that he was back with Meg, that was unlikely. I shook my head. "No. I can't think of any."

When Craig returned from the back room—the notecard in his hand—he stopped before going out the front door. "Your father won't mind if I stop by, will he?"

"Are you kidding?" I laughed. "He's still counting on you becoming a permanent member of the family. Besides, he'll probably spend the night at the hospital again with my mom. He doesn't trust the police to guard her as well as he can."

I sighed. "He only came home last night to shower because Crystal and Mel made him. They had to promise that they'd stay with Mom until he got back. So, long answer to your question: no, even if he's home, I don't think he'll mind."

"All right then. Hopefully, I'll have some news to share with you."

"Cool! See ya!"

As the door swung shut behind Craig, I watched him disappear down the sidewalk. A feeling of joy settled over me, and suddenly, a chill ran down my spine.

I glanced at my hand.

I was trembling.

***

Driving to Rick's, I thought about Craig's concern that I was being reckless and could get arrested. He was right. But wasn't the risk worth it if I could prove Danny's innocence *and* protect my family?

The front door of Rick's brick ranch was ajar when I arrived, but the screen door was closed. I grasped the handle, pulling it with one hand while balancing my tray of Sugar Cookies and Butterscotch Brownies in the other. Just as the sweets began to slide off the plate toward me, I was glad I had gone home after work and changed from my dry clean-only dress into washable bell-bottomed jeans and a floral shirt.

My eyes darted away from the tray to inside the house when Rick yelled, "I'll get the door!" He ran down the hallway and held the door open as I entered. Crisis averted.

"Let me help you with that," he said as he snagged the platter from my hands. He popped a cookie into his mouth as we made our way toward the kitchen, his head bopping in perfect rhythm to Jefferson Starship's "Ride the Tiger."

After Rick set the tray on the counter, he asked about my mom, but I sensed there was something else on his mind and was not surprised when he said, "Hey, I've been meaning to ask you —"

But Rick's words were cut short when Lawrence, who was getting something to drink out of the cooler, said, "Michelle! Did Craig get a hold of you?"

"No. Not since this morning, but we're meeting up tonight." I glanced back at Rick, the sparkle in his eyes gone.

"Sounds important," Rick murmured, his gaze focused over my shoulder in Lawrence's direction. "I think he wants to talk to you."

I pivoted to see Lawrence, clad in his camo jacket, walking toward us.

Rick sighed. "I better go check on things in the living room. Catch ya later."

"You don't have to go," I said.

"It's okay. It can wait."

"Hey, I didn't mean to run him off." Lawrence shrugged as he pushed his glasses up the bridge of his nose.

"It's all right. I'll talk to him later. What's up?"

"I wasn't sure if you knew, but I wanted to fill you in if you hadn't talked to Craig. Detective Douglas read the report about your car and thinks there is a connection between the vandalism of your car, the note, and the deaths of Coach Wyatt and Sarah."

"That's what I think," I said, wishing for once that my hunch had been wrong.

"He sees a connection between the attack on your mother, the damage to your car, and the note—especially since it's similar in tone to the one you received last fall. It all fits too neatly."

I nodded and bit my bottom lip as Lawrence continued. "Add that to what I found out about the phone number and the address that Craig dropped off, and, well, you could be involved in something a lot darker than what you can handle."

"Did you tell Detective Douglas about the notecard?"

"Oh, yeah. And whatever you do, *do not* tell me how you got it. Douglas says it's better if we don't know."

"Fair enough," I said, relieved that I didn't have to admit I entered and searched the Hathaway House. One battle at a time. "So, what did you learn?"

"Douglas is still checking some things out, but so far, we know the phone number and the address belong to Marco Rossini. He lived in Boston until a year ago. After that, he fell off the radar. It seems that he, Johnathan Miller, and Sarah's husband, Ralph Bentley, were involved in some rather shady business dealings back in the day. The police believe Rossini is living in the Midwest under an alias. I've been thinking about it, and maybe Craig's P.I. can get a lead on him before we can. He won't have to deal with all the departmental red tape."

"I'll ask him." I paused for a moment. "Why do you think Eric had the notecard?"

"Now, mind you," Lawrence winked, "for the record, I have no idea how you got the notecard, but hypothetically speaking, let's say you got them from Eric's room. The thing is, that doesn't necessarily mean it belongs to him. Someone else could have put it in his room, or it could have been left by the current owner or a previous renter."

"I guess the only way to know for sure is to ask Eric, but how do I tell him I know about it without saying how I found it? That makes asking him a bit complicated, doesn't it?"

"Welcome to my world. And one more thing," Lawrence said, leaning toward me. "As much as Douglas would like you to distance yourself from the Wyatt investigation, which he knows you won't do, he wants you to understand how dangerous this is. And that you need to be careful. Don't let your guard down! Keep him apprised of any information you come across. I'll be the go-between. Got it? No stopping by the station to meet with him. No calling him unless it's an emergency. Douglas doesn't want to have to explain why you're giving him info. He feels like he is being watched, and he doesn't know who he can trust on the force. The fewer people that know, the safer we all are."

"I guess that makes sense." I shrugged. "So, if and when I find out anything, I'm supposed to tell you, and you'll let Detective Douglas know?"

"That's the idea."

Bob Dylan's "Tangled Up in Blue" faded, and Jimmy's voice boomed down the hallway. "You guys about done? Todd wants everyone in here so Yash can read the business plan he put together."

Lawrence and I went to the living group, grabbing a spot on the floor by the coffee table. Everyone from the Commuter

Lounge group seemed to be accounted for: Meg and T.J. lounged on the couch while Jimmy and Billy leaned against it, Todd relaxed in an oversized gold velvet chair, and Tasha and Amy perched on the arms of a matching chair with Yash on the cushion between them.

Amy's flirtatious laughter cut through the air as Yash beamed and divided the stack of papers on his lap into two piles—one for each of his two seating companions.

Amy and Tasha passed out the papers as Yash began his presentation. Looking at Yash, I couldn't help but chuckle. His clothes—a partially unbuttoned metallic silver shirt paired with black pants—were more akin to partying on the dance floor than presiding over a business meeting.

Regardless of his clothing choices, Yash exuded confidence and authority as he commanded our attention.

"I've drafted a comprehensive constitution, a solid business plan, and committee ideas. This is way more than Alice needs, but we'll blow her away with how organized we are. There's no way she can say 'no' after seeing our work."

The only noise in the room for the next few minutes was the rustling of papers as we flipped through them. Yash's thoroughness in crafting a business plan didn't surprise me. After all, he was a business major. However, the language in the Constitution didn't sound like Yash at all. It was remarkably sophisticated, and I wondered if Alice would need a lawyer to decipher the legal jargon before giving us permission to proceed.

Unable to contain my curiosity any longer, I asked, "So, where did you get the idea for everything you included in the Constitution?"

Yash flashed a mischievous grin. "I had a lawyer write it up because I wanted it done right. I think it's downright stellar, don't you?"

"How much did that cost?" I asked, raising an eyebrow.

"No worries. He's a friend of mine who recently passed

the bar, and he was happy to help. It only cost me a few pizzas and some beer."

"Looks like he covered all the bases." I nodded.

Jimmy, his blazer neatly folded beside him, chimed in. "I like that the club's mission is to provide coffee at an affordable price to the caffeine-seekers who frequent the Commuter Lounge. I take it your lawyer friend has a sense of humor?"

"Yeah, The Man hasn't squashed it out of him yet," Yash laughed.

"I suppose we should decide on a name for this club of ours," suggested Lawrence, looking around the room. "Any ideas?"

"How about the Stick it to the Man Coffee Club," Tasha proposed, smirking.

"Of course you would," muttered Lawrence, peering over his glasses. "I'm surprised you don't want to call it Peace. Love. Coffee."

Tasha tossed her long, dark hair behind her shoulders, revealing the intricate embroidery work on her peasant blouse. "Why, Lawrence, what a cool idea! That would be perfect on tie-dyed t-shirts for our club," she said, flashing a mischievous grin.

I took a deep breath, bracing myself for the lively verbal sparring match that was about to unfold between Tasha and Lawrence. Our Commuter Lounge group may have been small, but we were eclectic.

Tasha, our resident *make love, not war* hippie, was a peace-loving spirit. As the daughter of Romanian immigrants, she grew up on her parents' stories of oppression. Both professors at the University of Petersburg, they instilled in her an understanding of the sacrifices they made to escape tyranny so she could have a future that was not burdened by an oppressive government. Thus was born Tasha's deep-seated mistrust of authority and her passion for peace, justice, and equality.

In stark contrast to Tasha's skepticism stood Lawrence, a

Vietnam War veteran with his unwavering faith in the U.S. government and its leaders—a conviction that sustained him throughout the war.

Lawrence and Tasha couldn't resist sharing good-natured jabs regarding their differing political philosophies whenever they got together. Lawrence would usually comment on Tasha's idealism and toss in a sarcastic remark about flower power. She, in turn, would roll her eyes and then counter his support of military interventions with jabs about *peaceful solutions.*

Although listening to them always proved entertaining, I sensed that Billy didn't want the evening's purpose to get sidelined by their lively debate. Just as their conversation was about to digress into a political free-for-all, he cleared his throat and interjected, "Hey, what about this for a name? Black Market Coffee?"

Tasha turned her gaze to Billy, her eyes lighting up. "I like that. It has just the right amount of an anti-establishment vibe without being up in your face. Nice job!"

Billy beamed, his cheeks flushing as he brushed a strand of his auburn hair off his forehead.

The rest of us looked at each other, exchanging nods of agreement. "Sounds like a winner," Todd said. "But I've got a suggestion. Why don't we call it BMK for short?"

"Why K?" Meg challenged, leaning back into the sofa, crossing her arms. "Last time I checked, coffee began with a C."

"I don't know," Tasha mused. "I rather like being uncon-ventional with the spelling. It adds to that *breaking-the-rules* kind of vibe.

Meg shrugged. "I guess so. It does sound better than BMC."

"All right, if no one objects, BMK will be the official name," Todd announced, his smile rivaling the smiley face on his t-shirt.

"Now that we've got a name, let's move on to electing officers," said Yash. "I think Todd should be President since it was his idea, and the coffee maker belongs to him. Anyone disagree?" He scanned the group, receiving nods all around. "Okay. Next up. Any nominations for VP and Secretary?"

Jimmy raised his hand. "I'd like to throw my name in for VP. As the future President of the United States, I think this will look great on my resume and help me win votes."

Laughter erupted in the room. Who else but Jimmy would think of his political aspirations at a time like this?

"Any objections?" Yash asked, grinning at the ensuing chorus of "It's okay with me" and "Sure."

"Who wants to be Secretary?" Yash continued, but the room fell silent.

No one moved, and I couldn't decide if no one was as bold as Jimmy to put their name forward or if no one wanted the position.

"How 'bout we all write something on a piece of paper, and whoever has the best handwriting gets the job?" Rick quipped.

"Ingenious," Yash laughed.

Rick left but soon returned with a stack of 3x5 index cards and a handful of pens. "Write 'the cow jumped over the moon', and make sure you put your name on the other side of the card."

"That's a good idea," said Amy as she threw her arm around Yash. "Then we can lay them out and vote."

Everyone except Meg and Lawrence turned in cards. Meg explained that she wasn't really part of the Commuter Lounge group because she lived on campus. Lawrence muttered something about being too old and wise for such foolishness before adding, "I'm an old married man and might not be able to attend all the meetings. I'll let you young'uns handle this one."

After laying the cards on the table, T.J. wrote numbers on

them. Once the voting ended, T.J. proclaimed me the winner as if I had just won a beauty pageant. "And now, the new secretary of Black Market Coffee...the ever-talented Michelle Kilpatrick. Congratulations! Anything you'd like to say?"

My cheeks grew warm as I laughed at the round of applause, shaking my head. "No. I'm good."

We unanimously elected Yash as the club treasurer and decided he and Todd would handle buying and stocking the supplies for BMK.

As the clock chimed six o'clock, Yash suggested we look over the committee page.

Amy's hand shot into the air. "I want to be on the Party Committee."

Yash flashed her a smile. "The perfect spot for our resident party girl. Does anyone else have a committee they want to be on?"

T.J.'s arm went up, the brown stripes on his shirt perfectly matching his brown eyes. "I'll be on the Telephone Commit-tee. I always end up calling everyone, anyway," he grinned.

I nudged Rick. "I've got to get going. I'm supposed to meet Craig tonight to go over some things regarding Coach Wyatt."

"How 'bout I walk you to your car?" he offered.

"That's all right. You've got a house full of people," I replied.

He chuckled. "I think they'll survive without me." He stood up and announced, "Hey, why don't we take a quick break for some food? Say, about ten minutes."

Smiles spread across everyone's face as they rose and stretched their legs. As most of the group dashed toward the kitchen, Rick and I headed for the front door. A glance over my shoulder revealed T.J. watching us.

I stopped when he asked, "Where are you two off to?"

"I've got to get home, and Rick's going to walk me to my car," I explained.

T.J. suggested, "Hey, man, why don't you stay here since this is your party and you've got all these people in your house? I can walk Michelle to her car. I need to go that way, anyway. Meg remembered she left her purse in my car and, well, after what happened to Michelle's car the other night, she doesn't want to take any chances that someone might break into mine."

"If you're sure," Rick replied, his easy-going smile gone.

"Yeah, I'm on my way out now," T.J. assured him.

I turned to Rick. "You can still come."

"No, that's okay. Catch you later." He pivoted and walked toward the kitchen.

"Didn't mean to upset your escort," T.J. said.

I narrowed my eyes. "Really? You could have fooled me."

Without saying another word, T.J. opened the screen door. I glanced back, hoping to see Rick in the hallway, but instead, I saw Meg—glaring.

chapter nineteen

As I drove home, I repeated the name Marco Rossini, rolling it over my tongue like a line from *The Godfather II*. Mafia boss, clandestine deals—maybe even a deadly secret. I pictured him: olive skin, piercing dark eyes, black hair slicked back, an impeccably tailored suit, and shoes so polished they reflected your face back at you.

One thing I knew for sure was that if Rossini lived anywhere near Petersburg, he would be the talk of the town. Someone with that kind of mystique could not avoid being fodder for the local gossip grapevine.

Hmmmm....maybe the next time Mrs. Winterfield visits Mae's Gift Shop, I'll casually ask if she knows of any such men wandering our quiet town. If anyone will know, it'll be her. She knows everything.

I turned into my driveway and parked beside my '68 Plymouth Roadrunner, which I affectionately dubbed the Orange Bomb. Today, *Orange Bomb* was more than a nickname. The poor thing looked like it had survived an actual explosion. A sad cardboard bandage covered its shattered windshield.

Another week, another paycheck, and I can get it fixed.

I pushed the front door open, and Gidget was waiting for

me on the staircase, her tail swishing, eyes bright and focused.

I set my purse on the table in the entryway and then sat beside her.

"I'm sorry, girl," I murmured, scratching her behind the ears. "I know—I haven't had much time to play with you today. What with work, then Rick's house, and now Craig's coming over…"

Gidget rubbed her head against my arm as I glanced at my watch.

"How 'bout I get you some milk? If there's time before Craig gets here, we'll play string. If not, we'll do it after he leaves," I suggested.

She yawned dramatically—her way of saying *about time*— then trotted behind me into the kitchen.

I poured her milk into a saucer, then hurried to the living room, grabbing the vacuum cleaner.

Tidying up was a breeze. I had been the only one home this week, except for Crystal and Dad's short visits. Even then, I hadn't been home long enough to make much of a mess between school, work, and sleuthing.

But I had a thing for those visible vacuum lines on the orange shag carpet. Something about them felt…orderly. Predictable. Unlike the rest of my life right now.

Once the hum of the vacuum cleaner stopped, Gidget appeared next to me, ready for game time. I dragged the long string behind me as I walked around the living room, inspecting it one last time. Gidget followed, bouncing on the string, trying to hold it down as we played a game of Tug-of-War.

Our antics continued, and I started to relax until a sharp knock at the door shattered the moment.

Gidget ran upstairs, and although I was expecting Craig, late-night knocks always sent a chill down my spine—especially now.

I crept to the peephole.

I let out a sigh of relief.

It was Craig.

I swung the door open, and as he stood there grinning, he handed me a pizza box. "I took a chance you hadn't eaten yet."

The warm aroma of cheese and pepperoni hit me like a tidal wave, and suddenly, I realized how hungry I was.

"What are you, a mind reader?" I teased, stepping aside. "Rick had plenty of food, but I got so busy talking to Lawrence, and then our meeting started, and…well, I guess, after that, I was in such a hurry to leave…I forgot to eat.

"Couldn't wait to get home and see me, huh?" Craig teased.

"In your dreams," I shot back, leading him to the kitchen.

Little Miss Scaredy Cat reappeared, sniffing the air—her curiosity outweighing her fear.

I headed to the cupboard to get two glasses, and Craig asked, "Can I help with anything? Get some plates?"

"Sure. Can you grab some paper plates from the pantry?"

As he got the plates, I poured our soft drinks, telling him what I had learned from Lawrence about the Boston address, Marco Rossini, and Ralph Bentley.

Craig pulled a chair out for me and then settled into his seat. "I'll ask my mother in the morning and see what she can tell me about Rossini and Bentley."

He reached for a slice of pepperoni pizza, then raised his glass. "So, Sherlock, what's your take on this—if Danny didn't kill Wyatt, who did?"

I chewed slowly, savoring the tangy flavors of the pizza as I considered his question. "Right now, I'd put my money on Olga or Jason. They both had reasons to be upset with Coach Wyatt." I leaned back slightly, thinking of the facts as we knew them. "But let's not forget the coach that Wyatt suspected of starting the rumors about him. We need to find out more about that guy…we don't even know his name yet."

Craig smirked. "Well, tonight's your lucky night. That's what I wanted to discuss with you. My P.I. dug into it and made a few inquiries. The guy's name is Thomas Bates. No surprise that there was no love lost between him and Coach Wyatt. In fact, Bates filed an official complaint with the Figure Skating Council, claiming Wyatt was doping his athletes."

I stopped mid-bite. "Do you think the accusations were true?"

Craig shrugged. "Doesn't matter. Wyatt's dead. I doubt the Council will even bother looking into it."

I leaned forward. "Can this guy of yours find out if Bates was in town the night of Wyatt's murder?"

"He's already working on it." Craig wiped his hands on a napkin. "But get this—Bates made several calls to Mr. Hansen and Eric, the singles skater."

I frowned, mulling over his words as I tugged on a piece of pizza in the box, a string of cheese trailing behind it. "That's weird. Why would he be talking to them?"

"Perhaps digging for more dirt on Wyatt?"

"I suppose," I shrugged.

"So, what do you want to do next?" Craig asked.

I sighed, pushing my plate aside. "I'm not sure. We have suspects with motives and opportunities but no proof. It feels like we're just going in circles."

Gidget nuzzled against my leg, and I scooped her onto my lap, gently stroking her fur.

Craig took a sip from his glass, glanced around the room, and then returned his focus to me. "Aside from getting a confession, I'm at a loss for how we can prove Danny's innocence. No one witnessed anyone other than Danny entering the coach's office."

"That's true, but someone overheard an argument. If it wasn't Danny in the office with Coach, who was it?"

Craig tilted his head. "Do we know who said it was Danny arguing with Wyatt?"

I opened my mouth, then hesitated. "Now that you mention it, I don't think Lawrence ever told us."

"Interesting," Craig murmured. "We need to ask him."

I nodded.

"Good," he said. "Because right now, their testimony is the only solid evidence that Danny and the coach were fighting."

Gidget, apparently tired of either my constant attention or the limitations on her freedom, jumped off my lap and scurried out of the kitchen.

As I brushed the silver strands of cat hair from my blue jeans, I said, "There's one person we keep forgetting—Mr. Hansen. Remember, he dropped off some sharpened skates on the night of the murder? Naomi mentioned Mr. Hansen wanted to speak with Coach Wyatt, but after she told him that Coach was on the phone, he left."

I leaned back in my chair. "What I don't know is whether Naomi saw Mr. Hansen leave. What if, on his way out, he stopped by the office? Maybe he overheard something. I don't know. It's a long shot, but I never asked."

Craig sat up and crossed his arms, the lines on his forehead deepening. "I suppose it's worth asking him. Do you want to talk to him, or do you want me to?"

"I can do it in the morning after I visit my mom in the hospital." I paused. "Did I tell you my mom may get to come home tomorrow? Dad thinks they'll release her in the afternoon after the doctors finish their rounds."

"That's good news. I'm sure she'll be happy to get home."

"Yeah. Dad said she's supposed to take it easy for the next few weeks, but Crystal and Suzie have volunteered to help since I've got school and work."

I stopped. "Of course, I don't want them to know I'm still trying to clear Danny's name. Crystal and my dad still blame me for what happened to Mom. So, if you talk to them, don't mention that we're still working on it, okay?"

Craig grinned as he crossed his heart. "You got my word, Sherlock."

Just then, the phone rang.

I jumped.

Craig shot me a look. I knew what we were both thinking. *The hospital.*

I flew into the living room and lunged for the receiver. "Hello?"

Lawrence's voice came through—tight. Urgent.

A sharp chill crept up my spine. "What's wrong? Is it my mom?"

"No," he said. "It's Olga."

Relief hit me—then vanished as he continued.

"She's dead."

My heart stopped.

I gripped the phone tighter. "What do you mean dead? How?"

Craig tugged at my arm. "Your mom?" he whispered.

I shook my head, covering the mouthpiece. "Olga."

I twisted the Eiffel Tower charm between my fingers and continued to listen to Lawrence.

"She was shot. Point-blank." His voice dropped. "And that's not all. Detective Douglas went to Wyatt's house to talk to Olga. She had asked him to meet her there. But when Douglas didn't report back, Grogan sent some officers to check on him."

"And?"

"They found Olga. Dead. But Douglas—"

He paused.

"He's missing. His car was parked in front of the house, but there was no trace of him. The skaters said they never saw him."

I hung up the phone and sank onto the couch, barely

registering Craig slipping beside me, his arm draping around my shoulders.

Slowly, I recounted what Lawrence had said about Detective Douglas—Olga setting up the meeting, someone shooting her, and Douglas disappearing.

"I don't get it," I whispered. "Why? What does it all mean?"

Craig exhaled, his voice low but calm. "My guess is Olga knew something, and someone didn't want her talking."

"And Douglas?"

"Maybe he saw who shot Olga...or...what if he was the target all along and Olga was collateral damage?"

Craig pulled me closer. "Either way, someone wanted him gone."

chapter twenty

Sunday, April 20th

After Craig left, I headed straight to bed, but sleep did not come. Instead, I stayed awake as questions flooded my mind. *Who killed Olga? Why? Where was Detective Douglas? Was he okay? Was he still alive?* I rubbed the back of my aching neck. Would the madness ever end?

Accepting my insomnia, I sat up and tossed the comforter to one side as my feet met the coolness of the wooden floor. I made my way to my desk and opened my notebook to my Venn Diagram.

With a sinking feeling, I drew another circle, the ink smudging slightly as I wrote *Olga*. Yesterday, I suspected her of killing Coach Wyatt—the jilted lover getting her ultimate revenge, but now she was dead.

I tapped the pen against the paper, the rhythmic clicks filling the silence. *Had I misjudged her? Or was she both villain and victim? If she didn't strangle Coach Wyatt, did she know the coach's assailant, or was she simply at the wrong place at the wrong time?*

With the first light of morning streaming through my window, I closed my notebook, showered, and quietly dressed so as not to disturb Gidget. Earlier, she determined there was no reason both of us should be deprived of a good night's sleep, so she nestled next to the pillows, blissfully unaware of my anguish.

As I pulled my favorite faded sweater over my head, I breathed in the scent of my mother's lavender fabric softener —it almost felt like she was hugging me. I grabbed my stack of 3x5 notecards and my Political Theory 201 textbook and headed for the kitchen, fully intending to read the assigned pages while eating breakfast.

Yet, as I sipped my iced tea, my thoughts drifted to the recent murders. With midterms behind me and final exams weeks away, there would be plenty of time to catch up on my coursework if I quickly cleared Danny's name and found Coach Wyatt's killer. The problem was I was beginning to doubt that I could solve it. All I had was my determination to try to get to the truth.

I spread the 3x5s on the table and made cards for Marco Rossini and Thomas Bates. Although unsure of their part in Wyatt's death, my instincts told me they were involved. Thomas Bates, in particular, bothered me. *Why did he call Mr. Hansen and Eric? Was he trying to cause trouble for Coach Wyatt at his new rink?*

I leaned back, twisting the charm around my neck. *What other reason could there be?*

My mind drifted to my plan for the day: visit my mom in the hospital before heading to the ice arena and then go to the police station. I had to speak with Mr. Hansen. He might have insight into who was arguing with Coach that fateful night. I also wanted to ask him about the phone calls. After that, perhaps Lawrence could fill me in on the latest regarding Detective Douglas's disappearance and Olga's murder.

When I got home, I had to finish my bio on Coach Wyatt. Keith, the assistant editor of the *Wildcats' Daily News*, needed it by tomorrow morning. He wanted to run my piece in Tuesday's edition and include a sidebar about the local memorial service sponsored by the family and the university.

A Celebration of Life service was being arranged by Coach's brother and the National Skating Council at their headquarters in Boston next month.

The rooster clock on the wall ticked past 7:00 a.m. Time was slipping away, as were my chances of finding the truth before someone else got hurt. I dumped my dishes in the sink, grabbed my notebook, and headed for the car.

First stop—the hospital.

***

The officer stationed outside my mother's room wore a grim expression. Fearing the worst, I asked about Detective Douglas, but he had no updates. The detective's disappearance was still a mystery.

As my fingers curled around the doorknob, I paused to take a deep breath, resolved not to let my heavy heart overshadow my visit with Mom.

I had no need to worry. As soon as the door swung open, her radiant smile melted away my sadness.

"Come in. Come in." Mom beamed. "With any luck, I'll be going home this afternoon."

Her smile faded as my father placed his hand on hers. "Let's wait and see what the doctor says," he cautioned, his gaze heavy with concern. "We don't want you leaving here if you're not well enough."

"Since Michelle's here, you should grab some breakfast," Mom said, her voice light but her eyes flickering toward Dad's hunched shoulders. "Who knows how long it will be before the doctor comes in?"

After the door closed behind him, Mom sighed and said, "Your father's so exhausted. He hasn't had a good night's sleep since the…accident." She patted the bed, motioning for me to sit beside her. "Even with a police officer outside my door, he won't leave my side unless Crystal or Mike is here. When I was in ICU, he slept in the waiting room, just to be close."

I smiled. "I know it's been rough on him, but it's kind of sweet that he cares so much."

"Yes," she nodded. "But I worry he's going to have a stroke or a heart attack. He can't keep going like this. I need to be at home. Your father can't handle planting season without me, even with Mike and Crystal's help."

Tension gripped me as I braced for a lecture about letting school take precedence over my family or, worse, how my actions had adversely affected everyone.

Trying to be upbeat, I said, "We're all going to help Dad. Even Craig has offered his help, but the important thing is for you to feel better. We want you back home, but we don't want you to risk a relapse. That won't help anyone, especially you." I patted her hand.

Mom chuckled, "Oh, I think the doctor will let me go home today. Just to make sure, I put on my makeup and plenty of rouge. Gives me a healthy glow, doesn't it?" She picked up the small mirror on her tray. "Doctors see a rosy complexion, and they think you're ready to run a marathon." She smirked, smoothing the blush on her cheeks.

When Dad returned, he slumped into the chair, his eyelids heavy. Sensing that he was on the verge of drifting off, I kissed Mom on the cheek. "I'll go now so Dad can get some sleep. Fingers crossed, I'll see you at home tonight."

***

As I drove into the ice arena's parking lot, I hummed along to the Beatles' *Sgt. Pepper's Lonely Hearts Club Band* drifting from the radio. It didn't take long to spot an open space. The lot was virtually deserted—it was Sunday morning. Campus life seldom came alive before noon on weekends.

I parked and took a moment to glance through my notes. As I scanned through my list of suspects and their alibis, a line from Agatha Christie's *The Murder of Roger Ackroyd* echoed in my mind—spoken by the brilliant detective Poirot: 'the person who speaks may be lying.'"

That's it! Someone on this list is either outright lying or lying by omission. No wonder I'm going in circles.

I resolved then and there not to accept any fact as truth unless I verified it with multiple sources, just like my journalism professors had taught me to do with a news article.

As I entered the ice arena, my footsteps reverberated softly in the quiet hallway. I strolled down the sloping ramp and headed for the skate rental desk, where I waited, hoping Mr. Hansen would appear.

After a few minutes, I rang the bell on the counter, but when no one came, I turned to leave, halted only by a familiar voice calling out, "Michelle. What brings you here?"

It was Yash standing in the doorway. "I didn't expect to see you today."

"I wanted to ask Mr. Hansen a few questions about Coach Wyatt. Is he working today?"

"Yeah. He's in his office, but good luck getting him to answer your questions. Every time I ask him about Danny or the coach, he just repeats what he told the police."

"I was afraid of that, but I'd like to ask him, anyway. You never know."

"Give me a minute, and I'll go get him." He paused, and his expression grew somber. "Did you hear about Olga?"

"Yeah, I can't believe she's dead." My voice dropped. "And…did you hear about Detective Douglas? He's missing."

His eyes grew wide. "What happened?"

I shook my head. "He went to the Hathaway House to meet with Olga but never returned to the station. Beyond that, I haven't heard anything. I thought I'd swing by the station after I leave here and see if Lawrence has any new information."

"Man, this just keeps getting crazier. Keep me posted, okay?" Yash gave me a quick nod. "I'll see if I can track down Mr. Hansen."

He vanished down the hallway, leaving me alone with my thoughts of Coach, Olga, and the detective.

Moments later, Mr. Hansen was standing in front of me. "Yash said you had some questions about the night of the murder?"

"Yes, I do," I said, trying to keep my voice even.

Remember—don't push too hard. Keep it together.

"What can I help you with?" Mr. Hansen crossed his arms and raised his chin slightly as his posture stiffened.

"On the night of Coach Wyatt's murder, Naomi said you dropped off the skates and had wanted to talk to Coach, but he was on the phone. So, to clarify, you didn't have a chance to talk to him that night, right?"

"Yes." He nodded. "Naomi told me Charles—Coach Wyatt—had gone to his office to take a call. I stopped by to see if he was available, but it sounded like he was still on the phone, so I decided to leave."

I leaned in closer. "Are you sure he was on the phone? Any chance he could have been arguing with someone?"

Mr. Hansen exhaled sharply, rubbing his hands together. "When the police questioned me, I told them what I just told you… but I left something out."

He hesitated.

"Charles might have been on the phone, sure. But Danny was in that office with him." He took a deep breath. "I like Danny. He's a decent kid, but with his scarf used to strangle Charles, it doesn't look good for him. I didn't want to give the police any more evidence to use against him."

I nodded. "I can understand that, but how can you be sure it was Danny in the office with Coach?"

"I'm positive it was Danny," Mr. Hansen replied resolutely. "I've worked with Danny long enough to recognize his voice."

"Okay," I shrugged. "I just wanted to double-check. You called Coach Wyatt by his first name. How well did you know him?"

A flicker of nostalgia crossed his face. "Believe it or not, once upon a time, I was a figure skater and a good one at that —had hopes of going to the Olympics until an accident ended my—well, that's a different story for a different time. Charles and I trained with the same coach, and despite being competitors, we were friends—not that unusual when you train together every day for three years."

"Wow!" I exclaimed. "No wonder you offered him a place to train his team when you found out he was having trouble at the other rink."

"That's what friends are for. I only wish inviting him here didn't result in his death." His eyes drifted toward the floor.

"It's not your fault. Whoever killed Coach could have just as easily murdered him at the other rink. Someone was out to get him." I took a breath. "Did you see anyone suspicious when you were at the house that night?"

"No. Naomi let me in. I dropped off the skates, went to the office, and ran into Olga on my way out. She walked with me to the door. Other than Naomi or Olga, I didn't see anyone else."

"Do you have any idea who would want to kill him?" I paused. "What about that coach…Thomas Bates?"

Mr. Hansen reared back. "Bates wouldn't hurt anyone. Sure, from time to time, he gets paranoid about his team not doing as well as he wants. But when you're going up against a successful coach like Charles, it's easy to think name recognition carries more weight with the judges than the abilities of your skaters. But he's harmless."

"Yet," I countered, "he filed a complaint with the National Skating Council about Coach Wyatt and spread some pretty malicious rumors. That doesn't sound harmless to me."

"Sure, Tom can be a troublemaker, but that doesn't make him a murderer. Besides, a rumor is only a rumor if it isn't true." He rubbed his chin. "I'm not convinced Charles was as innocent as we'd all like to believe."

"Did Mr. Bates ever contact you?"

Mr. Hansen narrowed his eyes. "When Tom found out Charles was at my rink, he called to warn me and suggested I keep my eyes open for anything suspicious."

"And was there?"

He exhaled, shaking his head. "I hate speaking ill of the dead, but... I saw things, Michelle. Things that made me uneasy. The last thing I wanted was for Danny to get tangled up in any of Charles's antics. I felt responsible for keeping Danny out of trouble. After all, I was the one who got the two of them together."

He paused. "That's why I wanted to talk to Charles that night. I needed to ask him about the rumors—to get to the truth once and for all."

He shrugged, a hint of regret in his voice. "But I never got the chance to ask him, and now look what happened to Danny…if only I had waited for Charles to finish his call…"

chapter twenty-one

When I arrived at the police station, I found Lawrence and Craig standing by the front desk, their voices low.

"Craig! What are you doing here?" I asked, stepping up to the desk.

"I thought I'd stop by and see if there was any news on Detective Douglas," Craig replied.

"Anything?" I asked, though Craig's weary tone already gave me the answer.

Lawrence shook his head. "A neighbor saw three guys getting into a car parked in the driveway at the Hathaway House." He hesitated, eyes darting around the room. "We checked with all the skaters, and they said Olga was the only one who went out that night. So we're assuming the woman witnessed two men abducting Douglas."

"Did anyone hear gunshots? Shouting?" I leaned in.

Lawrence shook his head. "No. Not a thing, except, get this." He raised an eyebrow and lowered his voice as if about to reveal a deep, dark secret. "That same neighbor saw a limo drive down the street about thirty minutes before the men appeared."

Craig asked, "Did she remember any part of the license plate?"

Lawrence shook his head. "Too dark. She didn't think much about it—just found it odd."

Following Lawrence's lead, I leaned on the counter and lowered my voice. "Do you think Detective Douglas's kidnapping is tied to his investigation of Sarah's death, or do you think it's connected to Coach Wyatt's murder?"

My eyes narrowed. "I'm asking because you said the other day that Douglas had talked to one of the guards assigned to Sarah's part of the prison. Do you think that guard told someone the detective was asking questions?"

Lawrence scanned the lobby before shaking his head. "At this point, I have no idea. I mean, for all we know, the abduction could be revenge by someone Douglas sent to prison and who's now back on the streets." He sighed deeply. "But with the limo showing up, my money is on Douglas's theory that there's a connection between the Coach's murder and Sarah's supposed suicide. The timing is too suspicious."

"What do you mean?" Craig asked.

"Yesterday afternoon, we ID'd our mystery guard. His name is Andrew Wilkins—a twenty-five-year-old ex-con who served eighteen months for larceny and illegal possession of drugs. And you'll never guess where the prison was?"

"Where?" I leaned closer.

"Deer Island Prison in Boston Harbor."

"Boston!" I exclaimed as chills ran down my spine. "Man, that place keeps popping up, doesn't it?"

Lawrence said, "Detective Douglas and Lt. Grogan are… well, I guess it's only Lt. Grogan now…is working on locating this dude." His gaze shifted to the floor.

"Let me know if you need my P.I. on this," Craig said." He's good. And speaking of my P.I., were you aware that Thomas Bates, the coach from Wyatt's home rink, has been in touch with Hansen and one of the skaters? Records show several phone calls between them," Craig said.

Lawrence's ears perked up. "Which skater?"

"Eric."

"I learned something else today," I jumped in. "Mr. Hansen used to be a competitive figure skater. He and Coach Wyatt trained with the same coach."

"Interesting," Lawrence mused. "I'll pass all that info to Grogan. I'm not sure it'll help Danny, if that's your hope. The DA's case against him is pretty strong."

"But if there is no other explanation for who killed Coach Wyatt," I countered, "why did Olga ask Detective Douglas to meet her at the house? Maybe she knew something, and that's why she was killed."

"But then why didn't they just shoot Douglas and get rid of him too?" Lawrence pressed as he picked up a stack of papers.

I clasped my Eiffel Tower charm and twisted it between my fingers, thinking. "I don't know, but there's something that we're missing. I just wish I knew what it was." I bit my bottom lip. "Do you know if Detective Douglas discovered anything about the limo by the coach's house?"

"Nothing. The limo company said their fleet wasn't near the Hathaway House that night. When one of our officers checked the mileage logs for each vehicle, he didn't find any discrepancies."

Craig chimed in. "Which means the limo is privately owned and wasn't rented that night—that complicates things unless we can get a plate number."

"When the skaters said Olga went out last night, did they say where she was going?" I pressed.

"Naomi said Olga went to Professor Constantin's house for dinner earlier that night. My guess is Olga had just gotten home when she was murdered. She never made it inside the house."

"Constantin." I rolled the word over in my mind. "That's Tasha's last name. I bet her parents had Olga over."

"I wonder why?" Craig asked.

"Probably because Tasha's parents and Olga's parents are from Romania." I mused, pausing momentarily. "Have the police talked to the Constantins?"

"Grogan and an officer went over this morning, but they're not back yet."

"I think I'll call Tasha and find out what she knows," I suggested. "Maybe Olga said something that will give us a lead on who killed her or kidnapped the detective."

Lawrence frowned and crossed his arms. "Let Grogan handle it, okay? I'm sure he got all the information he needed when he questioned Tasha's parents." Lawrence's gaze hardened. "Let us do our job. We know what we're doing. Plus, you need to keep a low profile. Someone is watching you, and they're not above taking people out who get in their way."

"I know, but...could I see the police report on Coach Wyatt's death?"

Lawrence took a deep breath and rolled his eyes. "Didn't you listen to anything I said?"

"Yes, and I appreciate your concern, but I'm just curious about something."

Lawrence raised an eyebrow. "Just curious, huh?"

"Yeah. That's all." I shrugged.

Lawrence gave an exasperated sigh before retrieving the file and sliding it to me. "Make it quick, okay?"

I went straight to the summary of events for that night, committing the details to memory before handing it back.

"Thanks.... I guess I better get going. See you later."

Craig decided it was time to go too, and walked with me to the parking lot. When we reached my car, he turned to me, concern etched on his face, and asked, "What was that all about?"

"What? Oh, you mean wanting to see the file?"

Craig nodded.

"We based our motives and opportunities chart on where

we remembered everyone being that evening. I wanted to make sure we had it all right. Getting even the smallest fact wrong could change the entire picture."

Craig's brows furrowed, his jaw tightening ever so slightly. "You're still planning to call Tasha, aren't you?"

I grinned. "Of course I am. I'm not leaving it up to Grogan to ask the right questions."

I saw the worry in Craig's eyes. "Promise me you'll be careful. If she tells you something that needs investigating, will you let me know before you do anything?"

"Unless I'm hot on the trail of a two-headed monster," I joked, nudging him playfully.

"All right, wise guy, you know what I mean. It's always good to have someone to bounce ideas off," he said, his gaze piercing as he placed his hand on my arm. "As much as I want to clear Danny's name for my mom's sake, I couldn't handle it if something happened to you."

Placing my hand over his, I squeezed it gently. "Nothing's going to happen to me. I promise I'll be careful." I paused. "But remember, I'm invested in this as well. Some guy tried to kill my mother, and they threatened my family and me. I want them found and stopped. I refuse to let them control my life with fear."

"But if you quit investigating Sarah's death or Coach's, they might leave you alone."

"And they might not. How do I know what sets them off? Whenever I investigate a story, I'll wonder if the dark powers that be will want to throw their weight around and threaten me again. I'll never be free as long as they call the shots. I will not live my life as a victim."

***

As I made my way home, my determination to find the

evil mastermind behind the murders and the threats to my family grew stronger. What was his connection to Mae Emerson—my boss and Craig's mother? Whatever his motivation, none of us were safe until he was caught.

I parked my Green Bomb beneath the basketball hoop and headed for the house, where Gidget greeted me by jumping off the stairway step. She leaped onto the end table next to the couch and pawed at the answering machine, its red light blinking. I scooped her into my arms and held her close while I listened to Dad's voice recounting the latest news about Mom. The doctor was running a few more tests, and if everything was all right, he'd let her come home tomorrow.

I sighed, relieved. Although I knew my mother would be disappointed about having to spend another night at the hospital, having more time to work on my investigation without the pressure of having to explain my whereabouts was exactly what I needed.

The urgency of finding Coach's killer settled around me.

The clock was ticking.

Gently setting Gidget down, I quickly dialed Tasha's number, eager to get straight to the point.

"Was Olga at your house last night?" I asked without hesitation.

"Yes!" Tasha replied. "Ever since the police left, I've been wondering—do you think Olga's murder is connected to the coach's?"

"Could be. Would your parents mind if I came over to ask them a few questions?"

"I'm sure they'd like to help. Let me check."

The telephone line was quiet for only a few moments before Tasha returned. "They have a meeting tonight, but said they'd have some time if you can come over now. Will that work?"

"That would be great! I'll be right over. What's your address?"

I grabbed my jacket and notebook. In less than twenty minutes, I sat across from Tasha and her parents in their living room, with its distinct Romanian aesthetic. The tapestry rug on the wooden floor, the hand-painted ceramics scattered on the side tables, and the colorful folk art adorning the walls emitted a warmth I hated to destroy by speaking of murder.

My eyes shifted from the lace curtains to Tasha, sitting cross-legged in an oversized chair, her floral skirt touching the floor. Glancing at her parents, I understood where she got her bohemian style. Her mother wore a flowing maxi dress in a bold psychedelic print and a pair of metallic gold sandals. Tasha's father opted for a more muted color palette. Yet, his hippie-free spirit was clear—mustard yellow corduroy pants paired with a coordinating blazer over a brown checked shirt with several buttons undone, revealing three gold chains around his neck.

"Olga was here last night," Dr. Emilia Constantin began, her voice calm. "After dinner, we had coffee and continued our conversation, but around 8:00 p.m., she asked if she could use our phone."

"Do you know who she called?" I asked, flipping open my notebook.

"No," Emilia explained. "I let her use the phone in the office, so I have no idea. But when she came back to the living room, she said she had to leave—there was a problem with one of the skaters she had to deal with."

"Did she say which one?" I asked.

"No, but she muttered something about wishing it wasn't her problem. I sensed there was something deeper going on. When I pressed her to explain, she didn't even look at me, pretending not to have heard me, but I'm convinced she did," Emilia asserted, her tone mixed with frustration and concern.

"Now, Emilia," interjected her husband, Dr. Anton Constantin. "You don't know that for sure."

"No. I do. She heard me. She just *chose* to ignore me. In retrospect, I now wonder if the trouble she was talking about had something to do with her death, or was it something else?"

I leaned in. "What do you mean?"

When Emilia hesitated to answer, Tasha chimed in. "I think my mother is referring to the fact that Olga's parents were part of a resistance movement in Romania. Those who support the government are not always ready to forgive and forget those who do not. What they view as treason comes with a price to be paid."

"You think one of them killed Olga?" I asked, images of assassins in dark trench coats running through my mind.

"Or," Anton leaned in, "it could be someone who is obsessed with the Cold War and believes anyone with ties to a Communist country is a spy waiting to betray the United States." He took in a deep breath. "People still eye us suspiciously, even after we have lived here close to twenty years."

He gazed out the window, his eyes narrowed as if scanning the shadows for watchful eyes. I could almost feel the weight of his world—constantly having to navigate an environment where he didn't know who he could trust. I understood that level of uncertainty. It had seeped into my life as well.

"I had no idea," I admitted, sorry for failing to consider the fear Tasha and her parents faced daily. I remembered the times I thought of Tasha as distant or standoffish, misinterpreting her caution as snobbery. At that moment, I realized perhaps she was simply being careful, aware that potential enemies could be anyone...anywhere. The paranoia her immigrant parents lived with had also woven itself into Tasha's life.

We chatted for a few more minutes, and then I excused myself, saying I had an errand to run. Tasha walked with me to my car. "So, what are you really doing?"

"What do you mean?" I smiled.

"You've got that look in your eye when you're about to do something you probably shouldn't," Tasha grinned.

"You got me," I chuckled. "I'm going to stop by the Hathaway House and talk to the skaters and……" I paused, carefully choosing my next words.

"And what?" Tasha tossed her waist-length chestnut brown hair behind her shoulders.

I leaned against the door. "And snoop around and hopefully find something that might help."

Tasha's eyes lit up. "I knew it. I knew you were up to something. What are you looking for?"

I shrugged. "Anything that seems off."

"Mind if I come?" She grinned. "I love a good mystery." Suddenly, her smile faded. "Besides, Olga was kind of like family. She was Romanian—like me. We have to stick together."

***

Ten minutes later, Naomi greeted Tasha and me at the Hathaway House. Cardboard boxes and suitcases filled the dining room. Stacks of papers were in the hallway, and plane tickets were scattered across the table by the door.

"What's all this?" I asked. "Is everyone leaving?"

Naomi replied. "Yes. We've all been on the phone today trying to find new coaches. Some of us wanted to stay together, but I don't think that's going to happen." She sighed. "It's hard to find someone like Coach Wyatt who works with singles *and* pairs skaters and is taking new students."

"Have you all been able to find a coach?" Tasha asked.

Naomi turned toward her but said nothing—questions in her eyes.

I chimed in. "Naomi, this is Tasha—a friend from school.

We were in the neighborhood and thought we'd stop by and see how you were all doing."

"Oh, that was nice of you. And to answer your question, Tasha, unfortunately, not everyone has found a coach. Those of us who haven't are going home and the rest of us are on to new rinks. Jason and I are leaving after the memorial service for Toronto. I might need to buy some warmer clothes before we leave," she chuckled.

I surveyed the table once again and counted six tickets. "Have some already left?"

"No. I think the entire team is here until Tuesday afternoon. Some are staying until the end of the week. Of course, Jason has been staying with his aunt since Coach's murder, so he has his stuff at her house, and Eric moved out this morning."

I cocked my head. "And where did he go?"

"His uncle is in town, so he went to stay at the hotel with him." She smiled. "Lucky guy. His uncle is also one of those rare coaches who has both singles and pairs skaters. He's not taking any new students, but I bet he'll make an exception for Eric." She paused. "I always thought it was strange that Eric didn't work with his uncle. I'd think the friends and family rate would be a lot less than what he was paying Coach Wyatt."

"Where does his uncle work?"

"At our old rink." She wrinkled her nose. "I can't imagine how weird it was to train with one coach while your uncle is looking on. I never understood it, but, oh, well."

In the most nonchalant tone I could muster, I asked, "What's his uncle's name?"

"Coach Bates…Thomas Bates."

With Thomas Bates' name ringing in my ears, I froze. Thoughts whirled in my head—should I search the house for more clues or change course and find Coach Bates and Eric?

"Uh…was there anything else I could help you with?" Naomi asked, bringing a halt to my inner battle.

Without thinking, I asked, "Would it be okay to look in Olga's room? I thought we might find something that could help figure out why someone killed her."

Naomi shrugged. "I suppose it'd be all right. The police already went through her room. They didn't say anything about not letting anyone go in. So, sure, why not? If you can find her killer, have at it."

"Thanks," I said as I started up the stairs, Tasha trailing behind.

Just before we vanished from Naomi's sight, I stopped, feigning ignorance, and asked, "Which room is it?"

"Oh, yeah, that might help," she bashfully chuckled. "It's the second door on the right."

A chill went down my spine as I opened the door to Olga's room. Despite knowing she was neither here nor would return, I felt her presence, if only in my imagination. I glanced at the bedside tables and the dresser, noting nothing of importance.

Time had worked against me during my frantic search of her room the other night, but now, I hoped it would be on my side.

"What do you want me to do?" Tasha asked as she scanned the room.

"Why don't you start in the closet?"

"What am I looking for?" Tasha asked as she threw the closet door open.

"Letters. Papers. Anything like that. Check her pockets too —she might have stuffed something in them."

As Tasha rummaged through Olga's clothes, I opened the drawer where I had found the love letters, but they were gone. *Perhaps the police have them.*

Something caught my eye when I started to close the drawer—a piece of paper lodged in the corner. I wiggled it free and held it under the lamp on the nightstand. It was a photo from an instant camera. Three figures bundled in white parkas with scarves around their necks stared back at me.

As I studied the photograph, Tasha came up behind me. "What'd you find? Who's in the picture?"

"It looks like Olga and Mr. Hansen. But the other guy—"

Tasha leaned closer, shaking her head. "Who do you think he is?"

I slipped the photo into my pocket, careful not to bend it. "I have no idea. But I'm going to find out."

I took a breath. "Did you find anything?"

"Not yet. I need to look on the shelves. Suppose it's all right if I stand on this?" Tasha asked, her hand on the wooden chair by the window.

"Sure," I shrugged. "While you do that, I'll check under the bed."

Nothing.

I lifted the mattress and looked underneath it.

Again, nothing.

Tasha came up empty-handed as well. Our big find was the photograph. Hopefully, it would help with our investigation.

Lost in thought while trying to decide our next move, I jumped when I heard Naomi's voice.

"Can I help with anything?" An apologetic smile crossed her face. "I'm sorry. I didn't mean to scare you. It is kind of creepy being in a dead person's room, isn't it?"

"Yeah," I mumbled. "I don't think I'll ever get used to it."

I scanned the room one last time. "I think we're done here, but do you know anything about a problem Olga was having with one of the skaters?

Naomi took in a deep breath. "Nothing more than usual. Jason was frustrated about some changes she made to our footwork sequence. And Eric was miffed because she added another jump to his program, and he didn't think it worked. Like I said, just normal stuff."

"Did she seem bothered by their reactions?"

Naomi shook her head. "No. Olga was used to us arguing about any changes she made, but it never seemed to faze her." She shrugged nonchalantly. "She never backed down."

I started to leave but stopped. "Just one more thing. Do you have any idea where Eric and his uncle are staying?"

chapter twenty-two

Tasha rode with me to the hotel, where we hoped to find Eric and his uncle. My mind raced with questions for Coach Bates. How long had he been in town? Why had he been in contact with Mr. Hansen? Did he recognize the third person in the photograph? And, although I hadn't quite figured out how to phrase it—did he hate Coach Wyatt enough to kill him?

With any luck, I'd get some answers.

I should call Craig and let him know what I'm doing. But if I do, he'll want to meet me at the hotel, and I don't want to waste his time in case Eric and his uncle have already checked out. I can bring him up to speed later. Besides, it's not like I'm alone—Tasha's with me.

After parking, I took a deep breath.

"Are you okay?" Tasha asked.

"Yeah, just a little nervous. I'm not sure how willing this Thomas Bates will be to talk to me, but I guess we'll find out."

"You'll be fine." She smiled. "Besides, if he gives you any trouble, I'll use my Krav Maga to stop him."

"Krav Maga?"

"It's a type of martial arts. My parents wanted me to know how to protect myself, just in case I ever needed to." She grinned. "It's quite effective. Trust me, I've got your back."

Grateful for the backup, we went inside the hotel with its décor of dark wood paneling and orange carpeting. At the mahogany desk, I asked if Thomas Bates was still a guest. As the young man looked for the info, I spotted Eric stepping off the elevator near the water fountain at the edge of the lobby. His eyes widened in surprise when he saw me.

"Michelle! What are you doing here?"

"Hi, Eric. I just wanted to see how you were holding up," I said, trying to sound casual.

"I'm fine, just trying to figure out what's next," he replied, his gaze shifting to Tasha.

"Eric, this is Tasha—a friend from school. By any chance, is your uncle here? I have a few questions I'd like to ask him."

"Sorry, he's not here. He had some errands to run before we go home. Was there something I could help you with?"

Tasha glanced around, then grinned. "While you two talk, I'm going to walk around the hotel and check out their banquet rooms. My mom's already planning my graduation party. Never mind it's two years away." She touched my arm. "I won't be gone long."

As Tasha wandered down the hallway, I gestured to a pair of empty chairs by the fireplace.

As we settled into the overstuffed chairs, a group of young men in bell-bottom jeans and polyester shirts gathered near a piano in the corner. One of them pounded out "Saturday Night's Alright (For Fighting)" while the others attempted harmony—failing miserably.

"When are you leaving?" I asked.

"Tomorrow morning," he replied, his fingers fidgeting with the edge of his jacket.

"You're not staying for the memorial service?"

Eric's posture straightened. "No. I don't see any reason to stay. It's not like it will make any difference."

I shrugged. "I guess I just thought you'd want to support your teammates."

He scoffed. "Just because we trained together doesn't mean we're like the best of friends. No. I need to do what's best for me—and that's to leave this place."

"How's it going with your uncle? When did he get to Petersburg?"

Eric crossed his arms. Things are fine with my uncle. I don't know when he got here. He didn't tell me, and I didn't ask. What's it matter?" His eyes narrowed. "You think he had something to do with Coach Wyatt's murder? Man, you'll do anything to take the heat off that scumbag, Danny, won't you?"

"That's not fair," I protested. "I'm just trying to get to the truth. If Danny killed Coach Wyatt, he'll pay for it. But he was in jail when someone murdered Olga, so we still have a killer on the loose. All I want to do is ask a few questions, that's all. Are we cool?"

"I suppose." He leaned back. "I just don't like you insinuating that my uncle had anything to do with either death."

"I understand. So how 'bout we just start at the beginning? It's no secret your uncle believed Coach Wyatt was giving his skaters performance-enhancing drugs."

Eric nodded, picking at the potted plant next to his chair.

"Did your uncle ever talk to you about Coach?"

"Sure. Uncle Thomas told me to be careful and to keep my eyes open. He didn't want me to get caught up in anything that could get me suspended from the National Skating Council."

"And did you see anything that made you think your uncle's suspicions were true?"

Eric hesitated, glancing around before lowering his voice. "I think Danny and Coach were in cahoots together."

"Why do you say that?" I leaned closer.

"There were rumors Coach was giving skaters something to boost endurance. Some of them got way better overnight. After Danny showed up, Coach stopped using local judges.

He moved up Ethan and Cherie's senior-level test by quite a bit and then flew in his own judges to officiate it."

"What happened at the test?"

"Ethan fell. Cherie missed two jumps. They shouldn't have passed, but they did. Then, a senior team dropped out of Nationals, and Ethan and Cherie took their spot. They won gold."

"That would explain the bribery rumors," I said. "But how does Danny fit in with all this?"

"Uncle Thomas looked into Danny's family. His parents were arrested for embezzlement, blackmail, and murder. As the saying goes, the apple doesn't fall far from the tree. I think Danny convinced Coach to bribe the judges for a guaranteed shot at the Olympics. He learned how to work the system from watching them."

"But they're in prison," I said. "Didn't exactly end well for them, did it?"

"I get that, but I still think Danny and Coach hatched this bribery scheme together. Danny knew how desperate Coach was to get back to the Olympics. It had been a while since his last trip, and I think he missed the attention that went with it. Coach Wyatt saw a way to make it happen again, and he seized the opportunity. You'll never convince me otherwise."

I raised an eyebrow. "Let me ask you this: do other coaches fly in judges?"

Eric shrugged. "Yeah, but—"

"And was there ever any proof that Coach gave drugs to his skaters?"

"No, but—"

I leaned in closer. "But what? It sounds like there's no conclusive evidence against either Coach or Danny."

Eric shifted in his seat. "Look, all I know is Uncle Thomas said he had it on good authority that the rumors were true. He said he would have solid proof by the time the National Skating Council needed it. He was just waiting for it."

"Waiting for the proof? What does that mean? Who was getting it for him?"

"He didn't go into detail, and I didn't ask," Eric admitted. "I trust my uncle. If he said there would be proof, there would be."

"This may sound like a crazy question, but why did you stay with Coach Wyatt when you suspected him of, shall we say, shady dealings? You could have easily switched coaches with your uncle coaching at the rink. Why didn't you?"

"Look. I love my uncle, and I'd do anything for him, but when it comes to skating, the coach standing behind the boards carries a lot of weight with the judges, and no one had the kind of clout that Coach Wyatt had. No way was I going to risk lowering my chances of making the Olympic team by changing coaches. But now, I don't know what my future holds."

Eric turned away briefly, but his demeanor was defiant when he faced me again. Judging from his rigid posture and clenched jaw, I knew he had just about had it with my questions, but I had one more I had to ask. I pulled out the photograph from my pocket.

"Do you recognize this man?" I pointed to the man with Olga and Mr. Hansen.

"Sure. That's my uncle," he said, his tone cautious.

"Any idea when it was taken?"

Eric studied the snapshot, and for one fleeting moment, I thought he might open up. Instead, he shook his head and shot up from his chair. "Nope."

He stormed off to the elevator and disappeared inside.

Tasha walked in, shaking her head. "What got him in such a huff?"

"Your guess is as good as mine. I asked him about this picture." I held it up. "And, well, you saw what happened."

Tasha raised an eyebrow. "I wonder what he's hiding?"

***

After dropping Tasha off at her house, I went home, where the deadline for my article on Coach Wyatt loomed over me. I had to get it finished—investigation or not.

As I closed the front door, Gidget darted down the stairs and rubbed against my legs. I bent down to pet her. Her loud purr making me smile.

"You're hungry? Me too. Let's go grab something to eat."

Gidget darted ahead, leading the way to the kitchen.

While she munched on her fresh, crunchy, dry food, I debated what to make for dinner. I still hadn't made it to the grocery store—not with the investigation and all.

I sighed. Peanut butter and jelly to the rescue again.

Opening the refrigerator to get the jelly, I gasped at the sight—it was full: two gallons of milk, two dozen eggs, a container each of orange juice and apple juice, cold cuts, sliced cheese, cream cheese, and a casserole with a note in Crystal's handwriting attached: "Supper for tomorrow when mom comes home. Two more in the freezer."

What a relief! Thanks to Crystal, at least one thing was under control.

With my sandwich and a glass of milk in hand, I retreated to my room. I set my plate on one side of my desk before placing my typewriter in the center. The opening paragraph for my article—the who, what, when, where, and why—came easily, but after that, the words stalled.

Did I understand the inner workings of Coach Wyatt? Was he a dedicated trainer or a manipulative cheat? Was he a victim or something darker?

It was common knowledge that Mr. Hansen invited Coach to train his team at the university's rink—that was easy enough to print. But what about the rumors and death threats against the coach? Was it my place to write an expose, or should I just produce a soft profile and gloss over the scandals?

As I sifted through my stack of magazines and newspaper clippings about Coach's life, I settled on the biographical approach. If the rumors were true, which was still a big *if*, there would be plenty of time to delve into them later.

While flipping through old articles about Coach Wyatt, I stumbled upon a feature about Doug Hansen from 1951 detailing his skating accident. An unnamed skater with whom he trained collided with him during practice, sending Doug crashing into the ice, unable to walk afterward. A long recovery followed, but with this doctor warning of permanent damage if he fell again, his dreams of making the 1952 U.S. Olympic figure skating team, as well as his skating career, ended.

My fingers found the Eiffel Tower charm around my neck. I had a hunch about the identity of the other skater involved, but I needed proof.

It was 10:15 p.m., but I couldn't wait.

If untangling this mystery would lead to Coach's killer and finding Detective Douglas, time was of the essence.

I picked up the phone.

"Craig? I need a favor. Could you have your P.I. look into Doug Hansen? He trained with Coach Wyatt. There was a skating accident. I think Wyatt was involved. I want to be sure."

"Oh, and can he look into Eric's uncle, Thomas Bates?" I glanced at the photograph of Coach Bates, Mr. Hansen, and Olga. "I think there's more to his story than we know."

chapter twenty-three

Monday, April 21, 1975

T.J. was uncharacteristically late picking me up for class. In all the time I'd known him, he had always been punctual, but today, he was clearly venturing into uncharted territory. I checked the answering machine, half-expecting a message that he was sick or there had been an emergency of some sort.

Nothing.

Just as I reached for the phone to call him, I spotted his car barreling down the driveway, gravel flying behind his tires as he seemingly raced to make up for lost time.

I darted out the door, rushed to his car, yanked the passenger door open, and jumped inside. "Everything okay?" I asked, trying to catch my breath.

T.J. adjusted his aviator sunglasses and shrugged. "Yeah, just running late. Meg had me over last night to meet her dad. We ended up watching a movie, and I lost track of the time. I must have been really tired because I forgot to set my alarm before going to bed. When I didn't get up this morning, my mom thought maybe I was sick or something, so she came to check on me."

"Wow, you had quite the night! So, tell me about her dad. What's he like?"

"I'm still not sure what he does—sales, marketing, stuff like that. Sounds like a combination of things, but it keeps him busy, and he's out of town a lot. It seems he has some high-stakes deals going on at the moment. While I was at their house, he had to take several phone calls to deal with some problems. Meg said he doesn't usually take care of business when he's home, so she figured it must have been important for whoever to call him."

"So…what's the deal with you and Meg? Are you back together?"

"Yeah, for now." T.J. shrugged again. "Honestly? I don't know. But at least my conscience is clear. I'm not hiding anything from her, and…she finally introduced me to her dad." He took a deep breath. "And get this. Her father was the one who told her to give me a second chance. He said keeping my promise to you proved that loyalty was important to me, and that was an admirable trait—not something to be cast aside. So, I guess we'll start with a clean slate and see where things go. You think that's a good idea…to give it another go?"

In my head, I was screaming, "No, *that's a horrible idea. She's not right for you.*" But the words that came out of my mouth sounded far more supportive: "I think you need to do what makes you happy."

"But what if I don't know what makes me happy?"

T.J. looked lost, and seeing him like that tugged at something deep inside me. More than anything, I wanted him to find happiness—even if it wasn't with me.

I laid my hand on T.J.'s arm. "The best thing to do is to try things with Meg again and see what happens. Find out how you feel about her, and how she feels about you."

"Is that really what you think?" he asked, looking deep into my eyes as if seeking a different answer.

Did he want me to say 'no'? Unable to read his thoughts or express my conflicting feelings, I said nothing and nodded in affirmation.

"Okay, then. I'll give my relationship with Meg another try," he said with great resolve. "If it's meant to be, it'll work out. If not, at least I will have tried."

As he spoke the words I didn't want to hear, the only thing I could do was to smile and say, "Hopefully, everything will turn out how you want."

He glanced in my direction. "So…changing subjects, how's it going with the Coach Wyatt case? Getting any closer to clearing Danny's name, or is it looking more like he's the one who killed the coach?"

"I've got a few new leads I'm following." I filled him in on Mr. Hansen's skating accident and my questions about Eric's uncle, Thomas Bates.

I ended with, "I called Craig last night to ask if his P.I. could dig up any info on those two. Thought that might speed things up. Sometimes, the required paperwork at the police station slows down the sharing of information."

"Thank goodness for good ol' Craig," T.J. muttered.

I nudged him playfully. "Oh, don't be like that. I need all the help I can get."

I pulled my hand away, the weight of his relationship with Meg making me hesitate. "By the way, have you heard about Olga and Detective Douglas?"

His brow furrowed. "No, what happened?"

I took a deep breath. "Someone shot and killed Olga, and some guys kidnapped Detective Douglas. I have no idea if the two crimes are connected, but they both occurred at the Hathaway House where the skaters are staying."

T.J.'s eyes widened in horror. "That's horrible! Why was Detective Douglas at the house?"

"Apparently, Olga called him and asked him to meet her there. No one knows why," I said.

"Do the police have any leads on who killed Olga or took Douglas?"

I shook my head. "No."

T.J.'s eyes narrowed with concern. "Are you sure you should be looking into all this stuff? I mean, you don't have a clue what you're mixed up in. People are getting killed and kidnapped…and your mom was almost one of their victims. Shouldn't you just let the police handle things?"

"It's not like they're doing such a great job," I argued.

"No offense, but neither are you. The only thing you're accomplishing is putting yourself and your family at risk."

I crossed my arms. "That's not fair. I'm trying to clear an innocent man's name, which is more than the police are doing. I'm sorry if I haven't cracked the case yet, but I'm not giving up on Danny or bringing down that mysterious man Sarah mentioned. He has to be stopped before he hurts anyone else. I have to protect my family."

"I understand that, but what makes you think you can stop him?" T.J. asked, raising an eyebrow.

"Because I won't quit until he's behind bars," I replied, more determined than ever.

T.J. reached over and cranked up the radio as Ringo Starr's "No No Song" filled the air. The music made the silence between us less noticeable and gave me time to collect my thoughts. But every time I thought of a rebuttal to his comment, I bit my tongue, deciding it was better to stay quiet than start an argument.

As T.J. turned into the commuter lot, B.J. Thomas' "(Hey Won't You Play) Another Somebody Done Somebody Wrong Song" started playing. I couldn't help but smile at the irony— T.J.'s lack of faith in my choices certainly felt like he had done me wrong.

Just as the chorus swelled, T.J. reached over and turned off the radio, his hand settling on my knee. "I get that you want to protect your family and save the world. But promise me you'll be careful. I don't want you to get hurt. I worry about you, that's all."

"I'm always careful," I replied with a slight smile.

T.J. grinned back, shaking his head. "That's what you say, but we both know that's not what usually happens."

***

Lunchtime couldn't come fast enough. My morning classes—Introduction to Accounting and 20th Century Political Thought—dragged on endlessly. While they checked the boxes for my graduation requirements and most days held my interest, today, they did not. My thoughts were focused on Coach Wyatt, Danny, Olga, and Detective Douglas. The life-and-death situations swirling around me were far more pressing than budgeting and capital expenditures or the political philosophy of ancient and medieval periods.

As I descended the stairs of Whitley Hall and stepped onto the floor of the Commuter Lounge, I glanced at our group's table. Lawrence was motioning for me to hurry.

"What's up?" I asked, dropping my books onto the table and slipping into the chair across from him.

"Detective Douglas called this morning," he said, leaning over the table.

"You're kidding! Where's he at? Is he okay?" I couldn't believe what I was hearing. Detective Douglas was alive!

"He's about fifty miles from here." Lawrence continued. "He escaped and made it to a restaurant, where he called 911. The sheriff picked him up and took him to the hospital where he's being treated. I guess he's been beaten up pretty badly. He's got a broken arm, and his nose is broken, and he has a concussion." He paused and drew a deep breath. "That's it for now until the hospital faxes the medical report to the Chief."

"Fax?" I asked, raising an eyebrow.

"Yeah, it's a way to send documents. I don't understand it, but the police stations in the state recently got fax machines. Now Chief just has to figure out how to use it."

"Sounds complicated, but how cool to send records that way. Kind of like a telegram, I guess," I said. "How'd you find out about Detective Douglas and the fax? Did you work this morning?"

"No. Lt. Grogan called me before I left for class and filled me in."

"I can't believe it. I'm so glad he's alive." I let out a sigh of relief. "Man, I was afraid whoever took him might have killed him. Any idea how he escaped?"

"Lt. Grogan didn't go into a lot of detail. Something about pretending to have a seizure and knocking his guard out when he came in to check on him."

"That was smart thinking. I wonder what he knows about his kidnappers?"

"I'll find out this afternoon when I go to the station. I'll keep you posted. Are you working tonight, or will you be at home?"

"I should be home. Mom's supposed to be released from the hospital today, so I took the night off."

"I'll call you after work and fill you in on the latest," Lawrence said, lifting his white foam coffee cup.

Behind him, Rick was exchanging one book for another at his locker. He ambled over to my side of the table and pulled out the chair next to me.

"How's it goin'?" he asked no one in particular.

Lawrence and I nodded, mumbling something about being fine, as Rick fished a quarter from his jeans pocket and slid it past me to Billy. "I'll take a coffee and keep the change," he said.

Lawrence chuckled. "Big spender today, huh?"

Rick leaned back, stretching his arms. "Man, I'm too tired to deal with more loose coins."

"Rough night?" Lawrence probed as he passed the coffee from Billy to Rick.

"A little. My mom needed some help at the fitness center. She's trying to set things up in the kitchen so she can offer cooking classes."

"Did you make it home in time to watch Ringo Starr on *The Smothers Brothers Show* or John Lennon's interview on the *Tomorrow* program?" I asked.

"No, I wanted to, but we worked late because she wouldn't go home until we finished the ballet room." He turned toward me and continued. "That reminds me, Mom's planning to hire a ballet instructor soon. She said if you're interested, you can take lessons for free—said it's a small way to repay you for saving her business."

Never in my wildest dreams did I ever think I'd be able to take ballet lessons, let alone for free. A huge smile spread across my face. "That's incredible! Yes, I'd love to. Tell her thanks."

Rick beamed, a slight blush creeping up his cheeks as he abruptly shifted his gaze away from me toward Billy and asked, "Hey, man, what's the latest with Alice and BMK? Are we legit or still goin' underground?"

Billy grinned, pouring himself another cup of coffee. "Yash turned in our paperwork this morning. Alice said it looked good, and we could brew and sell without hiding our wares under the table." He chuckled. "We never had her fooled, but Billy getting hurt made her realize she needed to cover her bases. Anyway, we have the green light to operate unless she hears otherwise from the higher-ups, but she didn't think there'd be any problems."

"Cool," said Rick, swirling the coffee in his cup. As our eyes met, a small smile crept across his face, but the moment ended when Lawrence chimed in.

"Yeah, it'll be nice to be legal. As a local law enforcement employee, I'd hate to have to haul everyone in for brewing coffee illegally. Although, running a coffee speakeasy could be kind of fun."

Yash settled into a chair next to Lawrence. "What? Are we opening a speakeasy?"

"Afraid not. Seems like your business plan ended our dreams," laughed Rick.

"Michelle, how's the Coach Wyatt case coming along? Is there anything you need me to do?" Yash asked.

"Have you gotten any leads on Danny's scarf?"

"No. Not one." He shook his head.

I shifted my gaze to Lawrence. "I was wondering if you could do me a favor?"

"Depends," he said.

"Can you check the autopsy report for any mention of fibers found around Coach's neck?"

"Sure, that shouldn't be too difficult. Why do you ask?"

"Just curious about something." I said, taking a breath before adding, "Any ideas about who killed Olga?"

Lawrence leaned forward, elbows resting on the table, his fingers intertwined. "Not yet, but I'm hoping Detective Douglas can tell us something that will help."

"Oh, and one more thing," I said. "Do you know if the police confiscated the love letters Olga had in her bedroom?"

"Wait. How do you know she had love letters in her bedroom?" he asked, peering at me over his round wire-rimmed glasses.

I wrinkled my nose. "Not sure you really want to know….but could you see if they have them?"

"I take it they're missing?"

I nodded.

He shook his head, a mixture of amusement and frustration crossing his face. "I won't even ask how you know that, but sure, I'll check into it."

A glance at the wall clock told me my time for intel-gathering was up—class was calling. I grabbed my books and hurried upstairs. Halfway up, I passed Craig, going down-stairs to the Lounge.

"Michelle, we need to talk," Craig said, his voice rising above the noise of students in the stairwell.

"Now? I've got class," I said.

"Right now. It's important," he insisted as the crowd behind him pushed him deeper down the stairs.

"Okay. Meet me out front."

The warm April breeze greeted me as I leaned against Whitley's brick wall, waiting for Craig. A surge of students poured onto the landing, with Craig trailing behind them.

"What's up?" I asked as I tried to decipher the urgency of his expression.

"I heard from my P.I. Turns out Eric's uncle, Thomas Bates, has ties to both the Peterson and Goodright families."

"How so?"

"Bates' father worked as a chef for my grandfather, Chauncey Peterson. That is until Steve had him fired."

"Why was he fired?"

"You'll love this—Steve accused him of padding the kitchen's expense account and pocketing the extra cash," Craig explained.

"If anyone knows about embezzling, it should be Steve."

"Exactly. But the elder Mr. Bates claimed he was innocent, insisting Steve set him up and that Steve was skimming the money himself."

"I can believe that." I nodded.

"Bates never got a job as a private chef after that because of Steve's accusations. He ended up cooking at a local diner, which, as you can imagine, put a real strain on the family's finances. The stress of it all took a toll on him mentally. He suffered from depression and turned to the bottle. Carson, my P.I., said the police were often called to the Bates household to deal with his aggressive behavior."

I let out a deep sigh. "That would have been Eric's grandfather, which explains why he doesn't like Danny or his family. Do you think any of this could be connected to Coach Wyatt's death?"

"At first, I didn't think so, but the more I thought about it, the more I wondered if killing Wyatt was part of a larger scheme to get revenge on the Goodright and Peterson families by framing Danny for the murder."

"If that's the case, we need to clear Danny's name and fast. His life could be in danger."

Craig continued: "As you know, I haven't always believed that my mother was right in saying Danny did not kill Coach Wyatt." Craig paused. "And, if I'm going to be honest, I didn't *want* to believe her. I was jealous because she seemed to care more about Danny than me."

I understood where Craig was coming from—when Mae, Craig's mother, moved to Petersburg six years ago, she and Craig were estranged. In fact, the first time he came to Petersburg was last fall when his aunt, Professor Anne Ladd, asked him to help her investigate the mystery surrounding his father's death. Though he and his mother reconciled after Anne's murder, the lost years could never be reclaimed. Watching his mother worry so much about Danny after his arrest made it clear Danny held a special place in her heart—a position that perhaps Craig wanted all for his own.

With a determined air, Craig seemed to shake off the past. "But that's all behind us. And the more I dig into the people tied to Coach Wyatt, the more I believe Danny was telling the truth. Someone set him up. The question is, who?"

"Do you think Danny knows who it could be?"

Craig shook his head. "I have no idea, but I know one way we can find out."

"How?"

"Let's ask him."

"Right now? I've got class."

"Okay. I can go by myself. I canceled my office hours, and

I'm taking the afternoon off. The perks of being a teaching grad student," he grinned. "I'll let you know what he tells me."

I inhaled deeply, weighing my options. I could sit through the lecture, but I knew my mind would wander, wondering what Danny was telling Craig. Or should I cut class, go with Craig, and get the information firsthand from Danny?

"You know what?" I decided, "Forget class. I'll borrow Melody's notes. Lawrence is downstairs. Let's ask him what we need to do to see Danny."

I grabbed Craig's arm. "Come on. Let's go. Time's a-wastin.'"

chapter twenty-four

Craig and I returned to the Commuter Lounge, where we filled Lawrence in on the connection between Coach Bates and the Goodright and Peterson families.

"I think there's a good chance someone framed Danny, but we need to talk to him and see what he knows about Bates," Craig concluded.

"Sounds like that would be a good idea," Lawrence said.

"Do you think we could see him now?" I asked.

Lawrence glanced at the clock. "Not likely. They don't usually let visitors in after hours unless it's been cleared ahead of time."

He pulled a pen and paper from his camo backpack, scribbled a note, folded it, and handed it to me. "Give this to Lt. Grogan—no one else."

"Sure," I said. "But why?"

"Sarah," he said quietly. "Need I say more?"

I nodded.

After everything that had happened, trust was a rare commodity, and Lt. Grogan was one of the few who had earned it.

I clutched the note as if my life depended on it and, in actuality, Danny's just might.

***

Craig and I approached the front desk at the station, where a weary-eyed officer glanced up. After listening to our request to speak to Lt. Grogan, he frowned and picked up the phone. Moments later, Lt. Grogan appeared.

"Michelle. Craig. What can I do for you?" He asked, his eyes shifting between Craig and me.

I handed him the folded note. "We need to talk to Danny."

Lt. Grogan read the note. "Wait here," he instructed before disappearing down the hall.

As we waited, I glanced around the lobby—nearly empty except for us and an officer stapling papers, clearly bored. Lawrence often complained about the monotony of working behind a desk and judging from the expression on the officer's face, he wasn't alone.

The sound of footsteps coming toward us shifted my attention to the hallway. Lt. Grogan handed me an envelope. "Give this to Officer Kent. He's expecting you. He'll make sure you see Danny."

"Thanks," I said. "By the way, have you heard any more about Detective—?"

He pressed a finger to his lips and whispered. "Not here. I'll have Lawrence get in touch with you later."

He glanced sideways and then returned his focus to me, speaking more loudly, "I hope this information about the Police Academy in Petersburg helps with your article. I look forward to reading it."

***

Craig and I sat at a table, waiting for Danny. He shuffled in wearing jeans and a chambray shirt, pale and hollow-eyed, the spark in him completely gone. A guard directed him to a chair across from us, a glass barrier between us.

"How are you holding up?" I asked.

"How do you think?" he snapped. "I'm accused of murder, and I'm scared I'm running out of time to prove I'm innocent."

"That's why we're here," Craig said, voice steady. "We're trying to find Coach Wyatt's killer. But we need your help."

Danny crossed his arms, his guarded stance doing little to hide his fear. "Mae said you two were looking into things, but she never said if you found anything. I just figured you weren't making any progress."

He hesitated. "Are you?"

"Not as much as we'd like," I said, trying not to discourage him. "But I think we have some new leads. We just need to ask you a few questions."

Danny leaned closer to the glass. "Ask away. I've got nothing to hide."

I drew a deep breath. "In your statement, you said you went to talk to Coach Wyatt, but he was on the phone, and he told you to wait on the porch until he finished his call. Is that right?"

Danny nodded.

"Did you hear anything the Coach said while he was on the phone?" I pressed.

"No. Not really." Danny shrugged. "Sounded like someone was demanding money, but I didn't catch the details."

"A witness claims they overheard you quarreling with Coach. Did you and Coach have a disagreement?"

He leaned back in his seat, saying nothing.

"Did you and Coach argue?" I asked again. "We can't help you if we don't have all the facts."

He moved as close to the glass as he could without touching it. "Coach got mad and yelled at me. That's probably why someone thought we were fighting, but it wasn't like that."

"What was it like?"

"When I was on the porch waiting for Coach, I heard Jason yelling at him…something about him showing favoritism to Ethan and Cherie. Anyway, it got pretty heated, so I stepped in and told Jason to back off. Then he and I got into it. Coach got mad at both of us and told us to leave. I stayed behind and tried to explain I was only trying to stop the fight between him and Jason and that he didn't need to be mad at me, but he wasn't having it. He told me to go back outside and cool off while he made a phone call—that he'd deal with me later."

"Did you tell the police?"

He shook his head. "No."

"Why not?" I leaned in, pressing him.

Danny's voice cracked, a mixture of anger and fear flickering in his eyes. "Because they already think I'm guilty. No way was I going to give them more ammo to use against me."

Despite understanding his rationale, I wished we had known about the disagreement earlier. My head buzzed as I tried to process what this meant—what else Danny might be holding back.

"Okay, what happened next?"

"I went outside to the porch like Coach told me. Then, I got bored and walked around the yard. A neighbor's dog started barking, and I thought I had upset him, so I went back toward the house. That's when I heard a scream, and I guess you know the rest."

Craig, with no sign of emotion, looked Danny straight in the eye. "Danny. Did you kill Coach Wyatt?"

Danny said emphatically, "No!"

"Then how did your scarf end up around Coach's neck?" I asked.

"I don't know," Danny said. "Like I told the police, I forgot my scarf at the rink. I have no idea how it got to the house. The only thing I can think of is that someone was trying to frame—"

I interjected, "Who? Who would want to frame you?"

Danny shook his head. "I don't know."

"You must have some idea," Craig said.

Danny sank into his seat. "Trust me. I have thought of little else. I know Eric and Jason don't like me, but I don't think either of them would kill Coach."

He thought for a moment, chewing his lip. "The only other person, and it's a long shot, would be that creepy coach from the other rink. I could never put my finger on what he was up to, but he was always watching me. Coach Wyatt noticed it too but told me to forget it."

"And the coach's name?" I asked.

"Coach Bates. Thomas Bates."

***

After Craig and I parted ways in the faculty parking lot— one perk of being a teaching grad student—I headed to the Commuter Lounge to wait until T.J. finished his class. While thumbing through my notes about Coach Wyatt's murder, Yash plopped into the seat next to me.

"Hey, foxy lady! How's it goin'?" He beamed.

"Pretty good, and you?"

"Not bad. Not bad at all, and—" The grin on his face grew wider. "—have I got some news for you."

"Oh, do tell."

"While balancing the rink's checkbook this morning, I stumbled on some old phone bills and discovered something that might interest you."

"What? The suspense is killing me." I chuckled.

"Back in October, around the time that Steve and Barb Goodright were arrested for Professor Ladd's murder and embezzling funds from the Peterson Lumber Company, someone was calling Mr. Hansen's private line every week from Boston. I checked earlier statements, and the number didn't show up in any of them."

"Really?" My pulse quickened. "Do you know who it was?"

Yash pulled a piece of paper from his pocket. "No clue, but I copied the number for you."

I stared at the telephone number. If memory served me correctly, it was the same number from the notecard I found in Eric's room.

It belonged to Marco Rossini.

***

After T.J.'s last class, we headed for the police station before going home. I filled him in on what Danny had told Craig and me about the disagreement he had with Coach on the night of the murder, as well as his thoughts on Thomas Bates.

When we got there, Lawrence was nowhere to be found. I asked the officer behind the desk about his whereabouts and learned he wouldn't be in until later that night.

Just as T.J. and I were about to leave, Lt. Grogan walked through the lobby.

"Lt. Grogan. Do you have a minute?" I called.

As he drew closer, I pulled out the card from Yash. "I know I'm supposed to go through Lawrence—"

"Not here," he said as he glanced around the lobby—two officers behind the front desk were talking to each other.

"Meet me in the backroom at the restaurant next door. Tell Nick I sent you. I'll be there in five."

T.J. and I followed his instructions, and, true to his word, Lt. Grogan walked in.

After taking his seat at our table, Lt. Grogan began. "I talked to Detective Douglas, and he said when he arrived at the skaters' house to meet with Olga, he saw a man shoot her in the front yard. When he tried to stop him, someone knocked him out from behind. The next thing he knew, he was locked in a room."

"That's horrible! Did he recognize the kidnappers or the guy who shot Olga?" I asked.

"No. The shooter's back was toward him the whole time. He never saw his face." He drew a long breath and continued. "His captors wore masks while they beat him. They wanted to know why he was still investigating Coach Wyatt's death—what he knew and what he was looking for."

Lt. Grogan leaned in. "But before I tell you anymore, I need you both to promise you won't tell anyone. T.J., I know you from the other cases you've worked on with Michelle, so I'm confident Detective Douglas would be okay with me sharing this information with you. Just understand that what I'm about to say can go no further. You can tell Craig, but no one else."

T.J. and I nodded.

"The men who abducted him wanted to know why he tracked down the guards assigned to the area by Sarah's cell on the night she died."

My heart pounded as I leaned back in my chair. "So we were right," I said. "The cases *are* connected."

"Yeah," said Lt. Grogan. "Which also means the investigation is more dangerous than we thought."

He took a moment, his eyes fixed on mine. "I know you want to help, but it's too risky. Detective Douglas wants you to lie low and let us handle the situation. I'm assigning patrols near your house until this matter is solved. If someone comes near, we'll grab him. But you need to stop investigating."

"Thank you," I said, feeling both gratitude and dread. "That will make my parents feel safer. By the way, my mom is coming home today."

"Yes, that's what I heard, which is another reason I'm having the area patrolled. I'm not convinced these people are done following through on their threats." Lt. Grogan's face grew somber. "Will you give me your word that you'll stop investigating Coach Wyatt's murder?"

I shook my head. "I'm sorry, but I can't do that. Not as long as my family is still at risk. Whoever's behind this has to be stopped. You can't protect us forever."

I looked to T.J. for backup, but he just rolled his eyes. "That's exactly what she said when I asked her to quit."

Lt. Grogan gave a resigned nod. "I'm not surprised. I told Douglas that's what you would say." He paused. "So, what do you have?"

I dug into my bag and pulled out one of Olga's love letters and the death threat I found in the secret drawer in Coach's desk. I handed them to Lt. Grogan.

He studied the notes as I continued. "At first, I thought they might be by the same person, but Craig's P.I. says they aren't. Is there any way you can find out who wrote the threatening note?"

Lt. Grogan raised a brow. "And may I ask how you got these?"

"I'd rather not say.".

He took a deep breath. "Let me see what I can do. Anything else?"

I rose to my feet and tugged on T.J.'s arm. "Uh... I'll have to think about that."

Before Lt. Grogan could ask another question, T.J. and I made a dash for the door.

"Don't you think you should tell him about the calls between Rossini and Hansen?" T.J. asked on our way to the car.

I sighed, knowing he was right but unwilling to admit it. "Not yet. I want to check on a few things first, and I don't want Rossini catching on. Subtlety's not exactly the police department's strong suit."

T.J. crossed his arms. "And if things get dangerous?"

I smirked. "For me or for them?"

"Michelle, this isn't a joke."

"I *am* serious," I said, even as my heart pounded. Someone out there was pulling strings.

And I was getting close.

chapter twenty-five

After my meeting with Lt. Grogan, T.J. drove me home. As we pulled into the driveway, I noticed his usual parking spot was taken. Crystal's bright red Dodge Colt, Mel's matching Chevy truck, Mike's '66 Ford pickup, and my Orange Bomb filled every inch of space on the cement pad beneath the basketball hoop.

"Looks like quite the family gathering," T.J. chuckled, arching an eyebrow.

"I bet the doctor let Mom come home today."

"That's what I'm thinking." He smirked at the house. "Wish I could stick around to celebrate, but homework's calling."

Granted, he probably did have homework, but we both knew the real reason he wasn't staying—my family was a lot to handle.

If tonight was like any other, my dad, Mel, and Mike would dive into one of their booming farm debates... about how to improve the farm, each trying to outdo the other. The three of them would soon be talking over each other in a verbal free-for-all that would have the rest of us laughing.

Then there was the fact that whenever T.J. braved a visit, Crystal grilled him about school and his love life. Despite having mastered the art of answering her inquiries without giving too much away, I had a hunch that he wasn't up for her inquisition today.

"Chicken," I teased, nudging his arm. "You just don't want to deal with them, do you?"

"Whatever gave you that idea?" T.J. smirked, feigning innocence.

"Oh, I don't know—maybe it's how quickly you backed up and turned the car around. If I didn't know better, I'd think you were in a hurry to get out of here," I laughed.

"You know me too well, Michelle Kilpatrick. Too well, indeed," he chuckled. "Tell your mom I'm glad she's doing better, and I'll stop by later when she doesn't have so much company."

I grinned as I climbed out of his car. "If you change your mind, she'd love to see you."

"I'll keep that in mind," he said.

"Sure you will," I chuckled.

As I stepped onto the porch, the hum of voices spilled through the door. I opened it and was hit by the usual chaos. My father gestured as he spoke while Mike, sunk deep into a corner chair, simultaneously shared his thoughts.

Meanwhile, Crystal and Mel sat crammed into the remaining chair, their mouths opening and closing as if waiting for the perfect moment to jump into the conversation.

Gidget was perched at the top of the stairs. I motioned for her to come down, but she remained steadfast—perched like a furry sentry, her ears twitching as she eavesdropped.

"There you are," my father said, glancing my way. "We were wondering when you would grace us with your presence. Your mother has been worried about you." His eyes flicked from me to the spot next to him on the couch.

I draped my jacket over the handrail and hurried into the living room, where my mother lay stretched out under her favorite afghan, a pillow under her head. I sat on the floor beside her, taking her hand in mine.

"I'm so glad you're home," I said, kissing her forehead. "How are you feeling? Can I get you anything?"

"No, I'm fine," she replied, struggling to keep her eyes open. "Your father's been an excellent caregiver. Do you have to work tonight?"

I squeezed her hand gently. "Nope. I took the night off. I was hoping the doctor would let you leave the hospital today, and I wanted to be here."

"Surprise. Surprise," Dad said with a snap. "You made time for your family. Is the world ending, and no one told me?"

"Give her a break," Mike interjected. "She's been busy with school—"

"And investigating things she has no business getting involved in," my father countered sharply. "Almost cost her mother her life."

"Dad," Crystal chimed in as she wrinkled her nose. "We can talk about this later. Mom doesn't want to listen to us squabbling. She needs peace and quiet."

Redirecting my focus to my mother, I could see the exhaustion etched on her face. "You look so tired. Would you be more comfortable in bed?"

"Yes," she replied softly. "I think I would." Mom glanced at Crystal, Mel, and Mike. "If you all wouldn't mind?"

"Of course not," Crystal said, rising from her seat. "Want me to help you up to your room?"

"I'd like that." She smiled weakly.

Mom held onto Crystal's arm as they went up the stairs. With my hand on my mom's back, I followed behind, supporting her balance. Once we got Mom into bed, I placed a bell on her nightstand for her to ring if she needed anything.

We kissed Mom goodnight and stepped back into the hallway. Crystal took a few steps forward but paused, glancing at me over her shoulder. "You might want to check your room. There was a letter in the mailbox and a big envelope stuck between the doors. I left them on your desk."

"Thanks. I'll be down in a minute," I replied.

As Crystal went downstairs, I headed to my room, where I found the letter and the large envelope. I pushed the letter aside as it was from the University of Petersburg and most likely news about summer and fall registration.

An unsettling curiosity washed over me as I flipped the large brown envelope over—no return address or markings showing who sent it or what it contained were visible.

With a surge of adrenaline, I tore it open—then froze.

In my hands was an 8x10 photograph of me sitting with Yash in the commuter lounge—a large red X across his face. Another photo depicted T.J.'s car parked at the police station, similarly defaced with an X. Four more photographs: Crystal grocery shopping, Mike filling his truck up with gas, my father in the hospital parking lot, and Craig coming out of Mae's gift shop—each image marred by an X covering the subject's face.

As if all those photos were not bad enough, the last one sent chills down my spine—Gidget curled up, sleeping beside me on my bed. Whoever took the photo had invaded my home in the middle of the night, watching us.

My hands shook as the photos slipped to the floor. Blood rushed to my head.

Crystal peeked into my room. "We're getting ready to— oh, my goodness, what's wrong? Are you okay? Let me help you sit down."

Her eyes darted to the pictures scattered on the floor. "What are these?" Crystal bent down and picked one up. "Michelle, who took these?"

Panic seeped into her voice as she gathered the rest of the pictures.

"I don't know," I said, my voice quaking. "I have no idea. But I'm scared."

Wrapping her arms around me, she whispered. "It's going to be okay, but we have to tell the police."

I straightened, shaking my head. "I'll call them, but please don't tell Dad. He'll go ballistic, and Mom doesn't need that right now."

"He needs to know—"

"Not yet. Dad just got Mom home. I'll go to the station and talk to Lt. Grogan. He said he's going to post an officer by the house, but maybe there's something else he can do."

"That's good, but what about the rest of us? The police can't protect us all," she said, pausing momentarily. "You're still not investigating that coach's murder, are you?"

I fell silent, unable to meet her gaze as guilt washed over me.

"Michelle, please tell me you stopped."

I said nothing.

"It's bad enough someone tried to kill Mom, and now they're threatening all of us. This has to end."

Fueled by anger, I stood up. "You're absolutely right. This has to stop."

After a deep breath, I said, "I'll go to the police station now. But before you leave, tell Mike what happened. Make sure you lock your doors and don't open them for anyone you don't recognize. Dad's good about keeping things locked...although locked doors didn't keep this crazy person out of my room."

I paused, the weight of the situation sinking in. "I guess you better tell Dad, but ask him not to tell Mom. She doesn't need to worry about this. She needs to focus on getting her strength back."

Crystal nodded, concern etched on her face. "Be careful, okay?"

"I will." I shrugged. "You should probably tell Dad I

might be out late so he doesn't stay up waiting for me. I've got my key."

Crystal raised an eyebrow. "I don't think that will stop him from worrying."

"I know, but everything will be all right. Trust me." I gave her a quick hug.

As Crystal closed the front door behind me, I heard my father asking, "Where's she—?"

I hurried to the car, glad it was Crystal and not me who had to deal with him.

The photographs reminded me that time was running out to catch Sarah's mystery man. Then, adding to my anxiety, a black limo was trailing behind me as I drove to the station. How could I keep up with everything when they always seemed to be one step ahead of me?

***

As I turned into the police station's parking lot, the limo slowed but did not stop. Whoever was driving had no intention of following me inside. They only wanted me to know they were watching me. I slammed my car door shut and rushed into the building, glancing over my shoulder for any signs of the ominous vehicle.

The station buzzed with activity as officers milled around in the lobby. Lt. Grogan and Lawrence stood behind the front desk, engaged in conversation.

"Michelle," Lawrence said. "What are you doing here? Rumor has it that your mom went home today. Is everything okay?"

I swallowed hard, the lump in my throat making it difficult to speak. "No—it's not. A limo followed me here. And someone left these at my house."

Lawrence and Lt. Grogan's expressions shifted from casual curiosity to deep concern as they flipped through the photos. Lt. Grogan's eyes narrowed as he picked up the one of me sleeping.

"I can't believe that someone was inside my house—in my bedroom," I said, my throat tightening.

"You better believe it," Lawrence said. "Someone is clearly sending a message that if you don't stop investigating, you, your family, and..." He held up the photo of T.J.'s car. "Everyone you care about is at risk."

"But how can I quit?" I shook my head. "I don't think Danny killed Coach Wyatt, and if you think I'm going to let an innocent person rot in prison, you're wrong. And, face it, even if I stop trying to prove Danny's innocence, there's no guarantee they won't keep coming after me and my family."

Lt. Grogan glanced around the busy lobby. "Lawrence, why don't you take Michelle to my office and take down her statement? I'll be down in a few minutes to help you finish."

The hum of chatter in the lobby faded as Lawrence led me down the corridor. His quick pace suggested he was in a hurry to get me away from listening ears.

"Are you all right?" he asked as we approached the office door.

"I'm fine," I replied, although I knew I wasn't—fear for myself, my family, and T.J. enveloped me.

We entered Lt. Grogan's small office. Piles of files and papers were scattered across his desk while two commendations and motivational posters adorned the walls.

"Have a seat," Lawrence instructed, gesturing to the worn leather chair opposite the desk as he settled into the other chair.

I clasped my quivering hands on my lap, the silence stretching as we waited.

Within a few minutes, the door creaked open, and Lt. Grogan stepped inside, taking his seat behind the desk. "As much as I don't think it's a good idea for you to be involved in this investigation, I know you're not going to stop," he began, his voice steady yet laced with concern. He said, "I got permission to have a patrol watch your house." After looking at the clock on the wall, he added, "They should be there now, and I'll keep someone nearby as long as I can."

Lt. Grogan let out a heavy sigh. "Look, even if I had all the resources in the world—which I don't—I still can't promise that you or your family will be safe every single moment. Right now, we're really stretched thin trying to track down Douglas's kidnappers, but we'll do our best to help. Keep your guard up, okay?"

"I get it," I murmured.

Lt. Grogan's tone shifted. "About Danny, I think you might be onto something."

"What do you mean?" I asked, a bit puzzled by his sudden change of perspective.

He hesitated, then held up the handwriting sample. "We got a match."

"You're joking. Who?"

"Thomas Bates."

"How'd you find that out?"

"Among the things we found in Coach Wyatt's desk was a copy of a handwritten statement Bates gave the National Skating Council about his doping and bribery allegations against the coach."

"Did you bring Coach Bates in for questioning? What did he say? Did you arrest him?"

"Hold on. One question at a time." Lt. Grogan paused, gathering his thoughts. "No, I have not questioned him. I sent two officers to the hotel to bring him in, but he and Eric had already checked out. Don't look at me like that. We'll find him."

Biting my lower lip, I pondered the implications. "Any idea which way they're heading?"

"I initially thought they might head back to California, where Bates coaches, but when I talked to the rink manager, he said Bates was taking an extended leave of absence. We're checking all the rental car places and transport terminals to see if either Bates' or Eric's name pops up."

"What if they used an alias?"

"That's a possibility, which is why I've got my guys showing pictures of Bates and his nephew. They'll turn up somewhere. They didn't just drop off the earth."

The loose string dangling from Lawrence's shirt reminded me of playing string with Gidget and sparked a memory of the yarn fiber wrapped around her nail.

"I know this sounds kind of random, but can I see the forensics report on Coach Wyatt?"

"Why?" Lt. Grogan asked, brows furrowed.

I pulled out the photograph of the three people in parkas stowed in my coat pocket. "I found this picture of Olga, Mr. Hansen, and Coach Bates. Notice they're all wearing scarves?"

"Yeah. What about it? Looks like they're all cold," Lawrence replied as he studied the picture.

"The thing is, scarves are made of different fabrics, right?"

They both nodded.

"Did the coroner mention the fibers found around Coach's neck? I mean, pulling the scarf tight enough to strangle Coach should have left some fibers."

"I see where you're going with this. Let me pull the report," Lt. Grogan said. He disappeared and soon returned with a folder. Flipping through its contents, he stopped and removed a paper, laying it on his desk. "Here it is."

After studying the paperwork, Lt. Grogan announced, "The report shows ivory wool fibers on the coach's neck."

I leaned over the desk, making sure I heard him correctly. "What was that again?"

"Ivory wool fibers were on his neck."

"Does it mention anything about silk fibers?"

Lt. Grogan cocked his head, puzzled. "As a matter of fact,

it does. It notes that off-white silk fibers were on the skin, but none were engrained. Why do you ask?"

"That means the killer used a wool scarf to strangle Coach Wyatt, and you can release Danny."

"And why would I do that?"

"Because Danny's scarf isn't wool—it's silk."

Lt. Grogan mulled over my statement. "That doesn't prove anything. He still could have killed the coach with a different scarf."

"And then take the time to remove the wool scarf and replace it with his own.?" I shook my head. "I highly doubt it."

Lt. Grogan nodded. "You might be right. Let me call the DA's office. You may have just cleared Danny's name...at least for now."

chapter twenty-six

I stared at the photograph of Olga, Mr. Hansen, and Coach Bates. They stood close, smiling easily—almost like old friends. But something about their posture made me pause. I tapped the photo's edge, eyes fixed on Bates and Hansen. I wondered—were they still that close?

I leaned closer. The scarves around their necks caught my eye.

Olga's scarf gleamed bright white, stark against the men's muted tones. Ivory? Wool? I needed to find out. If they were wool, could one have been used to strangle Coach Wyatt?

But right now, I had to focus on Eric and his uncle. If Hansen and Bates were still close, he might know where they'd gone. I started the engine, backed out of the police station's lot, and turned toward the campus ice rink. Hopefully, Mr. Hansen would be working tonight.

As I stepped into the lobby, excitement filled the air. Children, grinning from ear to ear, laughed and chattered as they got ready for their skating lessons.

Behind the counter, Mr. Hansen and Yash handed out rental skates to parents, who bent down to lace up the tiny skates for their little ones. A toddler waddled past, arms out for balance, and I couldn't help but smile. Sure, she had me beat off the ice, but could she pull off a T-stop?

Once the crowd thinned, I stepped up to the rental counter, ready to talk to Mr. Hansen. Voices drifted toward me from behind the skate racks. I thought about ringing the bell, but then I spotted Eric slipping out of Mr. Hansen's office, tucking a piece of paper into the pocket of his black windbreaker. He glanced down the hallway, eyes darting for witnesses, then dashed to the back door.

I followed him into the empty parking lot, dark except for a lone flickering lamppost. No way was I letting him slip away.

The door clanged shut behind me, and at that moment, Eric spun around.

"Who's there?" he said, panic in his voice.

"Eric… it's me. Michelle." I stepped into the flickering light.

His gaze flickered across the parking lot. "What are you doing here? You need to leave before you get hurt."

"Why? Are you going to hurt me?" I stepped closer.

He looked nervous, not threatening, just rattled.

His jaw tightened as if he wanted to say something but hesitated. "Not me, but…" His words trailed off into silence.

"I just want to talk to you," I pressed. "Do you know where your uncle is at?"

"No," he shot back. "And if I did, I wouldn't tell you."

"You know the police are looking for him," I countered. "They think he might have killed Coach Wyatt."

"That's insane!" Eric's voice cracked. "He may not have liked the guy, but he sure enough didn't kill him. Besides, they arrested Danny. Case closed."

I took a few more steps closer until we were face-to-face. "Maybe not. The police have additional evidence that proves Danny didn't strangle Coach."

Before I could say more, a voice sliced through the night behind me.

"New evidence? That's wonderful news!"

I turned to find Mr. Hansen and Yash emerging from the shadows.

Mr. Hansen's eyes shifted between Eric and me, a faint smile tugging at his lips. "When did all this happen?"

"Tonight," I said. "It's not official yet, but Lt. Grogan thinks there's a chance they'll drop the charges against Danny."

Mr. Hansen's grin widened. "What a relief. The poor boy has been through so much. First, his parents are arrested for murder, and then this mess with Coach Wyatt. Danny's been through more than anyone should. He's a good kid and he certainly didn't deserve any of this."

Mr. Hansen continued, "Yash thought he heard voices out here, so we came to see what was going on. Glad we did. After the last few days, it's nice to get some good news."

His eyes narrowed as he focused on Eric. "I thought you and your uncle were going back to California. What happened?"

Eric's posture stiffened. "Plans changed. My uncle left, but I had some unfinished business to take care of."

"I see." Mr. Hansen said, watching Eric closely. "Will you be around much longer?"

"No," Eric said, his voice low and defensive.

"Bad memories here, I'd imagine. Makes it hard to focus on training," Mr. Hansen said. He paused. "Where are you staying?"

"I'm not sure. I haven't decided yet."

"You're welcome to stay with me if you want. I've got plenty of room." Mr. Hansen offered.

"I'm fine," Eric snapped, stepping back as he shoved a piece of paper deeper into his jacket pocket. "I need to go."

Mr. Hansen's smile faltered. "Keep in touch."

"Whatever," Eric mumbled before turning and walking into the darkness.

With a sigh, Mr. Hansen turned to Yash. "Well, I suppose we should head back inside. I need to lock up and finish a few things before heading home. Did you two park out front?"

"Yes, sir," Yash answered, glancing at me.

I nodded.

We followed Mr. Hansen through the building and parted ways at his office.

As the door closed behind him, I couldn't help but wonder why Eric had been in Mr. Hansen's office.

And what was on that paper that Eric didn't want anyone to see?

Once we reached the parking lot, Yash leaned close, his voice barely above a murmur. "That was weird."

"What do you mean?" I asked, although I sensed it too.

"The way those two acted? I got the distinct feeling they *really* don't like each other. But why?"

I stopped.

"I don't know," I said slowly. "But there's definitely something going on between them. Let's go to my car. We shouldn't talk out here."

Yash zipped up his track jacket as we crossed the lot to my Orange Bomb. He slid into the passenger seat, shutting the door with a thud.

I took a deep breath. "I came to the rink tonight to ask Mr. Hansen a few questions. But while I was waiting, Eric came out of Mr. Hansen's office. It looked like he was sneaking out."

Yash raised his eyebrows. "Wait—he was *in* the office?"

"I don't think he was supposed to be in there," I said. "And after our little meet-up in the parking lot just now, I'm sure of it. But the question is, *why*?"

"You think he was looking for something?"

"That'd be my guess." I twisted my necklace. "While we were all in the back talking, Eric crammed a piece of paper into his pocket. Maybe he just didn't want to lose it, but I think it was because he didn't want anyone to see it."

Yash leaned back, thoughtful. "I wonder what it was."

I exhaled. "I don't know, but he's hiding something. We just need to figure out what."

***

When I returned home, my father met me, his figure looming in the doorway, arms crossed over his chest. "You were out investigating again, weren't you?"

I glanced down, avoiding his gaze.

"Your sister told me about the photographs and that you were taking them to the police," he said. "But that wasn't all you did, was it? Of course, it wasn't. Otherwise, you would have been home sooner."

He let out an exasperated breath. "What is it with you, Michelle? You just can't leave it alone, can you? Your mother was almost killed, and yet you continue to put your family in danger. What is it going to take to make you stop playing detective? Does someone have to die? Would you even quit then?"

The sharpness of his words cut through me, but I forced myself to respond calmly. "I never meant to cause trouble for anybody. You always taught me to stand up for what is right and to help those in need. Remember? Well, Danny needed me." I paused to gauge his reaction, but his expression did not soften.

"The police arrested him for a murder he didn't commit," I pressed. "And they finally agreed with me. It looks like they're going to drop the charges against him."

I hung up my jacket and steadied my nerves.

"So that's it then? You're done playing detective? Maybe now we can get our lives back to normal."

"That's what I want too. Believe me, I do," I insisted. "But there are some things I still have to do."

My father's jaw tightened, but before he could say anything, I said, "I'm going to be careful. I promise. But if I walk away now, there's a chance that more people are going to get hurt, possibly our own family and I can't let that happen. I can't explain it all. I just ask that you trust me on this."

His frown deepened. "You're not going to quit, are you?"

"No. I can't," I said.

He studied my face as if searching for the resolve behind my words. "You can be stubborn, you know that."

A small smile crept across my face as I attempted to lighten the moment. "I guess I come by it honestly."

My father sighed, the anger on his face replaced by something resembling concern, and for now, that felt like a small victory.

As he turned to go upstairs, I moved toward the phone in the living room.

"I need to call Craig. I'll only be a few minutes," I said.

My father halted on the staircase, gripping the banister. "Craig? Don't tell me you're dragging him into all this mess?"

"I'm going to tell him the news about Danny."

He shook his head. "I hope that's all."

I dialed Craig's number, twisting the cord in a knot as I waited for him to answer.

As soon as he did, I said, "Hey, it's me. I don't know if you've heard, but there's a pretty good chance the DA will drop the charges against Danny."

Craig listened as I recounted the events leading to the potential dismissal. "My mother will be relieved. But I think I will wait until it's official before I tell her. I don't want to get her hopes up and have something fall through. You did good,

Michelle," Craig continued. "I hope they catch Bates soon. It'll be a relief to have the actual killer behind bars and have this sordid mess over."

I paused, my fingers tightening around the phone. "If only it were that easy."

His voice sharpened. "What do you mean?"

"I'm not convinced Bates killed Coach Wyatt. Think about it. He hated Coach and wanted him out of the sport. But murder? That doesn't make sense. Bates was getting revenge by filing the grievances against Coach with the National Skating Council. Being banned from figure skating would have been a fate worse than death for Coach."

As I scratched Gidget behind her ears, her purring comforted me. "And then something happened tonight at the ice rink. I'm not sure what it means, but Eric snuck into Hansen's office, and I think he took something…a paper. I might be overthinking it, but what if Eric didn't leave town with his uncle so he could get it? What could be that important?

Craig was silent for a moment, and I imagined him leaning back in his chair, weighing the possibilities.

"Aren't you going to say anything?" I pressed.

"As much as I would like to disagree with you, I can't. Yet, at the same time, if I tell you I think you're right, you'll think I'm condoning your search for answers. Remember, we only got involved to clear Danny's name. You did that. Mission accomplished. It's time to let the police handle the rest."

"You're right, but I can't let it drop. What if they focus on the wrong person again? The real murderer will get away," I argued.

Craig sighed. "If Coach's murder is connected to Sarah's death, it could be far bigger and darker than we ever imagined. I care about you. I don't want anything to happen. You know that, right?"

"Yeah."

"You've got to be careful," Craig insisted.

"I'll try to be super careful," I said.

"You have to do better than try. Your life could depend on it. Don't take any chances."

"Okay, I got it. Satisfied?"

"As much as I can be. You better not have your fingers crossed?" he said with a reluctant chuckle. "Now, tell me everything you're thinking about looking into, and let's come up with a safe plan."

Craig listened as I laid out the facts and my suspicions. His steady voice and insights kept me grounded and focused, and when I hung up the phone, I knew exactly what I had to do—find Eric and get to the truth about why he was in Hansen's office.

chapter twenty-seven

Tuesday, April 22

The break between classes couldn't come fast enough. I hurried into the Commuter Lounge, scanning the large, crowded room the moment my feet hit the floor. No sign of Yash.

Instead, I spotted Todd at our table collecting money from a familiar face in the Commuter Lounge, though not someone from our group. Nearby, T.J. was pouring himself a cup of coffee.

As I approached, I glanced over my shoulder and caught sight of the student making his way to his table, proudly showing off his coffee to his friends and gesturing toward Todd.

Todd's grin said it all as he dropped the newly earned coins into a zippered pouch—business at BMK was booming.

I settled into the chair across from T.J. "Have you seen Yash today?"

"No," he said, glancing at the clock. "He's usually here by now. What's up?"

"I need his help with something," I said, fingers absently twisting the Eiffel Tower charm around my neck.

T.J. leaned in. "Can I help?" His voice carried a note of concern.

I leaned in and lowered my voice. "I want to get into Mr. Hansen's office at the rink. And I need to find Eric."

T.J. raised an brow. "I might not be able to help with the office thing, but if I'm not mistaken, I think Eric may have just walked in." He nodded toward the back door. "Yash pointed him out to me in that team photo the paper ran. That's the guy, right? The one with the uncle causing Coach Wyatt all that trouble?"

I turned. Sure enough—it was Eric.

When our eyes met, he quickened his pace, weaving through the rows of tables until he reached ours.

"Eric! I've been trying to figure out how to find you," I blurted.

"Well, I'm glad I found you. I wasn't sure where to look, but Naomi told me you hang out here sometimes, so I thought I'd take a chance. The fact is, I owe you an explanation. Actually, it's more than that. I need your help," Eric confessed.

"What's going on?"

"Can we talk someplace…private?" Eric asked, his eyes darting toward T.J.

T.J. cleared his throat, pulling my attention back to him. "I don't think that's a good idea."

"Why not?" I questioned, surprised by the sharpness in his voice.

T.J. crossed his arms and looked at Eric with a hard stare. "For all I know, he and his uncle are tangled up with Coach Wyatt's murder. And if I'm right, that means he knows more than what he's been saying. I think it's too dangerous to be alone with him."

Eric's jaw clenched. "Look, man, if I wanted to cause trouble, I wouldn't come looking for Michelle in front of everyone. Think about it—too many witnesses. I'm just trying to get to the truth. If my uncle killed Coach, he'll have to pay the price for it—family or not. But if he's innocent, I don't want him taking the fall for something he didn't do."

T.J. didn't budge. "Then why can't you talk to her here, where it's safe?"

"Because there are too many ears," Eric snapped, then turned to me, his voice softer but strained. "Maybe this was a mistake. If I can't talk to you alone, I'll figure it out myself. Maybe I don't even need your help."

He spun on his heel, striding toward the door.

"Wait, Eric!" I called, standing to my feet. "I'll go with you."

"Michelle, don't—" T.J. began, but I cut him off.

"It'll be fine," I said, already moving. I pushed through the back door and hurried after Eric.

***

As we walked toward the campus library, an uneasy silence settled between us, the tension grew with each step until I couldn't take it any longer.

"Where are we going? Can't we talk while we walk?" I asked.

Eric stopped abruptly and turned to face me, his eyes intense enough to make me regret speaking up. "I need to find someplace away from listening ears," he said quietly. Reading my confusion, he added, "When I tell you the whole story, you'll understand."

I nodded, but my mind filled with questions. "How about the cemetery? It's over there behind that building. I doubt anyone's eavesdropping in *there*."

Eric hesitated, my suggestion clearly catching him off guard. "The cemetery?"

"Do you have a better idea?"

A few minutes later, we were tucked beneath a sprawling

pear tree, its white blooms swaying gently in the spring breeze—an almost surreal backdrop for a conversation about murder.

I leaned against the trunk and waited, but when Eric didn't say anything, I broke the silence.

"So, what's so important that we need all this secrecy?"

Eric's eyes darted around the cemetery, scanning the quiet paths for movement. "Sorry," he said finally. "I don't mean to be so cryptic. It's just...I don't know who I can trust." He paused, looking deep into my eyes. "I'm taking a chance trusting you, but it's a risk I'm willing to take. I need to tell someone what's going on."

"So...what's going on?"

"It all started several months ago," Eric began, his voice shaky at first, then getting steadier. "My uncle got a call from Hansen. They go way back—used to skate together. Hansen, my uncle, and Coach Wyatt all trained at the same rink when they were competitive skaters. My uncle had a different coach, but they all hung out."

"Even though they competed against each other?" I asked, raising an eyebrow.

"Yeah. When you train every day together, the rink becomes your second home, and the people you train with like family. That's why when Hansen called my uncle and told him he had it on good authority that Coach Wyatt was giving performance-enhancing drugs to his skaters...my uncle believed him."

"Just like that...with no proof?"

Eric let out a bitter laugh. "He didn't need proof. Hansen was his friend. Besides, my uncle already suspected Coach of bribing judges, but this drug business—" His jaw tightened. "That crossed a line. Not just because his skaters couldn't beat Coach's, but because he was endangering their health. My uncle was furious. He told me about it right away. I defended Coach and told him I had never been offered any drugs."

"What did he say?"

Eric gave a faint, sad smile. "He said it was because I was good enough not to need them. But no matter what I said, he wouldn't let it go. He started digging, looking for his own proof that Hansen was right. And the more Coach's skaters dominated the podium while his own came in third or fourth, the more convinced he became that something shady was going on."

"Did he ever find anything?"

Eric's expression darkened. "My uncle said he would have it by the time he met with the National Skating Council. That's all I know. And that's where things get tricky." He lowered his voice, letting a conspiratorial edge creep in. "Apparently, Hansen has been getting his information about Coach Wyatt from someone else."

"Who?"

"He wouldn't say. Just—" Eric glanced around as if the shadows in the cemetery might be listening. "He didn't trust Hansen's source. Said he wasn't sure how far this guy would go to bring Coach down or anyone who got in his way. Uncle Thomas started worrying that he was being used." Eric's voice trembled, and I could sense his fear.

"And your uncle never gave you a name? Nothing?"

Eric shook his head. "Nope. He said the less I knew, the better. I have no idea who this dude is. He could be anyone. As the rink manager, Hansen deals with so many people from the community, the university, and who knows where all. He's got connections. And not just from now, but from when he skated competitively."

Eric hesitated, his gaze flickering away for a moment. "After you came to the hotel and started asking about my uncle, I knew you suspected him of killing Coach. And if you did, the police would too." A tremor ran through him as he spoke. "The thing is...I've wondered the same thing. Did my uncle kill Coach Wyatt?"

His admission caught me off guard. "What do you mean?"

Eric drew a deep breath, reaching into his inner jacket pocket. "I found this photograph in my uncle's suitcase. I took it and hid it in my skating bag." He pulled out a small photo, his fingers lingering on the edges as if he wasn't ready to let it go.

I studied the picture—Thomas Bates and Coach Wyatt, frozen in time, standing in front of three bookcases. Eric watched me closely. I was puzzled by his concern over the photo. Nothing jumped out at me. It all looked perfectly ordinary.

"It was taken in Coach's office at the Hathaway House," Eric said, his eyes wide. "That means my uncle was in town *before* Coach was murdered."

"Are you sure?" I pressed. "I mean, how can you tell this is Coach's office in Petersburg? It looks like any office."

"I'm positive," he insisted. "Look at the books on the shelves. That section there? Those are books on the history of Petersburg."

His revelation changed everything.

I looked again. "Okay, we know it was taken in Petersburg, but wouldn't you or one of the other skaters have seen your uncle in the house?"

"That's true, but—" Eric's face brightened. "Coach came out here early to get everything set up, and I remember my uncle was out of town at the same time. Maybe the picture was taken then and *not* right before the murder."

"That's definitely a possibility." I hesitated. "Can I hang on to this picture for a while?"

Eric nodded, but the wariness returned to his eyes when I added, "I hate to ask, but I need to. Was the notecard with a Boston address and phone number yours?"

Eric blinked in surprise. "How'd you find out about the notecard?"

"I'd rather not say. Just what can you tell me about the phone number?"

He frowned, clearly debating how much to share. "After Coach died, Olga gave it to me. She told me to keep it safe in case she needed it later—said she was afraid she'd lose it."

"Did she say who the address or number belonged to?'

He shook his head. "Nope. She didn't say."

My mind raced. "So, why were you in Mr. Hansen's office last night? What were you looking for?"

A tense silence fell between us. I watched as Eric weighed his words.

Finally, he said, "If someone else is really involved in all of this, I needed proof—something to show he exists, that he's working with Hansen, *anything*. My uncle won't tell me the whole story, so I had to start looking for answers myself. Hansen's office seemed like the best place to start."

"What were you looking for?"

"My uncle said Hansen made all the arrangements for him to come out here—his flight, hotel, and rental car. I figured he used a travel agent, so I was hoping to find a business card, a receipt, an itinerary…anything to prove when my uncle got to town. I needed to know for my own peace of mind, and he wouldn't tell me. I guess I was hoping for proof that my uncle wasn't in town when Coach was murdered."

"And did you find anything?"

"The only thing I found was Hansen's phone bill," Eric said, his voice dropping to a whisper. "It had all the long-distance calls he made and received last month. I grabbed it, hoping that this mystery guy had called and I could figure out who he was. And… there were several calls between Hansen and my uncle. I didn't want the police to see that."

I hesitated, then decided he needed to know. "The police already know your uncle and Hansen talked on the phone."

Eric's face fell, despair etching deeper across his face.

"Yeah, I'm not surprised. I guess they have access to that kind of info, don't they?"

"Did you put the bill in a safe place?"

"Sort of. I dropped it off at the Hathaway House before I came looking for you. It's in my suitcase." He glanced around the cemetery again, his shoulders tense. "My uncle mentioned once that Hansen was big on keeping a daily journal. I was also hoping to find it in his office, but I ran out of time."

"Why? What happened?"

"When I heard the kids leaving the rink, I figured Hansen might pop into his office. I didn't want to get caught, so I left. But I'm planning to go back."

"A journal, huh? That could be interesting." I considered the possibilities. "There's actually something I want to look for in his office too—his scarf. Since it's spring, he probably only wears it in the rink. So I'm hoping he keeps it in his office."

"Hansen's scarf? Eric flashed a puzzled look. "Why?"

"I'm just curious about something." I paused. "Do you know if your uncle still wears the scarf in the picture—the one with him, Mr. Hansen, and Olga?"

Eric squinted as if sifting through memories. "I'm not sure. Let me see the picture again."

I pulled it out of my purse and handed it to him.

Eric studied it for a moment and then nodded. "Yeah, that's the one my mom gave him for his birthday a couple of years ago. See the monogram on the end? He always wears it when he's teaching."

I leaned in. "Oh, that's what that is. I thought it was a smudge on the photo. Who knew?" I laughed lightly.

Eric smirked. "I only remember that because my mom went on and on about getting it monogrammed by someone in town. She was so proud."

"Do you know what material it's made from?" I asked, trying to keep my tone casual.

"Not a clue," Eric shrugged. "Does it matter?"

"It might. Can you ask her?"

"Sure," he agreed, still baffled by my insistence. Then his expression shifted. "You wanna go to Hansen's office now?"

"Right now?" I glanced at my watch. "Won't he be at the rink?"

"Nope. Club skating classes were last night, so he won't come in until later this afternoon—after the ice gets resurfaced."

"But his office will be locked," I pointed out.

Eric unleashed a mischievous grin. "Yeah, like that's ever stopped me."

"Good point." I laughed despite the knot forming in my stomach. I checked my watch again. "It's noon, and my next class isn't until two. I've got time. Let's do it."

A shiver ran down my spine as Eric and I followed the gravel path out of the cemetery. I had an. Uneasy feeling about this, but still I wanted to go.

Eric wanted to find the journal, and I needed a good look at Mr. Hansen's scarf.

Yet, no matter how many times I told myself everything would be okay, I couldn't shake the feeling that something was about to go very, very wrong.

chapter twenty-eight

Eric and I navigated our way across campus to the ice arena, glancing over our shoulders to make sure no one was following us.

When we arrived, his teammates were already practicing —likely their last session together before parting ways. The rest of the building was quiet. No curling, no club classes. The lobby and adjoining hallway to Hansen's office were empty, making our mission feel deceptively easy.

Still, with each step, I scanned corners and doorways, half-expecting someone to leap from the shadows. When we reached the office door, I gave one final sweep of the hallway and exhaled. We'd made it.

Eric pulled a thin piece of metal from his jacket pocket, bent over, and started working on the lock.

"Is that—wait, where did you get a lock pick?"

He shrugged. "Let's just say I like to be prepared."

"Prepared for what? You break into offices often?"

He smirked as the lock clicked open.

Inside, he moved straight to the desk drawers. I went to the black iron coat tree and lifted the parka, revealing a long white scarf. I rubbed its coarse fibers and found the tag.

"I found the journal," Eric announced, thumbing through

its pages. "Take a look in that cabinet in the corner. Maybe there's something in there that'll tell us who's been feeding Hansen information."

I nodded and draped the scarf over my arm.

The top drawer held a 1975 wall calendar. Flipping through it, I spotted several dates circled in red.

"Look at this." I handed it to Eric.

He pointed to April 15. "'Meeting at 4:00 p.m.—don't be late!'"

A shiver crawled up my spine. "That's the day Coach was murdered."

Eric narrowed his eyes and opened the journal. "I wonder if he wrote down who he met that day?"

"Maybe it was his accountant? April 15 is tax day."

"Maybe. But what about this?" He handed me the brown leather journal.

I skimmed the entries: Coach Wyatt's testing schedules, judges' names, hotel and flight numbers, and even notes about Coach's affair with Olga and her reaction when he ended it.

"This is insane," I muttered. "He's got dirt on everyone—skaters, parents, Olga…your uncle."

"Let me see that," Eric said, taking the journal. "Why would he keep track of all this?"

"Look at this entry," I said. "April 19: 'Matter with C must be resolved. M.'"

"That was Saturday," Eric said. "The day Olga was killed."

"Could C mean the choreographer? If he thought someone might read this, he'd write in code, right?"

"And M?" Eric asked.

"My guess? Marco Rossini."

"Who's that?"

"Some guy from Boston who—"

We froze..

Footsteps.

Eric shoved the journal into the back of his pants and tugged down his jacket just as the door creaked open.

A hand flipped on the lights.

The door closed.

"Well, well. What do we have here?" said a man dressed in black from head to toe, his eyes glinting beneath his ski mask.

A sudden adrenaline rush ran through my veins. "Who are you, and what do you want?" I demanded.

He leaned against the wall. "Let's just say I'm on assignment, and what about you? This isn't your office."

I reached for the phone. "You've got two seconds to get out of here before I call the police."

"The police? That won't do you any good," he sneered as he pulled out a gun, pointing it at Eric and me. "Now, why don't you just put the phone down and tell me what you're doing here before someone gets hurt."

"We were just looking for something my uncle left in Hansen's office," Eric said quickly.

"And did you find it?"

"No. It doesn't seem to be here."

"Too bad," the man said, a smirk playing at the corners of his lips. He waved his gun, motioning for us to step away from Hansen's desk. "Sit! And you—Blondie—drop the scarf. You're not going to need that."

Eric and I exchanged a tense glance as we sat down. The man kept his gun aimed at us—his gaze unwavering as he stepped behind the desk. He tugged open the drawers and began rifling through the papers, muttering, "Where'd he put it?"

"What are you looking for?" I asked, attempting to stall him in hopes someone—anyone—had seen him come into the office and aroused their suspicion.

"None of your business. But you know what? It doesn't

matter because if that journal's in here, I'm going to make sure no one ever finds it," he said, his eyes narrowing.

"What's so important about a journal?" I pressed.

He glared. "Anybody ever tell you that you ask too many questions?"

In a swift motion, he pulled a length of rope from the bulging pocket of his coat and tossed it to Eric. "Tie her hands behind her back."

Eric hesitated.

"I said, tie her hands, or I'll shoot you and do it myself."

With a resigned nod, Eric got up and began tying my wrists. Remembering a tip from my self-defense class, I spread my wrists apart so I could shimmy out of the rope. I hoped Eric would follow my lead and tie the knot loosely.

The man grabbed a yardstick and pushed it against the ceiling tile while keeping his gun pointed at us. As he lifted one end of the tile, a length of rope fell onto the desk. Reading the confusion in my expression, he chuckled, "The boss man told me he stashed some extra rope—just in case."

He tossed another length of rope to Eric and barked, "Now tie her to the chair."

Eric's jaw clenched. For a second, I thought he might leap over the desk, but then the gun turned on me. Eric froze, surrendering to the threat, and tied my wrists to the chair.

Eric returned to his seat, deflated. The grim reality of our situation settled around us like a suffocating shroud.

As the masked man secured Eric's hands, tethering them to the back of his chair, I caught a glimpse of a tattoo on his wrist. He noticed my focus and quickly turned his wrist over. Silently, he checked the knots binding my wrists and, finding them loose, forced my hands together and tied the knot securely.

Then, from his pocket, he pulled out two scarves. I struggled to resist as he tugged the first one over my mouth, but my attempts were futile. Eric's eyes widened in horror as he saw what was happening, but there was nothing he could do.

My heart pounded in my chest as I watched the man repeat the same cruel maneuver with Eric, silencing us both and muffling any cries for help.

Next, he withdrew a small bottle from his inner coat pocket, poured its contents onto a cloth, and pressed it against my face.

I twisted my head from side to side, trying not to breathe, but the sweet smell seeped in.

Darkness closed in around me.

***

When I regained consciousness, I was under a blanket on a stretcher with an EMT hovering over me. "She's coming to, sir," he called out.

Groggy and disoriented, I blinked several times, struggling to understand what was happening. Fragmented memories began to surface—the man, the gun, the smell… fear.

"Where's…Eric?" I croaked, my heart pounding. A sea of faces were gathered in the ice arena's parking lot, but Eric's face was not among them.

Lt. Grogan's face sharpened into focus. "Eric's safe, Michelle. Craig got you both out before the fire reached you, but you've inhaled some smoke. You're going to be okay."

"Fire?" I coughed. "What fire?"

"In Hansen's office—"

"There was a man…a man with a gun. He must have… started it. Did…did you catch him?"

Grogan's expression darkened. "We're still looking for him. A witness saw a man jump into a limousine. They couldn't recall much, but we're reviewing the surveillance footage in the parking lot and the office area. He should be on it."

Suddenly, the journal flashed in my mind, and my heartbeat quickened. "Eric found—"

Grogan nodded. "A journal—it's safe. The EMT's found it on Eric. I'll keep it for evidence, but Craig is looking through it now."

I closed my eyes, processing everything that had happened—searching Hansen's office, being tied to the chair…almost losing our lives. We nearly died. The enormity of it all began to consume me until a warm hand clasped mine, and I felt a wave of calmness. I opened my eyes—Craig.

"Hi, Sherlock," he said gently. "You hanging in there?"

"Better now," I whispered, squeezing his hand. "Thank you for saving us."

"I told you I wouldn't let anything happen to you," he said, his expression serious. "I had to keep my word."

"But how…how did you know?"

"Yash saw a guy go into Hansen's office. He was suspicious, so he followed him and heard voices coming from inside—he thought one of them was yours. He was on his way to call the police when he ran into me. I had just gotten here for my skating lesson. He told me what was happening, and while he called the police, I went to the office. When I saw smoke under the door—well, I did what any knight in shining armor would do. I rescued you."

"You're so modest," I chuckled weakly.

Craig's eyes didn't leave mine. "I'm just glad you're okay. That was way too close."

"But we got the journal," I said, with a hint of pride.

"That you did." He smiled.

At that moment, an EMT interrupted. "You can meet us at the hospital, sir. We're going to take them in to get checked over."

Craig released my hand. "I'll follow right behind you."

His eyes locked onto mine. "Do you want me to call your parents?"

"Yeah, I guess so," I said softly. "Just make sure you tell them I'm okay."

He nodded as the EMT wheeled me away.

Faces, clues, and journal entries swirled in my mind. If I could piece it all together, maybe we could catch whoever killed Coach Wyatt and Olga.

"Craig," I called.

"Yes?" he replied, turning back.

"Tell Lt. Grogan, I found Hansen's scarf... it's wool."

chapter twenty-nine

After what felt like forever, the doctors finally gave me the all-clear. No serious injuries—just rattled nerves and a bruised sense of safety. I pushed open the heavy ER door beneath the glowing EXIT sign and inhaled the cool air of the waiting room—grateful to be alive.

My dad and Craig sat near the front. Their faces lit up with relief the moment they spotted me.

"Michelle!" Dad shouted, jumping to his feet and walking quickly toward me.

"Dad, I'm okay," I said, my voice still hoarse. "I'm sorry…"

His expression shifted as his worry morphed into frustration. "You scared me half to death," he snapped, then caught himself, his voice softening. "You're one lucky girl. The doctor said you're no worse for wear."

Craig slipped an arm around my shoulder. "She's tougher than she looks," he said, but the worry in his eyes betrayed his tone.

My father's eyes darted from Craig's back to mine. "This was supposed to be over, Michelle. How many times do I have to tell you?"

"I know," I said, my voice wavering but firm. "But Eric

had a lead on information I thought could help find Coach's killer. I had to try."

My father heaved a heavy sigh, raking a hand through his dark hair, revealing a few silver strands. "At what cost? You could have died."

"But I didn't," I replied.

"Craig," my father said, shaking his head. "Maybe you can talk some sense into her."

Craig nodded slowly. "She can be a bit stubborn, that's for sure. My guess is she inherited it."

My dad sighed again, his gaze drifting toward the door, "Well, Craig said he'd drive you back to campus so you can pick up your car. Are you going to be okay to drive home?"

"Yeah, I'm fine, but—" I glanced at the clock on the wall. "What about T.J.? Is he still at school? Oh my, he doesn't know what's happened. He's probably worried or thinks I forgot about him."

"Everything's okay," Craig assured me. "I called the Commuter Lounge and explained everything to Alice. She promised to make sure T.J. had a way home, even if she had to drive him herself."

"Okay," my father muttered. "I'm going back home and letting your mom know you're okay."

A chill ran down my spine as I watched my dad's silhouette disappear. This time, I escaped danger because of Craig, but who would save me the next time, or could I do it alone? Craig's grip tightened around my shoulders. Was he wondering too?

I sank into the black leather seat of Craig's car and buckled in, the smell of faint cologne and old coffee grounding me in the moment. As we pulled out of the parking lot, I glanced at Craig.

Alive.

Safe.

And with someone I could trust.

For now, that was enough.

I turned to Craig, "Eric and I only had a few minutes to look at the journal before that guy came in, but it seemed like Mr. Hansen documented quite a bit about Coach Wyatt and, well, a lot of people. What did you find?"

Craig shifted his stance as his brow furrowed in thought. "It seems Hansen was getting information from someone and passing it along to Bates."

"Did he ever say who this other person was?" I asked, eager to connect the dots.

"Not by name, but I found the letter M written several times," Craig said.

I took a deep breath. "We saw that too. I think it refers to our elusive Marco Rossini."

"Exactly what I was thinking," Craig said, turning onto campus.

"After the fire, did anyone see Mr. Hansen? I mean, surely he was called about it," I asked.

Craig shrugged. "Good question. You would think so, but I don't remember seeing him. Odd, isn't it?"

I leaned back in my seat and closed my eyes, drifting off for a few minutes.

"Michelle," Craig nudged my arm. "Where did you park?"

"In Lot 3, but I want to go to the Commuter Lounge first and make sure T.J. got a ride home. It's 7:30 p.m., and Alice still might be there. Lawrence said she sometimes stays until classes end at 10:00 p.m."

"Are you sure you're okay to drive?" he asked, concern pinching his brow.

"Absolutely! A nice walk from the Lounge to my car will do me good—wake up the old senses," I said.

Craig pulled into the faculty parking lot closest to Whitely Hall, and as I reached for the door handle, he placed his hand on my shoulder. "You're only going to check on T.J., right?"

I grinned and crossed my heart. "I promise. I've had enough adventure for one day. All I want to do is see that T.J. got a ride. After that, I'm going home and heading to bed."

"Call me when you get home?" Craig asked, his voice laced with worry.

"I will," I smiled as I hopped out of his car, feeling warm and fuzzy inside—happy he was concerned about me.

When I stepped into the Commuter Lounge, the room was filled with the quiet chatter of a group of students unwinding before their evening classes. Our table was empty except for Lawrence, drumming his fingers on the surface.

"Hey," he said as I approached. "I've got news. The hospital released Detective Douglas, and he's back in town. He's doing well, considering his kidnappers broke his arm and nose, but it could have been worse. However, the chief reassigned him to a desk job, removing him from all investigations—especially Sarah's and Coach Wyatt's."

I let out a heavy sigh. "I guess I'm not surprised he's squashing Detective Douglas's investigations. Personally, I think the chief is involved in covering up Sarah's death and maybe even knows more about Coach Wyatt's murder. I bet that's why he wants Detective Douglas to back down."

Lawrence nodded, frowning. "Yeah, Grogan and I think the same—which is why we're going to help Douglas, even if he's off the case. Someone tried to silence him, which means he's onto something. There's no way Sarah took her own life."

Rising from his seat, Lawrence hefted his backpack, slipping his arms through its straps. "Oh, and when I was at the station this afternoon, Lt. Grogan asked me to tell you that Eric called his mother to tell her about the fire, and he asked her about the scarf. She said she thought it was wool."

My heart sank. "Well… that's not exactly what I wanted to hear."

"Why's that?" Lawrence asked, his eyes squinting behind his glasses.

"I was hoping to rule out Eric's uncle," I muttered, biting my lip. "But now I've got two suspects, two scarves, and one dead coach."

"So, you do suspect him?" Lawrence asked.

"Yeah, for now." I shrugged as I stood up.

Lawrence reached into his pocket and retrieved a piece of paper. "Here. Grogan said you should see this."

"What is it?" I asked as I unfolded the paper.

"The passenger list for the flight Bates was booked on."

I stared at the paper in my hands. "I think I'm going to run by the rink and see if Mr. Hansen is around."

"Do you want me to go with you?" Lawrence offered. "I don't think you should see him alone, especially after what I've heard he wrote in that journal of his. I don't trust him."

Shaking my head, I said, "No, I'll be fine. He's probably busy cleaning up his office after the fire and won't have a lot of time to talk. I just have a few questions about the travel arrangements for Bates, so I won't be long. Just want to make sure I'm on the right track."

"Okay, let me know what you find out."

"Will do."

***

By the time I walked into the ice arena, it was 8:00 p.m. A crooked sign hung on the doors stating that all club skating classes and Public Skate sessions had been canceled because of a fire in one of the offices. I tugged on the door, half-expecting it to be locked, but it opened.

When I stepped inside, the acrid scent of smoke greeted me and grew stronger as I made my way to the lobby, where I found the skate rental area locked up. There was no sign of Mr. Hansen or anyone else for that matter, so I decided to do the next best thing—check his office for answers, if any were still there.

I knocked on Mr. Hansen's office door, but no one answered so I slipped in, ducking beneath the strip of yellow caution tape. The smell of burnt paper and wood filled the room, and memories of the gunman momentarily made me pause.

Forcing myself to push such thoughts aside, I navigated through the debris behind Hansen's desk and scanned the wreckage for any clues. Papers were scattered across the floor, and a charred calendar was hanging from the edge of the desk. I sank into Hansen's oversized desk chair, reliving the horror of being bound and gagged just hours earlier.

Desperate for a distraction, I spun to face away from the chairs in which Eric and I almost died and replayed everything I had seen or heard about the night Coach was strangled.

Just then, a rustling sound broke the silence. I turned, my heart pounding.

"Michelle?" Hansen's voice cut through the silence. "What are you doing here?"

I stood up and stepped out from behind the desk. "Looking for answers—thought maybe you'd have some."

"Like what?"

"I wanted to ask you about the travel arrangements you made for Coach Bates, but—" I held up the singed calendar. "I remembered something about this calendar. You circled April 15. That's the day Coach Wyatt was killed."

"Yes, I guess it is. It's also Tax Day," Mr. Hansen said, his eyes locked on mine as a frown crossed his face and his posture stiffened. "Last time I checked, circling a date on your calendar wasn't a crime."

"I never said it was," I shot back, feeling a rush of confidence. "But since you brought it up, marking a date isn't illegal, but committing murder is."

With measured steps, Hansen approached the desk. "And why would I want to kill Charles? Let's not forget—it was Danny I heard arguing with Charles, and it was Danny's scarf around his neck, not mine."

"Now that's an interesting point. I'm glad you brought it up," I said, steadying my voice. "It seems there were wool fibers found in Coach's neck."

"Of course there were," Hansen said with a wave of his hand, as if brushing away the accusation. "Charles always wore a scarf when he taught. It makes sense that fibers from his scarf would be on his neck."

"Yeah, but that's the funny thing—Coach's scarf was white, like Olga's, but the fibers were ivory," I said. "What color is your scarf?"

He straightened his posture. "Now, listen here, if you're trying to pin Charles's murder on me, you've got it all wrong. A lot of people have off-white wool scarves. Just because I own one doesn't mean I killed Charles. In fact—"

"Bates has one just like yours, and he was in town at the time of the murder?" I interrupted.

"Of course he was," Hansen replied, pacing. "I organized his visit."

"I think you might have missed one detail," I challenged, cocking my head.

"What detail?" Irritation crept into his voice.

"The itsy, bitsy detail that the plane was overbooked, and he took a later flight, which got him into town the day *after* the murder."

"You know what?" Hansen said, advancing toward the door. "I'm giving you until the count of three to get out of my office, or I'm calling the cops. One, two—"

"Please do. I'd love to talk to them," I said, crossing my arms.

He spun on his heels. "That does it. I'm calling the police."

"So, tell me, why did you drop the skates off at the Hathaway House that night instead of letting the skaters pick them up at the rink like usual?"

Hansen stopped, his hand hovering over the doorknob. "Not that it's any of your business, but, like I told the police, I wanted to speak to Charles, and it made sense to take the skates with me when I went to his house."

"Did you also tell the police that you saw Olga before you left?" I pressed, my eyes narrowing.

His hand dropped away from the doorknob. "What are you talking about?"

"As I remember it, you told the police Naomi let you out that night, which she claims she did. But when we spoke, you said that Olga walked you to the door. Now, how could that be when everyone says Olga was in her room when you came to the house unless—" I drew a deep breath. "You went back inside, and she let you out the second time." I tilted my head, "Now, that would make sense, wouldn't it?"

"I suppose it would."

"Then what made you go back inside? You'd already dropped off the skates. You knew Coach had company. What was so important that you had to go back into the house?"

"I…I just forgot something," Mr. Hansen uttered.

"Did you forget something, or did you still have something to do? Perhaps something Marco Rossini asked you to do?"

All the color drained from Hansen's face at the mention of Rossini.

"How do you know about Rossini?" he asked, panic in his voice.

"It's not so hard to figure out. You and Rossini have been in contact. We have the phone records to prove it. And the police also know that Rossini just so happens to own the house you set up for Coach Wyatt to rent. I'm guessing Rossini had you kill Coach Wyatt. The only question I have is why? I get that Coach was responsible for the accident that ended your skating career, but after all these years, was murder really the only way you could get back at him? Wasn't ruining his career enough?"

Hansen's jaw tensed.For a split second, I thought I saw fear in his eyes. But then it was gone, replaced by a fierce anger.

"You don't know what you're talking about," he said.

"Then enlighten me," I said, leaning back in the scorched chair like it was a throne and this was my courtroom.

Hansen paced back and forth, nearly stepping into a heap of charred paper. "Charles has been ruining people's lives for years—first mine with the accident, and then I learned he was doping skaters to win. Someone had to stop him."

I raised an eyebrow. "This information you got… where'd you get it?"

"Rossini," he admitted.

"And you trusted him over your friend?"

"Charles and I lost touch. We were more like acquaintances than friends, and Rossini seemed to know what he was talking about."

"Where do you know him from anyway?" I pressed.

"I've never actually met him, but he's been a major donor for our skating club for several years, and the one who recommended me for the job of rink manager—said one of his friends told him about me, and he thought I'd be a good fit," Hansen explained.

"So, that's all it took to make you believe his allegations against Coach Wyatt were true?" I quipped.

"He said he had proof—that he had hired a private investigator to tail Charles, and there were photos. Why would I not believe him?"

"But to kill Coach? That makes no sense. Eric's uncle had filed a complaint against him with the National Skating Council. Wasn't that enough?"

"It should've been, but when Rossini ordered me to kill

Charles, and I refused, he threatened me—sent me photographs of my family. He said he'd hurt them if I didn't do what he wanted. I had no choice. I had to protect my wife and daughters and…and the skaters whose lives Charles was jeopardizing," Hansen said.

"Why didn't you go to the police? They could have helped?" I asked.

"Help? The way they *helped* Sarah Bentley? No way was I going to ask them for anything," he spat.

"And now what?" I said, a chill creeping into my stomach.

"I'm sorry, Michelle," he said, stepping closer. "You seem like a nice kid, but I can't have you going to the police."

"Planning another fire?" I asked, my voice steady despite the cold creeping into my spine.

"I had nothing to do with the fire in my office—it wasn't me. I assume Rossini sent someone—someone to take care of the evidence and anyone who got in his way. Had he done his job, you and Eric would no longer be a problem, but since he didn't and you're here, I guess it's up to me."

My instincts kicked in, and I bolted for the door—but he was faster. He shoved me back into the chair and wrapped his hands around my neck. Panic surged through my veins as his grip tightened.

Using what I'd learned from the last time I nearly died, I knew I had to stay clearheaded. I had to fight.

This wasn't about passing a self-defense class—this was about surviving.

Pressure points. I had to find his pressure points.

Twisting my body to the side, I broke his grip and drove my elbow into his ribs. He gasped.

I surged to my feet, pivoting to face him, fists clenched, adrenaline flooding my system. His eyes widened—he hadn't expected me to fight back.

"You picked the wrong person," I said, voice low and steady. *This girl wasn't going down without a fight.*

I kicked his knee hard in one swift motion. He stumbled back. In the split-second it took him to recover, I grabbed a lamp off the table and hurled it at him.

It hit.

He dropped.

I didn't wait.

I tore out the door, bursting through the police caution tape like it wasn't even there.

chapter thirty

I burst into the empty lobby, my breath ragged. Craig stood near the door to the rink, waving. His smile vanished when he saw my face.

"What's wrong?" he shouted.

I opened my mouth to answer, but a loud crash erupted behind me. I whirled around and saw Mr. Hansen stumbling from his office, his feet catching on the loose tape scattered across the floor.

Before I could react, Craig positioned himself between Hansen and me.

"Stop right there, Hansen. Don't take another step," Craig commanded.

Hansen sneered, "You shouldn't have come here."

Hansen lunged at Craig, but Craig sidestepped swiftly, catching his arm and twisting it behind his back. For a moment, it seemed like Craig had the upper hand—until Hansen broke free and, with a surge of force, slammed Craig against the wall.

I scanned the room, heart pounding. How could I help? Then I saw it—the bell on the rental counter. I snatched it and hurled it at Hansen. He flinched just enough.

I sprang forward and slammed my fist into his midsection.

Regaining his footing, Craig charged at Hansen, tackling him to the ground.

Just then, Lt. Grogan entered the lobby, leading a team of officers with their weapons drawn. The officers took in the scene, tense and alert, until Grogan's gaze locked on Hansen sprawled on the floor.

"You can let him go now, Craig," Lt. Grogan said. "We've got this."

As an officer cuffed Hansen and led him away, my knees threatened to give out as a wave of relief washed over me. I slumped onto a nearby bench, and Craig joined me, placing his hand on mine. "Are you okay?"

Laying my head on his shoulder, I let out a breath I didn't realize I had been holding. "Yeah, I am. Thanks to you… again."

"You didn't do so bad yourself, Sherlock. That was some mean punch you gave him," Craig chuckled.

I leaned in closer, feeling safe once again.

With Hansen on his way out of the building, Lt. Grogan turned his attention toward us.

Before he could say anything, I asked, "How did you know to come here? I didn't even have a chance to call the police."

"After Lawrence ran into Craig, he called me at the station and said you had gone to talk to Hansen. He had a bad feeling about it. What Lawrence didn't know was that Hansen was already on our radar as a suspect. When we got here, his car was in the parking lot, and, as they say, the rest is history." He smiled slightly, maintaining his professional demeanor. "I know you've had a long day, but I need to get your statements. Can you both stop by the station? Hopefully, I'll get some answers from Hansen regarding Coach Wyatt's death and maybe even Olga's."

Once Lt. Grogan disappeared up the stairs, I asked Craig,

"Where did you see Lawrence? For some reason, I thought you were going home."

"I had some paperwork to get caught up on in my office and was on my way to the Union to get some coffee. Lawrence was upset that you were heading to the rink and was debating about whether or not to call Lt. Grogan. I told him it'd probably be a good idea but that I would go and check on you," he explained.

He then added, "Why don't I call your father and let him know we got delayed? I'll tell him Coach Wyatt's killer is in custody.—he'll be happy to hear that. We'll leave your car here, go to the station, then I'll take you home after we grab something to eat. Sound like a plan?"

"Yeah." I nodded. "Sounds like the best plan I've heard all day."

***

Craig and I wandered around campus for a while, trying to unwind before heading to the police station. The quiet night air carried a refreshing calm, offering a brief escape from the chaos of the day.

When we finally arrived, Lt. Grogan was waiting in the lobby. He gave us a quick nod and motioned for us to follow him into Detective Douglas's office, where he gestured for us to take a seat.

After taking our statements, he said, "Hansen was reluctant to talk until I reminded him Rossini already knew where he was and that I *could* protect his family in exchange for his statement."

"And did he tell you anything?" I asked.

"He said Rossini orchestrated everything—Wyatt's murder, framing Danny. At first, Hansen thought Rossini was trying to help, that he was concerned about the skaters and the skating club. But by the time he realized what Rossini was really doing, it was too late."

"Why? What happened?" Craig inquired. "I don't understand."

Lt. Grogan exhaled. "It all started around the time Steve and Barb Goodright were arrested for Professor Ladd's murder. Hansen got a call from Marco Rossini, a major financial backer of the Petersburg Skating Club. Rossini claimed he was worried about the negative publicity surrounding the Goodrights and how it might reflect on the rink, especially with their son working there. He suggested it would be best for everyone if Danny left town. Said it would help the club. And help Danny, too. Then he offered to anonymously cover Danny's relocation costs to a rink that was hiring. Coincidentally, that rink was where Wyatt and Bates were coaching."

I leaned back in my chair, my arms crossed. "How did Danny and Coach Wyatt become such good friends?"

"Hansen reached out to Wyatt, explained Danny's situation, and asked him to look out for him."

"That was convenient," I remarked.

"Yes, it was," Lt. Grogan agreed. When Rossini confided in Hansen about the suspected doping issues with Wyatt's skaters, Hansen thought it was his duty to pass that information on to his friend, Bates, who then warned his nephew Eric, one of Wyatt's skaters."

"So, Rossini set the stage for Hansen and Bates to think Wyatt was up to no good, is that right?" Craig asked.

"Exactly. And to complicate matters, as soon as Danny arrived at the rink, tapes, and skates began disappearing, which earned him the label as a troublemaker with the other skaters," Lt. Grogan said.

"But why did Rossini go to such lengths to kill Coach?" I pressed.

"Coach Wyatt was an expendable means to an end. The plan, it seems, hinged on framing Danny for murder. That's why Rossini insisted Hansen use Danny's scarf to strangle Wyatt. The misstep came when Hansen wore his scarf that night and, in a moment of panic, accidentally used it instead. He then had to remove it and tie Danny's scarf around the coach's neck. Later, Hansen concocted a story about overhearing Danny arguing with Wyatt, which was easy for everyone to believe," Lt. Grogan explained.

"But why Danny? What did he ever do to this Rossini dude?" I asked.

"Hansen said when he asked Rossini, he would only say, 'Remittance dawns on the maiden of blooms.'"

"Remittance dawns on the maiden of blooms?" Craig pondered aloud. What in the world does that mean?"

"It's like a riddle," I replied. "Remittance is when you pay for something, right?"

Craig and Lt. Grogan nodded.

"And the maiden of blooms?" Craig asked.

"Let me think a minute," I said. "Spring, maybe? Blooming season?"

Craig nodded. "May."

We looked at each other.

"Mae," I whispered. "Your mother. Could Rossini be targeting her family—starting with her sister, then Shelly, now Danny?"

A heavy silence settled over us as we absorbed the full weight of Rossini's vengeance against Mae.

Then, another thought crossed my mind. "Olga. Was she part of Rossini's scheme—or just in the wrong place at the wrong time?"

Grogan took a deep breath, his gaze steady as he recounted what Hansen had told him during the interrogation.

"While Coach Wyatt was on the phone, Hansen slipped into the office through a revolving bookcase. He crept up behind Wyatt and strangled him. What Hansen didn't expect was Olga. She had wanted to talk to the coach and had just gotten to the office when she heard a commotion. She opened the door and saw Hansen standing over Coach's body. He told her to keep quiet—or she'd end up the same way. Then he left the way he came, circled around to his car, and drove off. Said he nearly panicked when the dog started barking, but no one saw him."

Grogan's voice dropped lower. "Later, Hansen told Rossini that Olga had witnessed everything. Rossini told him not to worry. He'd take care of it."

I leaned forward. "One more question. The phone call. Who made it? For this plan to work, Coach had to be lured to his office at just the right time."

Lt. Grogan shook his head. "That's still a mystery. It was a local call from a pay phone on the other side of town. Hansen claims he doesn't know who placed the call, only that Rossini guaranteed Wyatt would be in his office."

"Do you know if the allegations against Coach Wyatt were true?" I asked. "Was he really giving his skaters performance-enhancing drugs—or bribing judges?"

"No to both," Grogan said, shaking his head. "After the murder, Hansen spoke with Wyatt's team, and every one of them denied using any kind of drugs. At first, he wasn't surprised—they had every reason to lie—but they were so emphatic, it made him question the so-called evidence Rossini claimed he had."

Grogan paused, his expression darkening. "So Hansen called Rossini to press him about the rumors. Rossini just laughed. Said he never had any proof—admitted he was the one who started the rumors in the first place.

"Wow. What a waste. So, what happens to Hansen now? I mean, considering what happened to Sarah while she was waiting for trial, how do you protect him?"

"That's the million-dollar question. I'll probably get a reprimand, but I bypassed the chief and got permission to send Hansen to an out-of-state facility under an assumed name while he awaits trial. I'm not sure what I can do once the trial starts. We'll take it step by step. I'm also coordinating with the federal witness protection program to relocate Hansen's family and provide them a fresh start in exchange for Hansen's testimony against Rossini," Lt. Grogan said.

"Sounds like you've got your hands full." .

"Yes, I do. With Detective Douglas out of commission, I'm taking over as lead detective until he returns. Of course—" he lowered his voice. "It means I'll be able to help him from the inside by investigating Sarah's death and looking for this Marco Rossini. I only wish Prince Alexander of Orsino wasn't coming to town later this year. Now, besides everything else, I also have to put together a protection detail for him."

"Prince Alexander. That's pretty cool! Why's he coming to Petersburg?" I asked.

"It's part of his U.S. tour. He's visiting the university, the planetarium, and the cancer hospital. After that, I believe he's going to the Toledo Art Museum, and I don't remember where all. My job begins and ends while he's in Petersburg. When he leaves here, he's Toledo's problem," Lt. Grogan said with a slight smile.

As he spoke, I imagined the prince: tall, handsome, and surrounded by an entourage—just like out of a storybook. But then, a thought crossed my mind. Could there be more to his visit to Petersburg than Lt. Grogan was letting on?

Craig nudged my shoulder, snapping me back to reality. "Sounds like the perfect human interest story! You in?" His grin was infectious, sparking my sense of adventure and sweeping my worries aside.

"Yeah, it should be fun—a prince, a small town, a quick tour. A fun, easy assignment.

***

Craig and I left Lt. Grogan and made our way toward the lobby doors but stopped when we spotted T.J. pacing in front of the reception desk.

"Michelle!" T.J. shouted, striding toward us.

Before I could respond, Craig stepped in. "T.J., what brings you here?"

T.J. glanced at Craig and then back to me. "I wanted to make sure Michelle was okay—the fire...and then Hansen."

"I'm fine," I insisted, touched by his concern.

T.J. narrowed his eyes.

"Really," I smiled. "A little unnerved, but I'm all right." I took a breath. "How did you know I was here?"

"After Alice dropped me off, I called your father, and he said you had been released from the hospital, and Craig was driving you back to school to get your car. But I got worried when I never saw your car at the house. So, I called your father again to see what was up. That's when he told me Hansen attacked you, and the police arrested him for Coach Wyatt's murder."

He turned his eyes toward Craig. "I heard you saved Michelle from the fire and Hansen. Funny how you're always right where the danger is."

Craig didn't flinch. "Good thing I was. If not, Michelle and Eric might be dead."

T.J. lowered his eyes. "Sorry. I shouldn't take this out on you. I've just been worried about Michelle."

He turned back toward me, his voice softening as he took a step closer. "Are you okay? Really?"

"Yeah, just a little shaken," I replied, forcing a smile to reassure him.

Craig cleared his throat as he draped a protective arm around me. "Look, it's been a long day. She just needs to go home and unwind. But first, I'm going to get her some supper, and then I'll take her home."

T.J. stiffened, his jaw tightening in a way I hadn't seen

before. "Why don't I take her home? It'll save you a trip. After all, we're neighbors. I can get her some food on our way home—"

"It's no bother," Craig insisted, his voice firm. "I'm hungry too. Plus, driving out in the country will help me relax. It's been a rather stressful day."

I glanced at the two of them, the heat crawling up my cheeks as they waited for me to speak. My fingers found the Eiffel Tower charm at my neck, twisting it as I weighed my options, not wanting to hurt either of them.

If T.J. took me home, it might stir up more trouble with Meg. It would be innocent—he lived right across the street from me—but I couldn't forget Meg's complaints about our friendship. The last thing I wanted was to make things harder for him.

To further complicate things, I might hurt Craig if I chose T.J., especially after Craig had offered to take me home first. When I looked into his eyes, I saw how much he'd come to mean to me. He grounded me and brought balance to my relentless pursuit of the truth. The thought of risking our friendship—or maybe something more—weighed heavily on my heart.

"Guys, let's not fight about this," I said, having made my decision. "All I want to do is get something to eat, go home, and go to bed. So why don't we stick with the original plan? Craig and I can grab some food, and then he can take me home." My voice wavered as I turned my gaze on T.J. "And if you wouldn't mind letting my father know you found me and that I'll be home soon, I would appreciate it."

As I spoke, hurt flashed across T.J.'s face, though he quickly masked it with a smile.

Craig gave a slight nod, clearly relieved but trying to play it cool. "Well, if you're sure—"

T.J. opened his mouth to speak, but I cut in before he could, "Yeah, I'm sure."

Yet, even as I said the words, guilt swept over me. I hated being caught in the middle of whatever tension was simmering between them—especially when I cared about them both. I glanced down at the amber-colored stone in my mood ring. It nailed it: unsettled, torn between conflicting emotions.

T.J. sighed, his gaze a mix of resignation and frustration. "Okay, but promise me you'll call when you get home."

"I will," I reassured him, but I had to admit, I was a little disappointed at how quickly he lost his resolve to change my mind.

I exhaled slowly. There were bigger things to worry about than my tangled feelings—Sarah's death, Rossini's next move. This mystery wasn't over. Not even close.

about the author

SHARON KAY grew up in Ohio and earned a degree in photojournalism from Bowling Green State University. Her experience as a commuting college student in the 1970s—complete with rushed breakfasts, vending machine lunches, and far too many hours spent searching for a decent parking spot—loosely inspired *The Michelle Kilpatrick Mysteries*.

When she's not plotting fictional murders (strictly on paper, of course), Sharon enjoys organic gardening, devouring mysteries and historical fiction, and indulging in cheesecake—because life is too short to skip dessert. She has three adult children and is a proud grandma to their ever-growing collection of fur babies.

***

Be the first to hear about new book releases and special promotions. And get insider access to book club discussion questions, Michelle's favorite recipes, and the ultimate 1970s playlist. Because, let's face it, solving mysteries is even better with snacks and groovy tunes.

Don't miss out—visit https://thesharonkay.com

If you enjoyed *Icy Secrets, Scandalous Lies*, please consider leaving a review. Thank you!